Pinktoes

THE OUTRAGEOUSLY RACY RIOT FOR CIVIL RIGHTS IN THE BEDROOM

CHESTER HIMES

Pinktoes

PUBLISHED BY
DELL PUBLISHING CO., INC.
AND
G. P. PUTNAM'S SONS.

Published by

DELL PUBLISHING CO., INC. and G. P. PUTNAM'S SONS

Copyright © 1961, 1965 by Chester Himes

Dell ® TM 681510, Dell Publishing Co., Inc.

Reprinted by arrangement with

G. P. Putnam's Sons/Stein and Day, New York, N.Y.

First Dell-Putnam Printing—July, 1966
Second Dell-Putnam Printing—September, 1966
Third Dell-Putnam Printing—November, 1966
Fourth Dell-Putnam Printing—November, 1966
Fifth Dell-Putnam Printing—January, 1967
Sixth Dell-Putnam Printing—May, 1967
Seventh Dell-Putnam Printing—November, 1967
Eighth Dell-Putnam Printing—December, 1968
Ninth Dell-Putnam Printing—December, 1969

Printed in U.S.A.

Pinktoes

*Pinktoes is a term of indulgent affection
applied to white women by Negro men, and
sometimes conversely by Negro women to
white men, but never adversely by either.*

INTRODUCTION
EXCURSION IN PARADOX

NOTHING *ever goes right. Nothing ever turns out as one
has planned. How many times have you heard that said?
How many times have you said it? And yet, it is never an
expression of cynicism, defeatism or nihilism. It is always
a confession of faith.*

*Despite the fact that nothing ever goes right, life goes
right on. And, even though nothing ever turns out as one
has planned it, the human race increases, develops, pro-
gresses. Mankind becomes wiser, healthier and happier;
and all the various mechanisms it persists in developing
for its own destruction do not one whit deter this steady
movement toward the millennium, whatever and wherever
that might be. So everything goes right for Some One, and
everything turns out as Some One has planned. We our-
selves, the billions of people who inhabit this earth, the un-
adorned fact of our existence, that during each and every
day, every hour of the day, somewhere on earth there are
people of all colors and races, all creeds and breeds, engaged
in propagating, furnish the incontrovertible and absolute
proof of our faith in the fact that everything turns out as
Some One has planned it. Isn't it wonderful!*

*Take, for instance, the night Billie Hall fell in the Copa.
Billie wanted to make a sensational entrance, capture
everyone's full attention, became a cynosure of all eyes—*

The Cynosure. *She wanted to inspire passionate inclinations, instigate magnificent propositions, be envied and coveted, as what girl doesn't?*

The Copa, in case you do not know, is a big plush night club in Manhattan where the pinkest of Pinktoes dripping with furs and diamonds congregate in the late hours of the evening to seek and be sought, accompanied by male escorts whose chief function is to pay the bill—and at the Copa, this is not a minor consideration.

Billie, in case you don't remember her, was the star of an all-colored musical that was then having a brief success on Broadway. Naturally, Billie was a colored girl; it is only in the Opera further downtown that you will find white persons playing colored roles. Or does that make sense? "Colored roles" sounds like some way of doing it exclusive to the colored race.

Billie had jet black curls molded and polished by a Harlem coiffeur, and big dark eyes with a red underglow. Her skin was of the soft creamy texture of caramel pudding, and she had the beautiful, lovely, easy-to-take curves usually attributed to the Merritt Parkway. But no architect on earth, by whatever name, had designed her curves, regardless of who had made them. Because she felt the need to prove this about her curves to compensate for the color of her indescribably lovely skin, of which, naturally, she was somewhat ashamed, she wore only a fragile slip beneath her skin-tight rose silk evening gown.

Billie's escort for this occasion was a millionaire, the greenest, a white man-about-town who, during his nightlife career, had spent enough money in the Copa to be assured of deference, despite the color of his girl; and from the moment his limousine drew up before the Copa entrance the Copa flunkies began hotfooting about to reindoctrinate him with his own sense of importance.

Their timing was perfect. The Copa was overflowing with Pinktoes just waiting to be impressed. The Copa chorus had just left the floor and the lights had come on briefly so the diners could identify their filets and not find them-

selves chewing on their souvenirs. But after one brief glance in Billie's direction, everyone studiously ignored her. After all, everyone who goes to the Copa is a celebrity. In fact, once you have gained admission to the Copa, you have automatically become a celebrity. Only a celebrities' celebrity, such as having a king of the last great empire forsake his throne for your love, or yourself forsake the fabulous notoriety of your role as motion picture queen to become a legend in smoked glasses, shabby clothes and secrecy, could have overwhelmed that antagonistic audience.

Billie felt her nerves tighten. Sweat broke out between her legs. She steeled herself against trembling. But her body lost its graceful flow of motion and her high heels wobbled. She was trailing her mink coat on the floor, according to the rigid ritual in such places as the Copa. In the center of the dance floor, as they were crossing it to their table reserved at ring-side, her feet got caught in the soft folds of fabulous fur, and she fell forward toward the floor. Being an athletic girl, naturally she wasn't going to fall on her face, so she put forth her hands to catch herself. This posture of bending forward on her hands put too great a strain on the fabric of her dress, so that both her dress and her fragile slip ripped straight up the back, exposing to view the creamy hills of buttocks more captivating than ever seen in the Copa, or anywhere else in public for that matter. Needless to say, in such a posture it looked most inviting.

She had the instant attention of everyone present. Stovepipe pants became suddenly painful and young women were thrown into furious battle with their libidos. Old guys and nearsighted dames fumbled hastily in their pockets and purses for their glasses, mouths dribbling from the overflow of great gushes of saliva. There were several cases of hiccups and strangulation as gobs of half-chewed food went down the wrong pipes, and one old gentleman bit his tongue so severely he lost the services of his young chorus girl indefinitely.

It went as far wrong as it could possibly go. Nothing

*could have been further removed from the way Billie had
planned it. Nevertheless, she accomplished what she had
set out to do. She produced the most sensational entrance
in the history of the Copa, an entrance that has become
a legend.*

On the other hand, consider the case of Henry Hill. All
he wanted to do was make a little joke. He was one of five
porters cleaning a new Horn & Hardart lunchette in Manhattan for the opening next day. They had all been laughing at old Fats, who had come to work all juiced up and kept
trying to argue with the man. The man kept telling Fats
to do this and Fats kept asking the man in a belligerent
tone of voice, You mean do this? And the man would get
mad and say, That's what I said, do this, don't you want
to work? And Fats would say more belligerently than ever,
Yessuh, I wants to work, of course I wants to work, that's
why I'm here; if I didn't want to work I wouldn't have
come to work. Then the man would say, Then what's the
matter with you, if you want to work why don't you go to
work and do some work. Fats would say, That's what I'm
trying to do, is get to work. The man would ask, What's
stopping you then? Fats would reply, I'm just trying to
find out what you mean when you keep saying go to work,
ain't I come to work?

Old Fats is a pistol, the other porters said.

Finally the man saw he wasn't going to get any work
out of old Fats so he told Fats to take a ladder down into
the basement, hoping Fats would have sense enough to stay
down there out of sight. But Fats looked at the ladder and
then looked at the man and said, You mean this ladder,
boss? What other ladder is there, the man said disgustedly.
Fats looked back at the ladder and said, Boss, it wasn't me
who brought this ladder up here.

That knocked out the other porters. Even the man had
to laugh.

All the rest of the night they kept laughing at old Fats
and four o'clock the next morning, when they had about

got the joint cleaned, the man told them to get some buck-
ets of soapy water and go outside and wash the marble
posts alongside the old building. It was cold as hell outside
and the porters looked at the man as though he had gone
crazy. It was then Henry Hill thought he would make a
little joke, being as they had to wash the posts anyway,
so he said to the man, Boss, it weren't us who dirtied them
posts, it was them dogs that live around here.

Didn't nobody laugh. Like the spiritual says, "Way down
yonder by myself, an' Ah couldn' hear nobody pray . . ."
Old Henry couldn't hear nobody laugh. In fact, the other
porters, all of them being colored, got mad at him for
insinuating before the white man that they would stoop to
dirtying posts in the broad open street in the middle of
Manhattan. And the white man got mad at Henry for insinuating that he had ever even thought of any of the
colored fellows dirtying the posts. So one word led to another and the man told Henry he had been working with
colored fellows ever since he had come into the organization, and in all that time he had never once seen a colored
fellow dirty anywhere but in the lavatory and never once
in all that time had he ever had any trouble with the
colored fellows who worked under him, and it was people
like Henry always agitating that caused the Negro Problem anyway. Henry told the man it didn't have anything
to do with the Negro Problem, it was just that any time
anything ever came up about some colored fellows dirtying
some street posts it was people like the man who was always
trying to make out as if nobody but some colored fellows
would dirty a post, whereas over on Third Avenue and
down on the Bowery he had seen white guys dirtying all
over the street; and if he wanted to get down to the nitty-
gritty it was only white guys he had ever seen dirtying in
the street or against a post at all, because the average
colored man had more respect for himself and those about
him, and nine times out of ten he would either go into
a dark alley or duck into a doorway out of sight so nobody
could see him when he had to dirty. The man was getting

madder and madder, and said that was the entire trouble with the Negro Problem; colored people like Henry was always trying to draw a difference between white fellows and colored fellows, when people was just people, colored people was just people like white people was just people. Henry was getting madder and madder too and he said to the man, You don't act like colored people is just people, like white people is just people, and I'd be willing to bet if we was white people instead of colored people you wouldn't ask us to go out there in the cold and wash them dirty posts.

The man got so mad at this he said, Give me a bucket and I'll go out and wash the posts myself, intending to prove by this that a white man would do anything he would ask a colored man to do.

But naturally the colored fellows wouldn't think of letting the white man go out into the cold and wash the posts while they stood inside and watched, so they went out grumbling and shivering and scrubbed down the posts and rinsed them with hot water until they shone white. Then Henry looked up and down the street and, seeing no one in sight, took out his black sprinkler and proceeded to dirty the marble white post he had just cleaned. The other porters did likewise, their black sprinklers silhouetted against the marble white posts and emitting streams of steaming water as though baptizing gigantic white legs in some inherited ritual of fertility. They were laughing to beat all hell when they returned inside.

The man wondered what they found so funny about washing the posts out in the cold, but being as they were black, and the posts were white, he was too sensible to ask. Instead he let them knock off and go home a half hour earlier, and after that Henry became his right-hand man.

Or for that matter, one may study the incident of two cats meeting one dark night in Harlem. It was on a side

*street in the Valley, and not a sound could be heard but
the rustling of rats in the garbage cans; not a light could
be seen but the dim red glow through the cracks in window shades.*

*The white cat looked east and west and north and south,
then started catfooting obliquely toward the northern curb.
The black cat waited until the white cat got in the middle
of the street, then started walking toward the white cat,
staggering as though drunk, and deliberately bumped into
the white cat.*

*Why don'tcha watch where you're going? the black cat
snarled.*

*The white cat saw right off that the black cat was look-
ing for trouble, being as this was not the first time he had
been in Harlem, so he hastened to apologize, I begs your
pardon, sir, and tried to get past the black cat.*

*But the black cat wouldn't let him pass. Whatcha tryna
do? he snarled. You tryna take all the street? I got as much
right to this street as you is. This ain't Arkansas.*

*I'm sorry, the white cat kept apologizing. I didn't see
you.*

*The black cat bristled. Whatcha mean you didn't see
me? You tryna say I'm so black you can't see me in the
dark?*

*Why don't you let me go about my business, buddy; I
ain't looking for trouble, the white cat miaowed pacifically.*

*Don't call me your buddy; I ain't your buddy, you white
son of a puss, the black cat spat.*

*The white cat began getting mad too. Don't call me a
son of a puss, you black son of a bitch, he snarled.*

*You calling me a son of a bitch! the black cat yowled,
whipping out his claws. This is where I'm gonna cut your
throat, saying I'm mixed with dog!*

*Naturally, the white cat whipped out his own claws, and
for a moment they stood there, yowling at each other.*

*Some of the colored residents along the way were awak-
ened by all the caterwauling and opened their windows to
throw some whiskey bottles at the cats. But when they saw*

it was a black cat squared off with a white cat they jumped into their clothes and rushed down into the street to see the black cat beat the hell out of the white cat.

But seeing the white cat with his claws unsheathed also, and in all four paws to boot, the black cat was not so anxious to fight anymore, so he asked the white cat chummily, Say, man, ain't you from Cincinnati, being as when home folks from places like Cincinnati ran across one another in New York they acted like bosom friends, regardless of color, and went off somewhere to get drunk.

The white cat was not anxious to fight either, so he replied with lots of enthusiasm, Yeah, man, I'm from Cincy, how could you tell? Although frankly this white cat was born and raised in Jersey City, and merely slipped across the river into Harlem every now and then to find some black pussy and change his luck.

But the black cat was so relieved to get out of fighting he replied with equal enthusiasm, Man, I could tell you was from Cincy the way you squared off there like Ezzard Charles; you know old Ez, don't you?

Do I know Ez! the white cat exclaimed. He wants to know do I know Ez. Me and Ez is running buddies.

By this time the colored spectators were impatient for some action. Come on and fight, they demanded. What's this supposed to be, a hugging match? You two cats ain't funny that way, are you?

But these two cats weren't paying any attention to these colored people urging them to fight. The white cat had his jive going about Cincinnati, where he had never been, and seeing how good it was taking asked the black cat jubilantly, You know old Smokey Joe? figuring that was going to be the clincher.

But he didn't figure on how sensitive black cats were about being black. Smokey Joe? Who he? the black cat snarled indignantly. How come I got to know somebody named Smokey Joe? You must figure all us black cats knows is somebody called Smokey.

So all of a sudden they were yowling at each other again, slashing the air with their claws and carrying on like two cats who really might want to fight if they could find anything to fight about.

The audience of black people figured they were seeing some action, and began jumping up and down and saying how that black cat was going to put together a Sugar Ray Robinson combination, and fold that white cat like all good cookbooks say "fold whipped egg whites into batter." But being as nothing happened, someone said finally, Them cats ain't fighting, them cats is just loving, them is fairy cats, or else they is bulldiking. These colored people got so mad at being cheated out of seeing the black cat whip hell out of the white cat they jumped on both of these cats and whaled them good.

Those cats took off north on Lenox Avenue and didn't stop running until they'd reached 135th Street.

Brother, the white cat said to the black cat as they were sitting on a stoop, catching their breath and licking their wounds, I don't mean to insinuate anything, but what made them black people get so mad at you, as black as you is too?

The black cat looked at the white cat sorrowfully and said, Brother, that's what the trouble is: them is people and us is cats. So let's leave them people to their peopling and us cats go catting. I know where there is a cathouse near here with nothing but good pussies.

Pussy is all a tomcat needs, the white cat said, falling in beside the black cat as they catfooted for the cathouse.

Although Mama Meow, the madame, or landprop as they say in that part of the world, conducts a cathouse in a land of black cats, she is not at all opposed to serving white cats, which is more than can be said of the attitude of many white cats toward serving black cats. In fact, Mama Meow prefers serving white cats to black cats. If she were not a black pussy herself, cats might say she is prejudiced. But such is not the case. It is merely that she has found *white cats easier to serve; they pay more for the pussy, demand less from the pussy, and are not always trying to take the pussy home.*

So naturally Mama Meow greeted this white cat effusively, and even tolerated this black cat because he had brought such a fine white cat to buy some pussy. In fact, being as business was slow at that time she exhibited her whole stable of pussies.

These tomcats had never seen such an extraordinary collection of fine pussies. In fact there was such a variety of pussies offered, these tomcats could not make up their mind which they wanted. Obviously this aroused great suspicions in Mama Meow and she asked to see some green before these tomcats have come on a freeby. When it came out that this white cat was flat, and this black cat not even that, she threw them out into the alley.

Brother, the black cat said as they picked their way over the cold wet bricks, you know one thing, it's getting so nowadays the only friend a black cat's got is a pocketful of catnip.

Brother, the white cat said, it's just the same with us, only we got more pussies to feed.

All of which goes to demonstrate that nothing ever goes right for cats either.

Still cats keep right on catting, just the same as all these old bats one sees around keep right on batting, and as everyone knows who reads the daily newspapers, rats keep right on ratting.

FOR THE MOST PART *the American Negroes are descendants in whole or in fractions of African Negroes who were brought from Africa to the Western Hemisphere as slaves during the two centuries preceding the Civil War. Some, however, are descended from Negroes who came, and were not brought, from various countries in Africa, Europe and South America, as did emigrants of other races.*

There are no available statistics on the percentage of American Negroes who still retain the unmixed blood of their ancestors. Perhaps less than half. Many Negroes have only a minor fraction of Negro blood: one-fourth, one-eighth, one-sixteenth, one-thirty-second. Not so long ago, the American newspapers eulogized a great "Negro" leader, of whom they said had only "one-sixty-fourth part of Negro blood," for remaining in "his race" and fighting the battles of "his people."

"Are they produced by osmosis?" a visitor from Mars might reasonably ask. "Are some of them bleached?"

Upon receiving a negative reply, he might still desire to know, "But what is his race? Who are his people?"

Which brings us to the question of: Who is a Negro? Among the English there is the belief, "God made the Negro in the night, and forgot to paint him white." But in the United States, we do not ascribe these deficiencies to God. The legal definition of a Negro in the U.S.A. is anyone who has any Negro blood. Webster defines a Negro thusly: "1. A person of the typical African branch of the black race (formerly called the Ethiopian) inhabiting the Sudan, or loosely, of any of the black races of Africa, including, besides the Negroes proper, Bantus, Pygmies, Hot-

tentots, and Bushmen. 2. (usually not cap) A black man: esp., a person having more or less Negro blood." In the southern part of the United States, any person having as much, or as little, as one drop of Negro blood is accredited as being a bona fide Negro. However, this drop of blood is presumed to be mixed throughout all the remaining white blood contained in the Negro's bloodstream. And how is this brought about? Easily. Webster defines mix thusly: "1. To unite or blend into one mass of compound, as by stirring together . . . 2. To unite with in company . . . hold intercourse. 3. To form by mingling . . ."

But if one were to search for Negro blood along such lines, my God, imagine the confusion. Why, one might discover many bona fide white persons with more than one drop of Negro blood, and many bona fide Negroes with less. Therefore, the only valid definition of a Negro is a person who, for one reason or another, is known to be a Negro, whether he is white or not. One had better not go about calling dark-skinned white persons Negroes just because they might have a few drops of Negro blood running around in their bloodstreams, when they are known to be white. For the purpose of this journal, we must adhere to this definition and designate persons as Negroes who are known to be Negroes. How else could we seriously consider the Negro problem, if white people kept popping up in subsequent chapters carrying drops of Negro blood.

There is no question in the United States as to whether known Negroes are citizens, providing they fulfill the requirements of the Constitution on this point. The question is what does citizenship mean as applied to Negroes. In all areas of the United States we find these Negro citizens being segregated and discriminated against in various circumstances of life as though they were not citizens at all; which, if not downright illegal, is certainly most confusing.

As a consequence of all this confusion, throughout all the United States, most Negroes live together, side by side, in their own communities, such being known as black-belts, dark-towns, nigger-slums, fly-burgs, smoke-villes or simply

*colored districts; or by some name deriving from local
history, real estate developments or special racial delica-
cies, as for instance "Catfish Row" and "Possum Run,"
and "Chitterling Switch."*

*There are persons who contend that Negroes desire to live
together in this manner, and others who contend they do not.
This, however, has the oracular appeal of those debates, so
popular in southern Negro colleges, on "which is the more
destructive, fire or water?" The fact is that Negroes have to
live together in their own communities because there is no
other place.*

*Harlem, U.S.A., is such a community. It is located in
upper Manhattan, and at the beginning was bounded on the
south by 110th Street which borders Central Park, on the
east loosely by Fifth Avenue, and on the west loosely by
Amsterdam Avenue. At one time in the memory of war
veterans 135th Street formed its northern boundary, then it
pushed up to 145th Street, to 155th Street, and now it's to
hell and gone in all directions, north, east, south and west,
from the Harlem River to the Hudson, its black tentacles
reaching deep into the white sections of Washington
Heights, not to mention its other black parts; and on hot
summer Sunday afternoons the upper regions of Central
Park, bordering the Lagoon, take on the distinctive aspects
of a Mississippi swimming hole.*

*Upwards of half a million Negroes live there. That makes
it a city of an impressive population, a city of black, brown
and yellow-skinned people, known as Negroes. How many
cities are there in the world with a population of over half a
million? However, there are many other differences between
Harlem and other large cities than just the color of its inhabitants. One difference is that Harlem is not incorporated as a
city, but is a part of Manhattan, which in turn is a borough
of New York City. However the chief difference is in the
character of its people.*

*The inhabitants of Harlem have faith. They believe in the
Lord and they believe in the Jew and they believe in the dollar. The Lord and the Jews they have, but the dollar they*

have not; but this does not diminish their faith in it. In fact, more than any other people in the world, they believe that the dollar, like the great whore of legend, will give them everything.

They know, of course, that the Lord is the source of all good things—well, most, anyway. But the Lord is in heaven, and what with all the big international shooting and cutting and really important sinning all over this earth, the Lord is too busy to give much time to their immediate problems. But the dollar is right down here on earth, right here in the City of New York; Wall Street is overflowing with them. The trouble is the white folks have got them locked up. But if you keep pestering the white folks you might get enough of those almighty dollars back to back so you won't have to keep pestering the Lord.

They believe in other things too. They believe in bright-colored clothes and in the efficacy of intoxicating beverages and in the wonderful exhilaration derived from screwing. One desires to employ a term less idiomatic than screwing *in this historical treatise, such as fornicating, cohabiting, or even plain propagating, but there is nothing plain about this propagating; one is limited by a language that was not designed to describe the acrobatics and athletics involved in this contest.*

Let us point out that Webster defines the verb screw *thusly: "—v.t. 1. To turn as a screw; to apply a screw to; to press, insert, move, or the like, by a screw or screws. 2 a. To twist; contort; as, to screw the eyes (how do you do that, Danny?). b. To twist or strain, esp. to suit one's purposes. 3. To fasten with or as with a screw . . . 4. To force as if by pressure of screws; as, to screw a shopkeeper . . .—v.i. 1. To turn as or like a screw. 2. To turn with a twisting motion . . ."*

And the beautiful part about screwing is that it does not require the assistance of either the Lord or the Jew, although in recent years the dollar is becoming more and more meddlesome. But the faith is still there. As long as one screws, one hopes to screw again. Throughout the history of man-

kind, screwing has been the greatest boon to the poor and the oppressed. When nothing else will do, a good screw will renew. That's why there are so damn many of us.

There are those who believe that Father Divine is God. And those who believe that white women prefer black men. And those who believe that chewing the dried root of a certain weed (see Nathan the root man) will protect one from being poisoned by wood alcohol. Some who believe profoundly that dreams foretell the winning numbers in the lottery. Others who believe that Negroes are just naturally stronger than white people. Still others who believe that Negro men are bigger privately than white men and Negro women are better privately than white women. And even those who believe if you drink sweet milk while eating watermelon it will kill you.

That is why there are more liquor stores, more churches, more whorehouses, more lying, more laughter, more screwing, fighting and footracing, more numbers players, more freeloaders, more sports, more bars, more jukeboxes, more jazz, more crime, more chitterlings eaten, more singing and dancing, more knife-toting and loud-mouthing, more praying and shouting, more credit-buying, more ducking and dodging the collectors, more worrying and complaining, and with all of that more fun to be had than in any other city in the world. The people have faith. Why else would a forty-five-dollar-a-week porter go out on a Saturday night and blow his whole pay on a pickup in a bar? He's got faith.

White people go up to Harlem to warm themselves at this faith. They bask before it. There is nothing more inspiring to a fifteen-thousand-dollar-a-year white man, depressed by taxes and debts and ulcers and fear of impotence and a nagging wife, than a trip to Mamie Mason's in Harlem and seeing how Negroes manage on one-third of that income and listening to them laughing. Not only laughing at what is considered funny, but laughing at all the things considered unfunny, laughing at the white people and laughing at themselves, laughing at the strange forms injustice takes and at the ofttimes ridiculousness of righteousness. What is more cheering than laughter? Aphrodisiacal too.

Once a famous white man, explaining his enthusiasm for Mamie Mason's parties, said, "When I go there I forget all my problems, my worries, my burdens; I forget my wife and children and my stock market losses; I feel so warm and comfortable and relaxed that I don't want to do anything but fornicate."

So you can see that this faith is not only historical but also hysterical, not only inspiring and uplifting and enriching, but also catching. And Mamie Mason had faith.

REALLY, all Mamie Mason ever wanted was just to be the "Hostess with the Mostess." And also to serve the Negro Problem in whatever way she could; and if this called for the serving of Negroes, to white people, of course, that's the only reason she wanted to be the "hostess with the mostess." That's all she ever wanted, just to serve the Negro Problem up to white people and be loved by white people for this service; sex didn't really matter, and that's the real reason she wanted to be slim and chic and svelte and live adventurously and dangerously and be recognized as the undisputed social leader of Harlem, U.S.A., regardless of what envious people said. Just to be able to wear her black satin sheath dress, size twelve, and look lovable, the better to entertain all the important race leaders and their white sponsors at fabulous parties in her Harlem apartment, control their lives, separate husband and wife, free white women from the chains of racist tradition and spread the joy from male white buck hunters, and naturally make them all so miserable they'd have to come to her for love. Just to keep faith in the goodness of loving and being loved and to convert others to this faith, both white people and colored people, and thereby inspire such an abundance of interracial loving as to solve the Negro Problem—if not solve it, at least tire it out. And if because of such zealous service to the Negro Problem, her picture appeared regularly in all the Negro newspapers above the caption *Mrs. Mamie Mason, the celebrated Harlem hostess, entertained* . . . it wasn't her fault. You can't blame the girl for wanting to give her bit, although some jealous women claimed it was more than a bit, in fact, a great deal more.

The trouble was that Mamie was by rights a fat woman. And no one loves a fat woman, if they can do better. So for Mamie to be able to wear her black satin sheath dress, size twelve, and achieve that Paris silhouette, required keeping to a rigid diet under her doctor's supervision at incalculable personal torture and at a cost that could easily have maintained her in promiscuous gluttony. There were times when just a glimpse of big juicy frankfurters set her glands to working so furiously she wondered if it was worth it.

Mamie was a strikingly attractive woman whose features in repose reminded one of the colored lithographs of East Indian Maharanees. Her complexion was of a color termed "yellow" by other Negroes and "tan" by white people. She had raven black hair, slightly curled, which she often wore parted in the center and gathered in a bun at the back in what was considered a Spanish style. And she had huge dark slumbrous eyes colored a muddy maroon and curtained by fringes of black lashes incredibly thick and long: the kind of eyes generally described as "bedroom" eyes. One begins to understand how Webster felt when writing his definition, "to *screw* the eyes," but one still wonders how it's done.

White people marveled at her wonderful good humor. Isn't that Mamie sweet? they would say. She's always so happy. But do you think she should diet so much? Wouldn't she be exquisite if she were really fat? Of course, these ones thinking about how fine it would be if she were really fat were obviously jealous wives.

Few persons outside of her husband had ever seen Mamie when she was neither smiling nor laughing, both of which she could perform convincingly while in a state of raging fury. This was a great tribute to her courage because her constant hunger kept her in a constant state of evil.

And as hungry as she was all of the time, it was a downright dirty shame for overfed, well-screwed and seemingly contented wives to entertain such evil opinions of her and express them so maliciously. After all, it's quite an accomplishment for a thirty-nine-year-old, big-boned, hard-drinking, ambitious, energetic woman with the instincts of a lecherous glutton to get into a black satin sheath dress size twelve, much less wear the damn thing with any degree of assurance. It should have inspired only the highest admiration, even awe; no doubt it did inspire considerable awe. But it should never have produced the envy and fear and jealousy that it did, nor all the diabolical machinations to which she was subjected. The dirty little sugar-coated feminine tricks, such as the one Zoe played on her, were really unforgivable.

Zoe was Mamie's best friend, too; or rather one of her best friends; her best friend in Chicago, say, because all women who were important to her in any way, or married to important men, were her "best friends." Zoe's husband, Zeke, was treasurer of a big Negro insurance corporation in Chicago, and they owned a big brick house stuffed with wonderfully fascinating furniture from science fiction and two big diamond-back Cadillacs. Naturally, Zoe was Mamie's best friend.

Mamie always stayed with them when she visited Chicago, but she never had any intention whatsoever, then or at any other time, of trying to steal Zoe's husband. How could she, when she already had one husband, and he and Zeke were the best of friends, too?

All she wanted was to wear her black satin sheath dress and go with Zeke in one of his diamond-back Cadillacs to the exclusive party being given by Cornell Crane III, the big white newspaper publisher and department store tycoon, for the mayor's Committee on Race Relations. And the only reason she wanted to go with Zeke was to serve the Negro Problem, being as Zeke was a very distinguished and important man, big man too, over six feet tall and weighing more than two hundred pounds and giving the impression of great competence, and just the type of Negro man needed for the service. And no doubt there would be many white women there desirous of his services, making it not only inevitable but absolutely essential that she exchange him for some equally big and important white man desirous of her own services, perhaps Cornell Crane III himself.

After all, it had been Zoe's idea for Zeke to take her to the party, her only contribution to this idea was not to waste him.

It was practically the first thing Zoe had said when Mamie arrived that afternoon unexpectedly, after having kept to a rigid diet for the past thirty days, with not a thought of Zeke taking her to the function: "Honey, I'm so glad you came, you can go to Corney's party with Zeke and shoo away those bitches who keep curling their tails at him."

Mamie had really come to see Zoe off on a two-week trip to Los Angeles to cover the sunrise wedding of two Negro movie celebrities for the Negro newspaper for which she was society editor. She was very much surprised to find Zeke attending this function. "I thought he and Corney couldn't hit it off," she said.

"Honey, you know Zeke wouldn't cross the street to see Corney, but the Committee asked him especially to attend. They want to show a united front."

"Zoe, sugar, why don't you stay over and come too; we three could have some fun."

"Don't tempt me, Mamie honey, you know how I positively loathe going to the West Coast to watch those clowns perform," she rattled on innocently. "But they asked for me especially and the groom, bless his sweet heart, is paying me a thousand dollars and all my expenses for the publicity."

Up to that point the whole thing was just a natural coincidence. So it was perfectly natural for Mamie to suddenly remember to exclaim, Oh, sugar, I almost forgot, and that's all I've been thinking about is a new satin dress I got at Lord & Taylor's on sale for sixty dollars. Being a woman Zoe couldn't resist insisting that Mamie put on the dress right away, as though all the wild horses in Wyoming could have stopped her. It follows that Zoe was instantly envious of the sleek shiny satin-sheathed size-twelve shape the dress gave Mamie, since she required the services of shoehorns, sledgehammers and brute force to get all of her own pampered, overnourished, well-screwed flesh wedged into a size sixteen. And this envy would make her say maliciously, Oh, honey, it's perfectly stunning, a dream, absolutely a knockout, I just wonder what happens if you sneeze. And at that Mamie would reply coyly, I'll have it off before coming in a draft. And that Zoe would suddenly realize Mamie hadn't been fasting as hard as Mahatma Gandhi just for freedom, and begin wondering just what did Mamie mean by all this coming. And next she would start putting two and two together, or rather one and the other together, and come up with the conclusion that this was just too much coincidence to come naturally, and if Mamie thought that Zeke would look at anyone like her, she'd just tell her a thing or two, such as, Oh honey, what happens to your breasts when you diet like that, do they shrink up like dried bladders or just hang down like lean snakes? It goes without saying that this allusion to her weakest charm would get Mamie's nigger up too, as they say in that part of the world, and she would retort with sweet acid bile, Oh, sugar, hasn't Zeke ever told you that big men like titties that fit right into their mouths so they can feel like babies when they return to the womb.

Naturally this put Zoe into such a raging fury that she rushed downstairs and took a twenty-two-pound turkey cock out of the deep freezer, stuffed it with a highly seasoned mixture of onions, eggs, oysters, butter and bread crumbs, and slammed it into the oven to roast.

When Zeke came home he found Zoe in the kitchen, basting a turkey and looking hot, sweating and mad; and Mamie reclining on her bed in the guest room upstairs clad in a red silk robe and pale green pajamas, holding a perfume-drenched handkerchief to her nose, and looking pale, hungry and sad.

Zoe set the table for three and called Mamie to dinner, saying she had roasted a big milk-fed turkey cock especially for her, knowing how much she liked er, ah, turkey. When Mamie declined, Zoe insisted that she sit to the table out of politeness and if she didn't want to eat it for fear of spoiling her intriguing look she was sorry but she couldn't provide one for her to suck, and she could just have a drink with them. So Mamie had to sit there with the good Scotch highball setting fire to her hunger and watch big male Zeke biting big succulent chunks of black meat out of a big juicy turkey leg with his big strong white teeth and think of his big black potency to keep her thoughts distracted. She suffered the tortures of the damned.

But the meanest trick of all was for Zoe to take all the whiskey from the cabinet in the living room to the kitchen and then set the cock on the warmer out in plain sight on top of the stove, so in case anybody should want a drink of whiskey they would be perfectly welcome to sample the cock.

When Zeke left to drive Zoe to the airport to catch her plane, Mamie rushed back upstairs and drenched the guest room with perfume and locked herself in. But the room was situated directly above the kitchen and she didn't know the hot air duct had an opening into the kitchen and that Zoe had opened it. All she knew was that damned tantalizing smell of roast cock was outpowering the almost suffocating scent of thirty dollars' worth of perfume. She just had to have a drink to pacify her mind.

But there wasn't a drop of whiskey to be had anywhere but in the kitchen. So she was forced to go into the kitchen against her will. After she'd had a highball she was forced against her will to nibble a piece of crisp turkey cock skin and take a forkful, no, two, of stuffing to keep from getting drunk. But that was all. She was a very strong-willed woman and by exercising the full strength of her will she managed to turn her back on the tempting turkey cock and start back upstairs to her room to dress. The trouble was, the big brown roasted cock was too tempting and she never made it. Halfway up the stairs she was assailed, no, assaulted by such brutal, ferocious, merciless, insensate hunger, she couldn't mount another step. Out of sheer physical necessity she had to go back and sample a small helping of both white meat and black meat, with a small serving of stuffing thrown in, and just enough gravy to make it nice and slippery.

After that she was all right. She made it back to her room without difficulty. She was still ravenous for some turkey cock, but she had herself well under control and the weakness had left. The only thing now was that her empty stomach, suddenly confronted by a small token of cock, had pounced on it with all its juices, and had become woefully inflated, such as happens to the female stomach when it samples too much cock. She was still able to get into her dress, but it appeared as though she were a virgin trying to hide her shame. She could still go, of course, but no thirty-nine-year-old promiscuous woman wants to go to a swank party at Cornell Crane III's looking like a teen-ager seven months after her first session with a cock.

Suddenly she was overcome by such uncontrollable rage at allowing herself to be tricked, she staggered weakly down to the kitchen and gobbled an enormous piece of turkey before realizing she still had on her black satin sheath dress, size twelve, which she had boasted she'd have off before coming. She jerked it off savagely, and none too soon, because the seams were beginning to burst from all the cock she had in her and she couldn't stop cramming herself because she felt herself getting sick and she had to keep rapidly taking more cock to keep the cock in her which she already had. She was moaning and gasping until abruptly she felt all her glands open and turkey came gushing from her mouth at the same instant of a great gushing from all sources. She barely made it to the sink. For a time she hung there, too weak to move, but when her strength returned she drank a stiff Scotch highball and seated herself comfortably at the table, looking smug and pleased. It was so good the first time, daddy, she said to the cock, you got to do it to me again.

When Zeke returned from the airport he found her sitting there in her lace-edged black nylon slip, stomach bulged and eyes glazed with satiation, and a smile of complete satisfaction curled about her greasy lips. Couldn't take it, eh, girl? he said sympathetically. I can take it, she said, but I took too much. He looked at the turkey carcass and grinned know-ingly. You ain't the first woman to be screwed by a bird, he said. So he went to the party alone.

And Mamie wasn't mad at anyone. It was just a case of a month of privation confronted with a tremendous cock. The only thing Mamie Mason could never forgive was for some Negro woman to boycott her parties, thinking she was aping white women by building a wall about her black privacy when if the truth be known those old Confederate States' walls about white privacy had already come tumbling down. Mamie could forgive everything else anyone did. And there was only one Negro woman who had ever dared commit such a reckless breach of etiquette, acting like her black privacy was too good for white interference. That Negro woman was one Juanita Wright, the wife of the great Negro race leader, Wallace Wright, who ought to be the first Ne-gro woman in the great fornication for racial equality in-stead of thinking she was being screwed by a white man just because Wallace claimed only one-sixty-fourth Negro blood. Mamie's one ambition was to get even with Juanita by prov-ing to everybody it wasn't disdain that kept Juanita from her parties but shame because she had used so much alum to shrink her privacy it had dried up. As for Zoe, Mamie gave Zoe her due and looked forward eagerly to having her and Zeke as house guests and taking another crack at swapping Zeke for some big white man. Mamie Mason had faith. If she hadn't, why would she have returned to Harlem and started dieting all over again?

THIS FAITH OF MAMIE MASON shone so brightly it oftentimes illuminated areas as far away as Midtown.

No one who was there will ever forget that night when the mere presence of three Negroes from uptown caused so many people to become lit, people who had no intention of becoming lit, and others who, under the circumstances, had no right to get lit. And just because of Mamie Mason's faith in the efficacy of radio.

She believed so profoundly in its miraculous effects that, during a moment of tender intimacy, she arranged with her very dear white friend, Paul Patterson, who conducted the famous radio book review program, *Author Talks Back,* for the guest appearances of those two Negro authors, Edward Schooley and H. Randal Pine. It had nothing to do with the fact that afterwards she arranged a rendez-vous that night for herself with another famous white gentleman, an elderly and compassionate man who had contributed so abundantly of his time and energies, not to mention his money, to better relations between the black and white races. When this gentleman came to her in his declining years to taste the fruits of his travail, and naturally the fruit juice, how could she refuse? It just seemed such a pity to waste a perfectly valid excuse for being out all night by actually attending the festivities.

Edward Schooley and H. Randal Pine were co-authors of a book on drug addiction entitled *Dreamland,* which had been written twenty years previous by anonymous persons on a WPA project. The book had been recently published by the New York firm of Thomas Hightower and Son. It was a Hightower book. And Lou Reynolds, another of Mamie's fine upstanding white friends, was the editor.

To get his boys warmed up for the coming battle of wits, Lou had staged a little cocktail party in his East 50th Street apartment. Naturally Julius Mason was there. Julius was Joe Mason's brother, and Joe Mason was Mamie Mason's husband, therefore Julius had a perfect right to be there, whether Lou Reynolds thought so or not.

Julius had arrived in the company of his future boss, Art Wills, another of Mamie's fine upstanding white friends. The fact that they had not been invited did not bother them in the least, especially in view of the fact they had consumed several martinis before arriving and were now looking for some fine hot cunny, as what man isn't who attends cocktail parties?

Julius was a hard-working married journalist, although for the time being he had parked his wife in San Francisco and was now following his natural inclinations. He had come to New York to work on the editorial staff of the new Negro picture magazine scheduled to begin publication the following month.

Art Wills was currently employed as an editor for the publishing firm that competed fiercely with Lou's firm. However, he was supposed to resign his job to become managing editor of the Negro picture magazine, when and if sufficient funds were raised to begin publication, or, more to the point, to pay his salary.

During another of her moments of tender intimacy with a big fine white man, which, if all were put together, would make a Swiss watch, Mamie had persuaded Art to employ Julius as his star reporter. Naturally Art was only too willing to comply, being as she asked him in advance. After all, it wasn't his money; in fact, there wasn't any money.

Of course Mamie's motives had nothing to do with the intention of assuring herself the monthly publication of her picture in the proposed magazine. Naturally not! It was all for the Negro Problem. Julius was a Negro, wasn't he; and being underfoot all the time he was certainly a problem.

Therefore, as a consequence of these accumulated assurances, Art banged on Lou's door with the greatest of confidence.

Lou opened the door and gave him a jaundiced look. "This ain't the house," he said.

"That's all right, I wasn't invited," Art replied.

Since Art was a great deal bigger than Lou, Julius pushed into the apartment unperturbed and left the two white men to fight it out.

"Who's he?" Lou asked.

"He's a writer too."

"My God, another one. Who's going to be left to chop the cotton and sing 'Old Man River'?"

Art chuckled. "You and me."

By then Julius had already found the cocktail tray and was looking about for some fine woman to join him in a toast. He saw a bushy-headed colored man conversing intellectually with an academic-looking white woman, and figuring no academic-looking white woman would voluntarily be conversing intellectually at a time like that, he headed in their direction. He took a chance on the man being Schooley because the only name he could remember was "Eddy." But being as he was the world's worst guesser, naturally the colored gentleman was Pine.

The fact is Schooley had not yet arrived. Only his guests had put in their appearance. As for himself, Schooley had spent all afternoon trying to revive his unaccountably reluctant ambassador of goodwill. When he had awakened that noon in bed with his anxious white hostess, Merto, he had been greatly humiliated and chagrined to find that member of his entourage unable to perform the expected return of courtesy for her hospitality. Needless to say, his anxious white hostess was not a little put out, especially after such a feverish night of anticipation. Not to mention his white host, Maurice, who had been patiently peeking through the key-hole in hot expectation of what he would see. It goes without saying that his anxious white hostess applied all of the respiratory tricks she knew. But still the ungrateful member remained supine. Naturally, she was greatly astonished. The member looked sound enough. The size was right, it looked positively burly against her white thighs. And it was black enough, in fact it was considerably blacker than all the rest of Schooley. But for some unknown reason it simply would not come to life.

And that is how it happened that Schooley's deflated ego developed such a great thirst for strong liquor. Ever since he had been rushing from one smart Midtown bar to another, forgetful of his pocketbook; but fortunately his anxious white hostess had had the foresight to remember hers. However he did not forget to invite all his newly acquired white friends to Lou's cocktail party, possibly in the hope of finding a specialist among them to revive his member.

But the strange part about it is that not once during those long hours of drinking had he been assailed by a doubt as to the affinity of drug addiction to the Negro Problem, which goes to show how far-reaching the Negro Problem is in all its ramifications. Schooley swore he was going to knock the white folks' racial preconceptions to hell and gone, limp member or no limp member. By God, he was going to shock the supremacy piss out of their white-livered bladders. He was going to knock them on their hypocritical asses and kick them in their guilt-ridden balls, which is more than he would have said if his limp member had got as aggressive as he had. The only trouble was he fought his great fight prematurely and gave the white folks such a scare they slipped a mickey into his drink. At least that's the way it appeared to him. But even so, he was not despaired. Pine would carry on. Not for nothing was Pine named after the sturdy tree that had supplied the world with so many mighty poles. Pine would pick up the great fight where he, Schooley, had fallen to the enemy.

But Pine had already exploded his big gun on Julius for calling him Eddy and it had precipitated such an articulate discussion of the Negro Problem as to sidetrack all affinity with dope addiction.

"All Negroes should stay mad," a white lady commended him. "The way you are treated."

"That wouldn't help," a white man contradicted. "Cool heads are needed to solve this problem."

"You've been cool long enough," a flushed white lady said to Julius in so pointed a manner he felt called upon to defend himself.

"I'm not cool—" he began, truthfully enough, but another white lady cut him off:

"Negroes must always keep a hard—"

She never got to finish, or maybe she had finished, when the angry shout of Lou Reynolds silenced the din: "Where's Schooley?"

The apartment was already packed with people whom Schooley had invited and still more were arriving, but as to Schooley's whereabouts, none knew or were willing to admit they knew. It was time for Lou and his boys to depart for the studio, but Schooley's guests were very reluctant to leave before their host arrived, especially as there were still cocktails to be drunk; and naturally Lou was even more reluctant to leave them in his apartment, especially as he was not acquainted with a single one of them. But with a sudden stroke of genius he announced that the liquor had given out, and they left of their own accord.

And was Lou horrified to learn that Schooley had also invited them to the studio, which was in walking distance, to witness the broadcast. So they started down the sidewalk in a long ragged procession headed by Lou and Pine.

Passers-by, doubtless white liberals interested in the Negro Problem, smelling the interesting interracial group and becoming excited by the frolicsome mood which seemed to prevail, joined the procession, thinking there might be some frustrations to be alleviated, and were delightfully surprised to find themselves being ushered into reserved seats in a big broadcasting studio. Only the first two rows of seats had been reserved and it was necessary to clear two additional rows to seat all the invited guests. Growing suspicious, the ushers began asking the tail-enders who invited them, and discovered many who could only reply, "Me too."

On the stage were a table and five chairs. It was a very large table and each place was equipped with microphone, ashtray, pencil and pad and water glass. The scene bore a striking resemblance to a stage set for a Congressional investigation. The two culprits charged with subversion would sit facing the audience, in the full glare of public condemnation. The chairman of the investigating committee would sit at the head of the table; across from him, at the foot, would sit the investigating attorney. While the defense attorney would sit with his back to the audience, so that his expressions and gestures would remain unobserved and his pleas unheard.

At least it seemed to have that effect on Pine. When he mounted the stage, accompanied by Lou, he gave the appearance of a prisoner probing his soul for the answer to whether he was then or had been a Communist, and whether or not it was a fact that his best friends were still Communists, answer yes or no.

However, what was actually to take place was the radio program *Author Talks Back*. It was the MC who sat at the head of the table, Mamie's intimate friend Paul Patterson, an amiable and forgiving man who condemned no author, be he black or white, for perpetrating an insult to public intelligence so long as he, Paul Patterson, got his own two thousand dollars weekly. And it was the night's invited critic who sat opposite to him, in this case Mr. S. P. Bile, book critic for the very conservative morning newspaper *The Daily Liar*. He was a small, bright-eyed man with a very red mouth surrounded by a thick dark brush of moustache and beard, which gave him a very suggestive appearance, to say the least. The "expert," a reformed drug addict from Drug Addicts Anonymous, referred to as "Mr. X," might have once been a white man but was now very definitely a member of the gray race. The two seats facing the audience were reserved, of course, for the authors, Mr. Pine and Mr. Schooley, but Mr. Schooley had not yet arrived. However, the program was not yet on the air.

"Where's Mr. Schooley?" Mr. Patterson asked the approaching editor and author.

Reluctantly and wordlessly, Mr. Pine sat down.

Lou gave a marvelous impersonation of a wife-killer confessing his crime. "He hasn't arrived."

"I can see that."

"His hostess telephoned that he was suffering severe attacks of nausea."

"Ha!" snorted Mr. Bile. "Trying to read his own book, was he?"

"But he might get here yet," Lou defended.

"Not if he was me," said Mr. Bile.

Mr. Patterson looked at his watch and said smilingly, "We'll just go ahead with Mr. Pine."

Mr. Pine looked as though that was what he had been thinking.

A red light glowed and an usher stepped to the front of the stage with a sign reading: WE'RE ON THE AIR. And then a sudden commotion was heard and Schooley reeled up the stairs and staggered across the stage and sat heavily in the vacant chair beside his rigid co-author. His glazed eyes looked unseeingly over the darkened auditorium and he smiled benignly into space.

Sitting in the middle of the front row, Julius Mason burst into enthusiastic applause, which stirred the audience to such an ovation one would have thought that Marilyn Monroe had disrobed. As a consequence not a word of Mr. Patterson's opening remarks was heard.

The first comprehensible words following the din formed a question by Mr. Bile directed to Mr. Schooley. "Where, may I ask, did you get your information, authority rather, for this, er, ah, thing?"

Schooley gave a start. "Thing! Whose thing!" Then he caught himself and smiled sternly as though the question were beneath his dignity. Turning to his collaborator he said, "You take it, Pine."

Pine took it.

Mr. Bile looked bored. Mr. Patterson smiled interestedly, as though his thoughts were concerned with distant pleasures, such as to screw the eyes. Every now and then the expert, Mr. X, came in with the same observation, "When I had that monkey on my back——" but no one about the table paid any attention to him and he was never able to get out what happened when he had that monkey on his back, much to the disappointment of several persons in the audience.

At the end of Mr. Pine's discourse, Mr. Patterson asked Mr. Bile, "Are you satisfied?"

Mr. Bile frowned angrily. "Satisfied! I haven't been banging with cocaine and morphine."

Mr. X laughed uproariously.

When he had finished, Mr. Bile asked Mr. Schooley, "Now that Mr. Pine has told us where you got the information for your, er, ah, book, why, may I ask, did you go to the trouble of writing it?"

"Trouble!" Schooley echoed. He tried mightily to get Mr. Bile's face into focus to find out what was the trouble, but Mr. Bile's bearded face somehow so embarrassed him he looked away in shame. "You take it, Pine," he said.

Pine took it. "A writer, any writer——"

"Any number of writers," Mr. Bile interrupted rudely.

"——takes the information that has come to his knowledge and presents it in terms of literature to the best of his, er, abilities."

"You tell 'em, Eddy!" Julius shouted from his front-row seat along with a loyal outburst of clapping, obviously inspired by something other than what Mr. Pine had said, perhaps by the insistent pressure of a feminine leg against his own.

Naturally, when they heard the name *Eddy,* all of Schooley's loyal white guests rallied to his support; and the others, although personally unacquainted with Mr. Schooley, felt constrained to conform, Mr. Schooley being one of the subjects of the Negro Problem, and this being the age of conformity. Thus Schooley was applauded long and lustily and with mounting enthusiasm by all the dedicated white people, for what no one knew, and when the program went off the air a great horde of his admirers swarmed upon the stage and mobbed him with acclamation. Schooley was so moved by their acclaim he felt impelled to invite them all to the little party at Café Society Uptown which Lou had planned in honor of his, er, ah, authors.

A short time later the hilarious gathering, augmented considerably by this lavish invitation, stomped happily into the resplendent confines of that expensive Midtown night club, anticipating the utmost in enjoyment, especially as it was free. The management was unprepared for such a gathering. Time was needed to assemble more tables.

During the interim, Lou Reynolds disappeared.

Mr. Bile hastened to the bar like a thirsting man toward an oasis, with Schooley and Pine at his heels like dark angels of vengeance. Mr. Bile ordered a Scotch whiskey straight and invited Mr. Schooley and Mr. Pine to have a drink like-wise. The bartender approached with the bottle and poured the three of them drinks. Someone standing on the other side of Mr. Bile tapped on the bar, and the bartender poured him a drink. Seeing how easily it worked, someone else tapped on the bar and the bartender poured him a drink. Then someone else tapped and he poured, and someone else tapped and he poured. When all of a sudden Mr. Bile looked up with a startled expression.

"Wait a minute! How many is that?"

"Eight, sir," the bartender responded politely.

Mr. Bile threw a twenty-dollar bill on the bar with an expression that lived up to his name, and when he didn't get back any change he had to fish up some more for a tip.

Julius was down toward the center of the bar and the drinks had run out before he had gotten any response to his own tapping. He looked longingly at the bottles on the shelves and thought of the fifteen cents he had in his pocket. A plump stylish white woman joined him and smiled pleasantly.

"I'd like to congratulate you on a very excellent polemic," she said.

He gave a start. "My polemic?"

She blushed embarrassedly. She didn't wish to put on her glasses for fear of offending him, but she was so near-sighted she couldn't tell one Negro from all the millions of others in the dim night club light.

"Oh, I'm so sorry. I thought you were one of the authors."

"No, I'm just a plain hard-working newspaper journalist."

"I'm just a plain hard-working book editor," she replied. Her gaze strayed toward the bartender who hovered near-by. "I work for the same firm as Lou. You know Lou Reynolds, don't you, the boys', er, two authors' editor?"

"Oh yes, I was at his cocktail party. But I don't see him around now."

"He had to leave."

Julius had been killing time to let her buy the drinks, being as she was white and white people had all the money, but by now his discourtesy was becoming painfully obvious, so he had to buy them himself. They talked pleas-antly of the excellent polemic while consuming three Scotch whiskeys each.

One of those strange pools of silence followed. From somewhere in the background a feminine voice was dis-tinctly heard to remark, "I've been told that Negroes feel superior to Chinese."

And another feminine voice was distinctly heard to re-ply, "Oh, but aren't they? You know what I mean."

Julius ordered two more drinks and smiled courageously, more like a man who didn't have a care in the world than one who didn't have but fifteen cents in his pocket, and meanwhile tried to convince the sympathetic white editor that in spite of her mistake as to his identity, his own po-lemic was nevertheless just as excellent. She seemed not to believe it, and he never got a chance to prove it, because at that moment, Lou Reynolds, fool that he was, chose to return.

And Lou went directly to the bar to join his co-editor who had been conversing with Julius. He was panting as though he had been, er, ah, running.

"Where did you go?" she asked.

"Grand Central Station."

"Oh. I thought you went for more money."

"Of course not. I went to get Schooley a ticket to Chicago."

She laughed and looked about to see if Julius had heard.

But Julius had taken advantage of the situation and had rushed upstairs to the men's lounge and used ten of his last fifteen cents to lock himself in one of the pay toilets.

By then the management had put six large tables end to end down the center of the dining room floor, and Art was calling, "Come on, Julius, they're sitting down."

Bottles of Scotch and Canadian Club were paired at short intervals down the many-legged table, accompanied by bowls of ice cubes and bottles of ginger ale and club soda.

Schooley and Pine occupied the places of honor at the head of the table. They were flanked by Lou Reynolds, who appeared at the critical stage of a fatal illness, and Mr. Bile, whose mouth was working as though he had a bone stuck down his throat, or was desirous of one.

Julius and Art sat facing a pair of whiskey bottles.

All seats were quickly occupied. Everyone ordered club steak sandwiches. The guests began introducing themselves to each other, mostly by first names. The orchestra played dance music and some got up to dance.

Julius danced with a long-legged brunette wearing a flaming red dress.

"I like Negroes," she said.

He tightened his grip on her. "What is it you like most about us?"

"I like your skin."

"Oh!" he said disappointedly. "Is that all?"

"It's so nice and brown and warm, like a good roast."

Speaking of roast made him hungry and he returned to his seat and ate another steak sandwich. Next he danced with a plump matronly blonde.

"You were superb," she said ecstatically.

"I was?" he asked in astonishment. "When was that?"

She giggled shyly. "You're so witty."

"I am? How did you know?"

"Which one are you, Eddy or Randy?"

"I'm Julius."

"I'm going to call you Jule," she said. "My life would make a wonderful book, Jule."

"It would?"

"I'll give you my phone number, if you want to write it."

The music stopped.

Art caught Julius by the arm and steered him across the dance floor and along the dim narrow aisle alongside the wall toward the rear of the dining room.

"They're passing around the hat," he whispered.

"They are? Let's get the hell out of here. All I've got is a nickel."

"Can't. The exit is guarded. We'll go to the john."

Chatting for all the world like two completely gone be-boppers avoiding a houseful of squares to blow a marijuana butt, they ascended the stairs to the lounge. Finding it momentarily deserted, they crouched down behind the balcony overlooking the dining room and watched the uninvited guests at the long banquet table digging disconcertedly for money.

Suddenly the bright lights came on to facilitate the collection, and the two renegades could distinctly see expressions of dismay on the faces of their erstwhile companions. It made them feel good all over.

The bill had come to $540. Lou didn't have but $180. And he had had no expectation of spending half of that. He informed the management that it was not his party, he had only made reservations for six.

The guests protested that Mr. Schooley had invited them. Those who had not caught Mr. Schooley's name called him

Dr. Fooley. Lou said in that case they were Mr. Schooley's
or Dr. Fooley's guests, however they wanted it.

Smiling benignly, Mr. Schooley arose and turned out his
empty pockets, as though to say, little good 'twill do you.

Some guests had to pay for others who didn't have
enough on hand. Some had to write checks. Identifications
were shown. Names and addresses were reluctantly exchanged. Quarrels broke out, but no fighting ensued. Even
after the bill had been settled, dazed financial adjustments
were still taking place.

Pine looked embarrassed. Lou had the appearance of a
stern judge pronouncing a severe but just sentence. Somehow Schooley gave the impression of a patron saint. Mr.
Bile showed the self-contained glee of a scorned man completely vindicated.

Which just goes to show, faith is not always what it appears to be to the uninitiated, but it's faith just the same.

(Author's note: In Harlem idiom a square is a
lain, a doe, a John, a mark—in other parlance
a fool, a chump, a sucker, a simpleton. A five-
cornered square is a square so square as to have
an extra corner; a five-cornered square is a
square's square.)

WHILE HIDING behind the balcony of the lounge, Julius
spotted a Negro doctor who was a good friend of Mamie's
sitting at a small table in the company of two luscious
brownskin babes. He had met Dr. and Mrs. Steele at Mamie's the previous week, and he now noted that neither of
Dr. Steele's present companions in any way whatsoever
resembled Mrs. Steele.

In fact, Julius had become very well acquainted with
Dora Steele only two nights previous when she had attended a meeting of *La Société des Mondaines du Monde
de Harlème* at Mamie's. It had grown rather late and,
being as the Steeles lived in Brooklyn, Mamie had suggested he walk to the subway stop with Dora. They had
gotten as far as the subway stop when Dora suggested
they stop at the Fat Man's, conveniently located directly
beside the kiosk for just such purpose, and have one for
the road. He insisted on treating her for the next round,
and naturally that called for another. Then Dora remembered she'd almost forgotten to see a girl friend who lived
in an apartment across the street. It was about a hat. The
girl was making Dora a hat. But the hat was not finished,
although this girl had been working on this hat ever since

Dora began dropping by with new male acquaintances. So while Julius and Dora were sipping their second highball, presumably waiting for the hat to be finished, the girl friend suddenly remembered she had run out of thread, and had to rush to the emporium posthaste to buy some more. What took her so long was no doubt due to the fact that she found all the emporiums closed at that hour, so she had had to go to a friend to try to borrow some thread. But the friend didn't have any thread either, being as the friend was a postman whose wife was visiting some relatives in the South, and he didn't use thread in his profession.

It happened that while the girl friend was looking for this thread Julius and Dora made the startling discovery that the couch on which they were sitting was really a bed, and it was a pity to let a bed go to waste as tired as Dora was. Sighing prettily, she lay back to rest for the long trip ahead to the continent of Brooklyn. Thinking a gently applied massage to the right places might enhance her rest, he pulled up her dress. It was not as though she were promiscuous, she pleaded gaspingly, but when she thought of her husband being impotent she just couldn't breathe. Happily, he had the presence of mind to pull off her panties to keep her from suffocating. But as it happened, all turned out fine. So when her friend returned from looking for some thread, all she found was the evidence on the couch, which was just as well because there was plenty of sewing yet to be done on the hat.

So that's why Julius felt he was actually a friend of the family; after all he had substituted for Dr. Steele in a marital emergency. But he was surprised to find the doctor, who was sterile, squiring two young women to a night club. He figured that Dr. Steele must surely need some help, even though he might not want it, so he pointed him out to Art and suggested they drop by his table and say hello.

Art was also acquainted with Dr. Steele, although he was not as well acquainted with Dr. Steele's wife as was Julius, and he had no idea that Dr. Steele was impotent.

Nevertheless he thought the suggestion valid, being as there were two babes, and they looked too much for one man to handle even though he be as potent as Pan. So they descended from the lounge and skirted the walls as though they'd just arrived fresh from the outside.

Julius clapped Dr. Steele on the back and shook his hand with gusto, in the prescribed fashion of treating an impotent man squiring two hot brown babes to a night club. "Hello, Johnny, old man. Imagine seeing you here. Me and Art just stopped in for a quick one and I saw you from the bar."

Dr. Steele smiled weakly, knowing he was caught. "I thought I saw you and Art at the party."

"What party?"

"Over there. They're having a big shindig for Schooley and Pine."

"Oh, is that what that is?"

There was only one empty chair at the table and Julius sat down. "Pull up a chair, Art."

Art hesitated until Dr. Steele said, "Hello, Art. Pull up a chair." What else could the man say?

Art pulled up a chair.

By the magic prevailing in such places, a waiter appeared. Dr. Steele's new guests ordered Scotch whiskeys. To be sociable the two young women ordered rum cooler refills. Dr. Steele was drinking bourbon whiskey and he quickly downed what was left and ordered a double on the rocks, from divination no doubt.

"Hello," Julius said to one of Dr. Steele's young babes.

"Hello," she replied.

Dr. Steele introduced them. "This is Bebe and this is Fifi. Julius and Art."

"Hello, Art," Fifi said. "Hello, Julius."

Bebe echoed. Julius echoed. Art echoed.

"What do you do?" Julius asked Fifi. He had tabbed her as the extra. Bebe seemed to be holding on to the doctor.

They were both luscious-looking girls with whole acres of smooth brown shoulders and bosoms exposed.

"I'm in show business," Fifi said.

Art gave Julius a look as though to say, what a question, what other business would such hot brown babes called Bebe and Fifi be in?

But Julius didn't notice. "You too?" he asked Bebe.

She smiled distantly.

Julius was unperturbed. He knew Dr. Steele was impotent. So he danced with Bebe.

Fifi waited for a moment, then asked Art, "Don't you dance?"

So Art danced with Fifi.

"Are you so big all over?" she asked.

Luckily the light was too low to show Art blushing.

Dr. Steele drank his bourbon, like a man of distinction.

Julius danced past the plump blonde whose life would make a wonderful story.

"Where did you go?" she asked. "I was looking for you."

He turned to reply but Bebe turned him back. "One at a time, buster. Unless you know the secret."

He didn't know the secret (neither does the author, girls; what is the secret?) so he decided to give her to Art. The next dance he had with Fifi. Art danced with Bebe. Maybe he knew the secret. Dr. Steele had another bourbon on the rocks, like the gentleman he was.

The dancers sat down and had another round of Scotch whiskeys and rum coolers.

"This sure is a dull place," Fifi said.

"Nothing's keeping us," Julius said. "Let's all go."

"Let's all come," Fifi said.

"Come where?" Julius asked, being as he was from the West and wasn't hip enough to dig this.

Art gave him a look as if to say, what a question.

"I'm all for it," Bebe said. "I'll come."

Dr. Steele looked blank, as a gentleman should.

So they all finished their drinks and stood up. Julius held Fifi's coat. Art held Bebe's coat. After being coated the girls started walking toward the exit. There wasn't anything left for Julius and Art to do but come along with them. No need of standing there and getting in the way of Dr. Steele paying the bill as a gentleman always does.

By the time Dr. Steele got the bill paid and got out into the street they were all waiting for him in a taxi.

"Come over here," Bebe called through the window as though he might come somewhere else.

Dr. Steele came over there. He and Art sat on the jump seats. Julius sat between the girls on the back seat. Fifi had given the driver an address on 145th Street. He drove up through Central Park.

No one seemed talkative, so Julius patted Fifi on the thigh. "Did you have a good time?"

"Oh, I had a good time, but it's always so dull there. Not like the Stork Club where you can really have a good time."

"I like the Stork Club better too," Bebe said.

Art didn't say a damn thing, being as he knew the Stork Club's prices, and ditto with Dr. Steele, being as he knew the Stork Club's segregation policies.

But Julius, being as he didn't know either, said expansively, "We'll go to the Stork Club next time."

"When's that?" Fifi asked.

"Oh, soon," Julius said evasively.

"I like to go out every night," Bebe said.

"So do I," Art said. "But I ain't a girl."

Fifi laughed.

"What show are you in?" Julius asked, to change the conversation.

"I'm at leisure now," Fifi said. "I was in *Rock Candy Babies*. Did you see it?"

"Oh, sure, I remember you now," Julius lied.

"You do? I look different without any clothes." She looked at Art suggestively.

"Me too," Art said.

She giggled and playfully explored his difference. "It's a big difference," she said.

The difference got even bigger.

No other differences were examined.

The taxi stopped before a walkup apartment on 145th Street, near St. Nicholas Avenue. They stood on the sidewalk while Dr. Steele, the perfect gentleman, paid the fare.

"I'm going to say good night," Art said. "Three's a crowd."

"Oh no, come on in," Fifi said. "It won't be crowded, unless you crowd it."

But Art still held out. "No, some other time." He shook hands with Dr. Steele. "I'll make it all right," he whispered, meaning he'd pay his share of the bill.

"It's right now," Fifi insisted. "Yours and mine too." She took him by the arm and said, "Come."

He looked ready enough.

"Just for a minute," he gave in.

They walked up a narrow stairway to the third floor and entered a crummy apartment. Julius steered Art to the john.

"Play it cool, man," he advised. "It's all right. I'm telling you."

Art figured it was all right, or even better, but he couldn't very well play it cool as hot as he was. But he said, "Okay, fine," whatever that was supposed to mean.

When they returned to the lounge Bebe was saying, "Don't be mad, Jimmy." She was sitting in Dr. Steele's lap in a manner which shouldn't happen to a man who was impotent.

But Julius didn't see a thing. "How goes it, Johnny?" he said exuberantly. All along he had been calling Dr. Steele Johnny while everyone else was calling him Jimmy, but he had paid no attention.

"How goes it with you, Julius?" Dr. Steele replied politely, in his gentlemanly manner.

"Fine, Johnny. Everything is fine with me."

He noticed Art sitting with Fifi on the sofa, so he sat

down on the other side and put an arm about her shoulders.

"How are things with you, baby?" he said.

"Cozy," she said. "And with you?"

Art stood up. "I guess I better go now," he said.

"You can't go now," Julius protested.

"He's ready to come now," Fifi said.

"No, I've got to go now," Art insisted.

"No, you can't start a fire and leave it burning," Fifi insisted.

But Julius didn't seem to hear her. "If you go, I'm going with you," he said, playing his trump card. He was certain the girls were going to protest.

But no one said anything.

Art went toward the door. "I'm going. Good night, everybody."

Dr. Steele stood up. "I'm going too. I've got a busy day tomorrow."

"If everybody's going I guess I'll go too," Julius said.

Everybody looked relieved.

The three men left together and walked down toward the subway stop.

"I'm going to take the subway uptown," Art said, shaking hands with Julius and Dr. Steele.

"I'm going to try to find a taxi," Dr. Steele said, turning downtown on St. Nicholas Avenue.

"I'll see you fellows soon," Julius said. "I'll straighten it out with you, Johnny."

He continued east on 145th Street. He lived at 409 Edgecombe Drive with Joe and Mamie, which was only five minutes' walk. But instead of turning into 409 he continued circling the Drive until he came to 155th Street, climbed the hill and doubled back to St. Nicholas Avenue and returned to 145th Street. When he turned the corner by the drugstore he nearly bumped into Art, who was standing half-hidden in the shadow, watching the entrance to the apartment building across the street where Fifi and Bebe lived. He drew back quickly before Art saw him and peeped about the corner to see what Art was looking at.

A taxi pulled up in front of the apartment building and Dr. Steele, gentleman to the last, got out and paid the bill and went quickly up the stairs. As soon as he had disappeared inside, Art hastened across the street and went quickly up the stairs and did likewise.

The only thing left for Julius to do was to go across the street too. But instead of going quickly up the stairs, knowing there was no damn use, he stood on the sidewalk and wrote carefully in the tiny address book he carried: "Fifi and Bebe. 145th Street. Third floor."

If that doesn't show faith, what does?

EDGECOMBE DRIVE begins at 145th Street and traces the extreme western edge of the stone ridge that forms the upper half of Manhattan Island, until confronted by a shabbier neighborhood at 168th Street, where it puts an end to itself. From 145th Street to the 155th Street bridge, there is a steep drop down through a rocky jungle to the flat squalid neighborhood of slums on the northern reaches of the Harlem River Valley. The bridge spans the Harlem River to the Bronx, and north the Drive curves inward, skirting Coogan's Bluff, and ambles leisurely northward past the old Jumel Mansion, now a museum, which George Washington once used as a military headquarters, if we have our history correct.

The whole vast side of the Drive is a cliff, overlooking the distant rooftops of the apartment houses far below on Broadhurst Avenue and the Polo Grounds to the north, and giving clear view to streets and buildings and the Yankee Stadium over in the Bronx.

Very nice apartment buildings line the west side of the Drive. There are trees and plots of grass and rows of benches bordering the sidewalks, and in summer it is very pleasant sitting in the shade and watching the crack New York Central trains flashing in the light as they race along on the other side of the river, far below.

All things taken into consideration, it seems a far more preferable residential neighborhood than Park Avenue, and one wonders how Negroes ever got to live there. The first ones to move in must have been very happy and excited, watching the sun rise over Flushing Bay, miles distant, and shining into their living room windows. Now it is all Negro and the thrill is gone.

Although many of the apartment buildings have names, practically all are known by numbers. The two tallest and most famous are known respectively as 409 and 555. It is to be imagined that, when Negroes moved into these two houses, all the numbers players in Harlem loaded up on those numbers.

Of the two, 409 is the more famous. Partly because it is better kept and partly because it is inhabited by more famous Negro people. It has two elevators operated day and night by efficient uniformed operators. And it has a uniformed doorman and sometimes another lackey whose duties are not entirely clear, called a "footman." One does not know exactly what a footman of an apartment house does that cannot be done just as efficiently by a doorman, except it be footing. But there you have it, doorman, footman, elevator operators, all clad in the apartment house colors. The apartments have Chinese red doors, and the building is fourteen stories high.

The Masons' apartment was on the tenth floor front. A hallway extended from the entrance, alongside the kitchen, to the living room. With the kitchen door closed a stranger would not have guessed the kitchen was there. Beyond the living room a short right-angled hallway led to the bathroom and two flanking bedrooms. The windows of the kitchen, living room, and the smaller bedroom looked out onto an inside court. This bedroom contained a three-quarter bed piled high with cushions to double as a couch, artistic bookcases which doubled as tables and lampstands, and a big red leather chair. It served in the modern sense of library, den and guest room. Julius slept there. The master bedroom across the hall was at the front of the house and its two large windows looked out over the Drive.

The kitchen was quite large and also served as dining room, and it was amazingly functional. A chest-high partition of shelves, divided by a middle passage, separated the cooking section from the dining section. The dining table was big and long, designed like an outdoor picnic table with built-on benches, and was made of dark unfinished mahogany.

Mamie and Joe and Julius were sitting at the table, having breakfast. Mamie's consisted of a glass of canned, unsweetened grapefruit juice, coffee sweetened with saccharine tablets and muddied with condensed de-fatted milk, and two slices of dry toast. She was on her perennial diet. Joe was having his customary oversweetened coffee, a soft-boiled egg and two slices of buttered toast. Julius was having six slices of soft-cooked bacon, three sunny-side eggs, and a stack of squashed toast dripping with butter, no doubt a consolation breakfast because he hadn't been doing anything to merit it. He hadn't gotten to his coffee.

Joe wore a blue flannel robe over striped pajamas. He was a powerfully built man of medium height with an egg-shaped head and features like an Arab's. His complexion was as black as is humanly possible for skin to be, and his egg-shaped head was shaved as smooth as a billiard ball. When he grinned, his white teeth flashed from his black face like lighthouses on the sea.

Both Mamie and Julius were dressed in the clothes they'd worn all night, or rather, in Mamie's case, part of the night. They'd just gotten home. They'd bumped into each other in the downstairs foyer and had arrived at the apartment door together.

And now Joe was slyly teasing his younger brother about having to come home at sunrise in the company of his sister-in-law.

"What's the matter, Jule, you running out of gas?"

"No, I, er, have been playing, er, third man."

"Oh, you're running out of lass."

"Joe, shame on you, talking that way to Julius."

"Jule's heard about it before. Jule's a regular tuft-hunter, aren't you, Jule?"

"You're embarrassing Julius," Mamie said. Her first glance at Julius as he came dragging into the foyer downstairs had been enough to convince her he had not caught any tuft that night, no matter how great a tuft-hunter he might have been in the past.

"I thought sure Schooley would have thrown something Jule's way. Out in Chicago they call Schooley Fire Engine No. 1."

Mamie laughed. Not because she was cognizant of the fact that Schooley's fire-extinguishing apparatus had broken down, but because laughing for her was a definitive reply when she knew of no other. She was one of those women who can laugh in a hundred different ways, none of which might denote she was tickled.

"Eddy Schooley was too busy orating to put out any fire," she said.

Joe flashed a grin. "Just starting them, eh?"

Julius stole a look at Mamie, but her face told him nothing. He started to say that Schooley was too juiced to start them or stop them, but Mamie turned her big inclusive grin on him. Instead he said, "Probably tuning up his engine."

This time Mamie laughed in a secretive way.

Julius stole another look at her, but she appeared perfectly guileless and completely comprehending. He supposed she knew what they were talking about, even though he didn't.

Joe chuckled. "How did it go? Did Schooley and Pine sniff snow or take a bang to demonstrate the evils?"

"You know Eddy Schooley, he always takes the whole show," Mamie said. "Pine's just his shadow."

"Oh," Julius let slip. He was about to say, "Were you there? I didn't see you."

But she continued blandly as though she hadn't heard his exclamation. "Schooley's only fault was he talked too much; he didn't give Pine a chance to say anything. Lou had cautioned him before, and was Lou mad."

"What'd you think of the great Schooley, Jule?" Joe asked. "You never met him before, did you?"

"No, I, er, he was all right, a little, er—" Julius floundered.

"Julius played it cool," Mamie said, smiling at him indulgently. "Afterwards a little party of us went to Café Society Uptown, and after that we went back to Lou's and cleaned up what was left from the cocktail party."

"The ends and leavings of the cock and tail, eh?"

"None was left," Mamie said. "They all took it home, eh, Julius?"

At last it dawned on Julius that Mamie was trying to convince Joe that she had been at both the broadcast and the party, and what was more, that she had been escorted by himself.

He rushed valiantly to her assistance. "We'd have still been at Lou's if the liquor hadn't given out. But Schooley was drinking so fast—"

Mamie gave her conniving laugh and headed him off. "Brother Julius was trying to keep up but Eddy Schooley outswallowed him. You know Schooley's big mouth."

"The ladies say it's formidable," Joe said.

Mamie gave her pseudo-embarrassed laugh. "They say it's his secret weapon," she supplemented.

Joe chuckled. "It's a real wonder he didn't get drunk before the broadcast, if I know Schooley."

"It's a wonder," Mamie agreed. "But he was as sober as I've ever seen him. You know Eddy Schooley can be brilliant when he wants to. When he started talking about the cold turkey treatment—"

"They talked a lot before they went on the air, and then afterwards there was a discussion period and—" Julius interrupted, trying to keep her from those dangerous shoals.

But she was lying so sensually it had gotten good to her. "He told about a fifteen-year-old girl who'd had the habit since she was five. Her father used to give her a shot to keep her from crying and by the time she was ten she was a confirmed addict. Eddy Schooley said—"

"How was it on the radio?" Julius asked Joe, cutting her off again. "You listened, didn't you?"

Mamie laughed nervously. "Oh, Joe was at a conference. But you'd have liked it, baby," she said to Joe fondly.

"No, I was here at home," Joe said.

"Oh, baby, you weren't!" Mamie gasped.

"They called off the conference. I phoned just before eight, but you and Jule were at the cocktail party by then."

"Oh, baby, I didn't fix you any dinner. You ate downtown, did you?" Mamie said desperately.

"No, I had a snack here. I just ate some leftovers. I wanted to catch the radio program so I came straight home—"

Now Mamie was laughing in an incoherent manner. "Oh, baby, you know how I am about broadcasts, don't even know—" she blabbered guiltily. "Hardly ever get things right. Would have phoned if I'd known. You could have joined us . . . course I was tied up with Vivian until . . . but Julius would have . . ."

"I thought of going to the studio," Joe said. "But after I'd had a highball and got off my shoes—"

"Oh, baby, you're lazy—" She bussed him noisily on the cheek. "You know it never sounds the same on the radio . . . sometimes half what one says . . . then whenever anyone says anything . . ."

"But you heard most of what Pine had to say," Julius cut in with one last desperate effort to save her. "Just like me, I didn't know Schooley from Pine until . . . I kept calling Pine Schooley . . . and then, er, well, that's how it was."

Joe was looking at him in surprise. "Didn't they announce it?"

"Announce what?" Mamie and Julius chorused in unison.

"Why, the program wasn't broadcast at all. They announced it was canceled because of technical difficulties. They substituted Hall Johnson's choir singing Negro spirituals."

"Couldn't hear nobody lie
Way down yonder by myself,
An' Ah couldn't hear nobody lie," Julius sang silently to himself.

Mamie began laughing hysterically. "Oh, baby—" She

gave Joe a wrestler's hug and a big fat juicy slobber. "You missed your dinner and the broadcast and everything. I'm going to give you a party to make up for it."

"Didn't miss my sleep," Joe said, grinning slyly.

Obviously, Joe Mason had faith.

WHAT MADE MAMIE MASON GREAT was she capitalized on coincidences. And she could capitalize on them in such a singular manner because she believed in them. She believed that all life from the womb to the grave was a coincidence. She knew that in the womb it was indubitably coincidence; in fact, everything about the womb was coincidence, from what went in it to what came out of it. She believed in coincidence as a pilot believes in air. He doesn't see it, but he's flying many tons of steel on it, so it must be there.

Her whole life was a series of coincidences, one stumbling after another.

If she had never gone to the reception given by Madame Walker in 1931 in honor of the minister to Liberia, and if she had never noticed Madame Walker look at her distastefully, and had never heard Madame Walker ask scornfully, "Who is that fat girl there?" she would never have become Harlem's most famous hostess many years later. Madame Walker was Harlem's most famous hostess of that time, and it cut Mamie to the quick to be called "that fat girl there." It was bad enough to be called fat, even though she was fat and, worse still, a girl, but the additional *there* was a gratuitous insult for which she never forgave Madame Walker. *There!* Oh, the contempt hidden in that innocent-sounding adverb. *There!* says the waiter as he throws you your drink. Whose horse is that *there?* Did you see those darkies *there?* No, this here is mine and that *there* is yourn! It was contempt added to the fat that started her toward greatness.

Because if her fat had not been contemptible she would never have had any need of dieting. And if she had never dieted she would never have suffered such prolonged tortures of hunger. And if she had never suffered such prolonged tortures of hunger she would never have become such a revengeful hostess. And if she had never become such a revengeful hostess she would never have spent so much money and time and energy giving parties to get people into her house and into her hands so she could make them suffer too.

If her fat had not been contemptuous she would have nourished it and delighted in it and would have been a good big-bottom wife, cooking and sewing and serving her husband's needs, and happy and excited every time she had a chance to give some away; and by this time she would have resembled those women whose pictures are employed in the advertisements of battercake flour, except that her complexion was lighter. She would have let all her interracial friends and enemies live their own lives and create their own miseries, and she would have only been able to serve the Negro Problem suet pudding.

No coincidence?

Then how does she account for her marriage to Joe Mason?

She was engaged to Sam Banks. The wedding date had been set. The invitations had been mailed. The reception had taken place. The time of the wedding had arrived. The church had been filled. The minister had gone to the pulpit. The groom had arrived at the altar. The wedding march had resounded. She had walked shyly down the aisle on the arm of her mother. Her eyes had been lowered demurely. She had arrived at the altar and had stood beside the groom, her eyes downcast with virginal modesty. The pastor had read the marriage litany. The old ladies in the front row had sighed vicariously. The fateful question had been asked:

"Do you take this woman to be your wife, etc.?"

"I do."

"Do you take this man to be your husband, etc.?"

She had lifted her glance shyly to steal a loving glance at the sweet loving countenance of the man who in the next moment would become her husband, the father of her children, for better or worse—*and good jumping Jesus!* She saw the wrong man standing there. It was no more Sam Banks than you or me. It was Joe Mason. And he was blind drunk. For a moment she was panic-stricken. But only for a moment. Her great sense of realism rallied to her support. One man was as good as another, perhaps better. Besides which, she had known them both, for a long time and in the same ways, and one had nothing on the other. And anyway, it was too late to run. She lowered her gaze and said demurely:

"I do."

And why was Joe Mason there, in that church, at that altar, at that time, clad in the traditional garments of a groom? Why, because Joe Mason was engaged to Eureka Banks, no relation to Sam Banks however. The wedding date had been set. The invitations had been mailed. The reception had taken place. The time of the wedding had arrived. The church had been filled. The pastor had gone to the pulpit. And there all similarity between the two services had ended. Because the groom never did arrive. Joe Mason was the intended groom and he had got so thoroughly drunk beforehand he had arrived at the right time but in the wrong church.

And what happened to Sam Banks? Sam Banks had got drunk beforehand, too. However, unlike Joe Mason, he had arrived at the right church, all right, but at the wrong time. In fact, by the time Sam arrived at the church to be married to Mamie, she was already the happy wife of Joe Mason, the church was empty, and the happy couple had departed on their honeymoon.

Well then, what happened to Eureka Banks? She waited and waited until the church had emptied and then she had phoned Joe's apartment again and again and had tried in every desperate manner to contact him before she finally gave up and went back to her lower-class lover. But she never did forgive Joe for jilting her. And she put out some very ugly stories about Mamie's childhood in Pittsburgh, Pa. One had it that Mamie's father was a white pimp who had conceived her accidentally while changing his luck one day with the colored maid in the whorehouse. Another had it that Mamie was actually the daughter of a white prostitute who had been accidentally knocked up by a Negro trick trying to win a home, and when the white prostitute had moved on to another house in Youngstown, Ohio, she had abandoned the half-black baby to the colored maid. The most vicious seems the one which Eureka could only be persuaded to relate when she was tight, that Mamie's father was a colored steel mill worker who'd picked up some white tramp and begun living with her. "That nigger used to come home from work every day and stomp up on the porch with his big dirty feet," Eureka would relate. "And before Mamie's mama could get the door open that nigger would start hollering as loud as he could, *'Baby, your twat better be hot!'* After she got pregnant she got tired of that nigger hollering every day about her twat better be hot so one day she waited for him with a red-hot poker and blazed that nigger's ass out of town. The last she ever seen of him he was highballing it toward Erie with a big hole burnt in the ass of his pants."

In considering the validity of these stories one must remember the old proverb about a woman scorned. To her intimates, Mamie herself put out the story that her father was a very rich and famous white man who had loved her mother ardently all of his life, but because he was already married and had a fine family, he could never marry her.

Did she know who he was? Of course she knew who he was. As a little girl she used to sit on his knee and play with his great beard, and her fondest memory was of the time he first took her riding in his new Rolls-Royce. He was still alive and they wrote to each other regularly and she visited him at every opportunity. But she didn't want Joe to know. She had never told Joe about her father; he might be shamed by her illegitimacy. She had told him her father was dead.

In any event, Mamie's father never appeared on the scene. Her mother visited her often, and as black as she was one may believe what one wishes. All it requires is faith.

JOE MASON was a politician. He had a desk in the state welfare department and an elegant salaried title. He had a favorite corner in the lobby of City Hall, known as Mason's Corner. And he had a private office on 125th Street near Seventh Avenue, in the heart of Harlem. His office consisted of a reception room and an inner sanctum with a couch. The couch was not for what you think, Joe never had dizzy spells. The outer door of his office bore the legend in gold script: JOSEPH P. MASON—PUBLIC RELATIONS. The reception room contained Joe's secretary, by name of Kathy Carter. Nasty-minded people called her Joe's piece. Joe spent most of his time in this office; he liked his piece.

Joe's big job, however, was that of consultant on interracial relations for the national committee of a major political party. Mamie claimed this was the only reason she gave so many parties. Where could one consult better on interracial relations than at interracial parties where interracial relations became even more related, she contended. Cynics claimed there was more consenting at these affairs than there was consulting. But they overlooked the obvious fact that people must consult in order to consent.

At eight-thirty o'clock each workday morning Joe left for work. At ten minutes to nine he let himself into his 125th Street office. At nine o'clock Kathy Carter arrived. While she was removing her coat, Joe locked the outer door. This done, they went to work.

So much for Joe Mason.

At two thirty that afternoon, hunger awakened Mamie Mason. She rushed to the kitchen, gulped a half bottle of skimmed milk, ate six raw eggs, a half pound of raw, partly frozen ground steak, two all-beef frankfurters, and six slices of boiled ham after peeling off the fat. Suddenly she was sick. She drank a stiff bourbon straight to keep it down, but it kept on coming up and she just made it to the bathroom to let it go. After it had gone she took a tablespoon of mineral oil, returned to the kitchen, ate three hard-boiled eggs, two slices of dry toast, a can of tuna fish, and a head of iceberg lettuce sans dressing. Everything stayed down. She mixed a Scotch highball and took it to her bedroom. Then she went to the bathroom and swallowed two tablespoons of a milk-of-magnesia laxative. She looked in at Julius asleep in the den. He was snoring in two octaves. She went back and got into bed and opened a small black notebook in which she kept a list of the names and addresses of visiting celebrities.

The list read:

> OWG Waldorf
> CVS New Yorker
> BBB & M ditto
> SK Commodore
> AT ask Joe

MS & B Theresa
WR call Fay
ES & P who cares

First she phoned the Waldorf-Astoria Hotel and asked to speak to Dr. Oliver Wendell Garrett. Dr. Garrett was the epitome of the type of distinguished white man whom Mamie just loved, not to mention just loved to be loved by. As president of the board of directors of the Rosenberg Foundation, a fund bequeathed by the late philanthropist, Sam Rosenberg, to promote love between Negroes and Southern whites, it was his lot to pass final judgment on such projections and inceptions of the aforementioned love as he deemed salutory. Needless to say, for such a responsible position one needs look the part, and indeed Dr. Garrett looked every inch the patriarch the work required. He was a giant of a fine-looking man with a mane of white hair and a bristling expensive goatee. However, his benevolent gray eyes through which he surveyed all racial chaos with infinite compassion relieved him of austerity.

"Are you alone?" Mamie greeted him.

"Why, Mamie dear, I was just thinking of your bottom."

She knew he was alone. "I'm having a little party tonight for Eddy Schooley to promote love between Negroes and Southern whites. He's just had a book published and—"

"Schooley. Never heard of him."

"—a lot of people are coming, old friends of yours. Stetson Kissock, Willard Overton, Wallace Wright—"

"Don't want to see any friends but you. I'm dying to spank your bottom."

"—and Lorenzo and Vincent," Mamie kept casting. "And Alice and Maiti—"

"Maiti! The one with the bosom? Is she here?"

Mamie was beginning to wonder when he'd bite.

"With Billy," she said. "They're at the New Yorker."

"It'll be nice to see the two of them, ha-ha, her bosoms;

and will I have the opportunity to whip your own lovable caramel pudding bottom?"

Mamie laughed. "You've been drinking."

"Indeed so."

"Come any time after ten, sugar."

Next she telephoned Dr. Stetson Kissock, Chairman of the Southern Committee for the Preservation of Justice, at the Commodore, and informed him she was giving a party in honor of Dr. Garrett. Dr. Kissock was a chubby, pink-skinned man with a shining pink ball head fringed by snow-white hair, who looked for all the world like an aging, but still shooting, cupid. Twinkling blue eyes looked out from his beaming cupid face with an exceptionally benign expression at all the sordidness of racial injustices. But Dr. Kissock was not the man to be beaten by the Negro Problem, as such. In more than forty years of dedicated devotion to the "cause" he had found no better way of preserving Southern justice in its pristine form than love between Southern whites and Negroes. Naturally he would come to see his old friend Dr. Garrett, fosterer of such love, as you might say.

Then she phoned Dr. Carl Vincent Stone, president emeritus and chairman of the board of a famous Negro college located in the Deep South, at the New Yorker, to let him know she was giving a party in honor of Dr. Kissock, and exchange ideas on how best to combat that greatest enemy to Southern education and Southern justice—desegregation. It goes without saying that Dr. Stone was a white man. In the South that exalted title of President Emeritus, worthless or not, is never wasted on a black man. The only trouble was that Dr. Stone had brown patches on his face and hands, due no doubt to either himself or one of his forebears carelessly rubbing against a black person, and before appearing in the presence of colored people he had to apply white pancake makeup. Along with his coarse black hair and thick black eyebrows and his strong prematurely human features, the white makeup made Dr. Stone look more white than many cynical Negroes thought necessary.

After which Mamie telephoned Dr. Baldwin Billings Brown, the noted Negro psychologist, Professor of Psychology at the Negro College of which Dr. Stone was President Emeritus, at the New Yorker also, and told him she was having a party in honor of Dr. Garrett. Dr. Brown said he wouldn't miss it, in fact he better hadn't.

Then in turn she telephoned:

Milt Shirley, publisher of a Negro weekly newspaper, and his wife, Bessie, at the Theresa Hotel in Harlem, and told them she was having a surprise party for Dr. Brown;

Will Robbins, the noted liberal white producer of that magnificent film on racial tolerance, entitled *Read and Run Nigger*, and subtitled *If You Can't Read Run Anyhow*, at the apartment of that blond, East Side divorcee, Fay Corson, where she was certain she would find them both, and buzzed to him that she was throwing a little shindig for Panama Paul, that fabulous Negro actor who immortalized the lead role, Hot Foot, in Robbins' film;

Lorenzo Llewellyn, the forty-nine-year-old leading young Negro author; Jonah Johnson, the famous Negro foreign correspondent; Moe Miller, the famous New York City blackhawk, er, ah, black newshawk; and Lou Reynolds, the harried white editor of Hightower's black books, were told that the party was for Schooley and Pine, those redoubtable authors of *Dreamland* and other, er, ah, things;

Willard B. Overton, president of a city-wide, privately endowed Negro welfare organization, Negro Aid Incorporated, and whispered to him that the party was for some very rich and important white people whom she was sure he would like to see but whose names she dared not mention prematurely for fear of inconveniencing them in some manner. Seemingly he understood this language perfectly for he assured her that his discretion would not be overwhelmed by his eagerness to meet these unmentioned people;

And it goes without saying that she telephoned Wallace Wright, the great Negro race leader of one-sixty-fourth Negro blood, to whom we have referred previously, Executive Chairman of the National Negro Political Society, NNPS (which some dirty-minded Harlem Negroes have dubbed Native Negro Pussy Seekers), and told him the party was in honor of himself, knowing it was the only reason it would never occur to him to doubt. And she insisted that he bring his wife, that pussy-hoarding bitch Juanita, who had sworn she would never set foot in her house. In fact, what other reason would Mamie have for giving such a perfectly spontaneous party if it wasn't to trick that droopy-drawered bitch into her house?

But even so, Wallace was hesitant. "I hope you won't have any reformed Communists and protest novelists there, Mamie."

"Oh, there will only be a dozen people, dear, including you and Juanita. Our Drs. Stone, Garrett and Kissock, of course—"

"Of course."

"And Billings Brown, perhaps Art Wills and maybe Lou Reynolds—"

"Lou Reynolds? Isn't he Schooley's editor? You're not having that degenerate Schooley, I hope."

She laughed. "Eddy Schooley is safely in Chicago, dear."

So naturally she had to phone Schooley after that, which she had not intended to do, and tell him that Julius wanted to get an interview and some pictures of him for the first issue of the proposed Negro picture magazine.

"Why don't you drop by tonight around eleven or twelve o'clock; Julius will be home by then and I'll have a few people in to meet you."

Schooley assured her he would be there, and forthwith began drinking to get all his members in working order.

Joe was the last person she telephoned. She told him some old friends were dropping by, naming the most important of her guests, and asked him to get in touch with Special Presidential Assistant Arthur Tucker, who she had heard was in town, and ask him to come too. Joe thought it was a fine idea and promised to do his best.

When he arrived home she gave him a wrestler's hug and stuck several inches of tongue down his mouth, then said: "You've got to shave and dress so you'll be pretty, baby. I'm giving a big surprise party for you."

By then it was six-thirty o'clock and she had to rush to the john. She had held it as long as she could.

NATURALLY JUANITA WRIGHT had no intention of coming to Mamie's party. But everyone who came thought the party was in honor of themselves, so it was a fine party anyway.

There was plenty of liquor and the conversation was brilliant. Joe Mason discoursed eloquently on the Negro vote and its true context as the balance of power.

"It's a matter of economics," said Dr. Stone, his dazzling white makeup shining in the muted light.

"What's a matter of economics?" asked Dr. Garrett, his white mane shaking and his goatee quivering.

"Why, the Negro Problem, of course," said Dr. Stone.

"More dollars sowed, more black votes growed," that black newshawk, Moe Miller, said cynically.

"I think it's more psychological," said Dr. Billings Brown.

"Education is the answer," said Dr. Kissock, his pink face flushed with goodwill and strong whiskey, not to mention the blood-warming proximity to Negroes.

"Mamie looks positively haggard," some woman said.

"She's been on a diet," her female companion replied.

"But I heard she eats all the time."

"Don't be silly, dear, she doesn't swallow them."

Mamie smiled maliciously.

"The Russians are worse to the Jews," said Lorenzo Llewellyn, who had recently denounced the Communist Party after having been a member for seventeen years.

"A distant relative of mine, third or fourth cousin, married a Russian once," Dr. Garrett confessed. "A prince of some sort, I believe, driving a taxicab—"

"White Russian?" Dr. Stone asked anxiously, looking as though he could lend him some white if he didn't have enough.

"Oh yes, definitely white. Are there any, er, ah, black Russians?"

"Ask Jonah Johnson, he's a foreign correspondent. Jonah, are there any, eh, er, black Russians?"

Jonah's black face assumed an expression of deference as is proper when replying to a distinguished white gentleman, especially on a question of Russians.

"Yes sir, plenty. A whole nation of black Russians. Georgia."

"Not *our* Georgia?" gasped an interested white woman.

"*Their* Georgia," said Jonah.

"Mamie, darling, you look positively stunning," Brown Sugar complimented.

"—from Lord & Taylor's, honey," Mamie mumbled incoherently, referring to the black satin sheath dress, size twelve, which she seemed about to burst out of.

"Black people everywhere!" Booker T. Henry, militant black union executive, said belligerently. "Black Frenchmen, black Englishmen, black Chinese—"

"Indeed? Black Chinese you say?" interrupted Dr. Kissock with a surprised expression on his pink cupid's face. "In the south of China?"

"I hear Mamie has cancer in her rectum," some woman whispered.

"That wouldn't surprise me, dear," her companion whispered back.

"She's been named correspondent in you-know-whose divorce."

"I know, it took place right here on this very sofa."

"I heard he was a homo."

"Little difference that makes to Mamie, as long as he is rich and white and has a thing."

"Don't be too sure about the thing, dear."

Her companion laughed cattily.

"Left her in six months for another woman," said Dr. Garrett. "We never learn not to trust them."

"Do you mean men or women?" Merto asked.

"Chick's jumping out of the pan!" Mamie's maid, Aquilla, shouted from the kitchen. "Come and eat it!"

Dr. Stone almost jumped out of his skin. Must have thought she meant him personally.

Edward Schooley arrived just in time for the fried chicken, but he was too drunk to eat any of it. He gave everyone a bemused smile and mumbled, "Thank you . . . one and all . . . Mamie, dear . . . consider it great honor . . ." Then he staggered across the living room and entered the bedroom and fell across the bed and went straight to sleep. There seemed to be an extra woman with a new face floating around, but no one considered it of much importance.

"You likes dark meat or light meat, honey?" Mamie's maid could be heard addressing one of the white ladies sitting at the kitchen table, more pointedly than seemed necessary.

This was a cue for Moe Miller to say, "I know what part Joe likes."

"Last part over the fence," Art Wills suggested helpfully.

"You don't know Joe. He starts with the white meat and eats down."

"Oh, breast," Art said.

Joe looked at Mamie slyly. "Turkey breast."

Mamie laughed indulgently.

Moe said, "Mamie, your husband is always starting something. Don't you have enough breast to keep him satisfied?"

"Eating breast," Joe reproved sweetly.

Drs. Garrett, Stone and Kissock were listening with grave attention.

"You told me that was breast you were eating and we

were a thousand miles from Turkey," Moe charged.

Joe blinked his eyes and said innocently, "When in Sweden eat Swedish."

"That ain't what you said then. You were making so much noise eating it you woke me up."

"Breast."

"That's what I mean. Mamie, I asked your husband what he was eating and he said breast and I asked him where he got turkey at that time of night and he said it wasn't Turkish, it was Swedish."

"I never said I didn't prefer turkey breast."

"You said Swedish breast was the best breast you'd ever eaten and you'd been raised on a turkey ranch."

Drs. Garrett, Stone and Kissock laughed.

"Reminds me of that story by Faulkner," Dr. Kissock said. "Fool about a horse."

"Eat your chicken with your hands, girl, where do you come from with all those airs?" Mamie's maid was scornfully directing Kit Samuels, the cute blond wife of athletic-looking Isaiah Samuels, professor of English literature in an upstate woman's college.

Off in a corner the gossips were still gossiping.

"It's a tapeworm she uses, dear."

"To reduce? My God, isn't that dangerous?"

"Oh no, she takes poisonous enemas to kill them."

"Heavens, won't that impair body tissue?"

"Nobody's tissue has been impaired as yet."

Brownskin Lucy Pitt, who had arrived with that great white liberal producer Will Robbins and blond divorcee Fay Corson, slipped on the kitchen linoleum and fell on her pratt. Her skirt flew up, clearly revealing the place from where babies come, regardless of what they say about the stork.

Dr. Garrett's goatee quivered convulsively and for a moment he seemed on the verge of, er, ah, beating the girl then and there.

But Dr. Stone was so busy lapping some imaginary juices

from some imaginary source he didn't notice his colleague's reaction.

The big black handsome minister of one of Harlem's most important churches, Reverend Doctor Mike Riddick, a very religious man who had been patiently ministering to a cramp in Kit Samuels' thigh, crunched his chicken leg with such force he crushed the bone to splinters and chipped the enamel of his dog tooth. "Lord, preserve her modesty," he gulped prayerfully, and at the same time his big black hand closed so protectively over white Kit's privacy she wondered whose modesty he meant.

"Baby hurt self," Mamie murmured solicitously, examining Lucy's smooth brown thighs so meticulously for bruises as to arouse suspicion. "Mike, help her up."

"Lord protect the helpless," Reverend Riddick said solemnly as he knelt before the child.

"Permit me to help you," offered Dr. Kissock, licking his wet red lips with a pointed tongue.

"Up!" Mamie said sharply. "Not up on!"

Whereupon Reverend Riddick lifted the helpless girl into a chair provided by the maid, not without painful consequences from his ecclesiastical trousers, which had not been tailored for such a contingency.

In the living room, affable Arthur Tucker, Special Presidential Assistant, the dark horse of Mamie's white celebrities, was standing over Maiti Brown, wife of Dr. Baldwin Billings Brown, and peering down inside the front of her décolleté gown with a fixed wet expression as though he were mesmerized.

"My heavens, but you have a wonderful bosom!" he shouted vehemently. "Marvelous! Never seen another like it! Perfectly extraordinary!" He rubbed his hands together with uncontrollable enthusiasm and roared, "Magnificent! Perfectly matched! Exquisitely colored! And, my stars, they are enormous. Every bit as big as elephant udders, I'll wager a year's pay. Here, let me measure them."

"No! No!" Maiti cried in alarm. Her big bright hook-nosed face resembled a startled eagle's.

"Arthur's tight," Mamie murmured happily.

"Only with my hands," he cajoled Maiti, wagging a finger. "No instruments."

"No you don't!" she cried, drawing back in horror.

"Stupendous!" he shouted ardently. "What a place to smother!"

"You get away, don't you dare touch me!" she cried in terror.

Mr. Tucker was a frail man and short, and Maiti was a big, powerful-looking, imposing and seemingly domineering light-complexioned colored woman weighing two hundred pounds and approaching fifty years of age. The idea of his smothering in her ample bosom was not so farfetched as it might seem.

"Ah, Maiti," he roared regretfully. "If I were Botticelli, what a feast! I could eat forever. Ah, what a boon to art! What a boon to humanity! You could feed the world's famished, on an assembly line. Let me show you—"

But Maiti heaved to her feet before he could demonstrate, dwarfing his frail figure by her awesome proportions and very nearly trampling the life from his passionate heart as she fled, panic-stricken, to the bedroom. Mr. Tucker followed with face aflame. What his intentions were no one ever discovered, for she slammed the door in his face and he reluctantly withdrew, muttering to himself, "My stars, what an armful."

Mamie winked at him as she went past to console her terrified guest.

"He was going to rape me," Maiti whispered breathlessly.

Schooley sat up suddenly and gave her a stern, indignant look. "No such thing," he denied. "I was just dreaming."

"He was going to rape me right out there before everyone," Maiti sobbed, ignoring the indignant Schooley. A tear slipped from her stern forbidding eye and trickled down her strong broad cheek past her beaked nose.

"Don't cry, dear," Mamie said. "Better luck next time."

"Never raped a woman in my life," Schooley protested.

Maiti fixed her eagle eye on him. "You couldn't, you drunkard!"

In total ignorance of this near tragedy, the gathering in the den was having a lying good time.

Julius was saying. "And he'd slip off from work three or four times every day and come home and stretch her legs wide apart and look in it to see if it had been used."

"What did he expect to find?" Art asked. "One that somebody had left?"

"Well, one day his landlady came in and caught him at it and wanted to know what in the world he was doing to his wife, and he said shamefacedly he was just blowing on it to cool it off."

Moe Miller passed the den on his way to the john. A moment later a small dapper man rushed past on his way to the john also. But by the time he arrived, Moe was just leaving.

"Oh!" said the small dapper man disappointedly. "I beg your pardon."

"Don't mention it," Moe said.

"Certainly not," the small dapper man replied.

In one corner of the living room Wallace Wright was recounting to Jonah Johnson his experiences on one of his air-hops to the European Theater during the war.

"I had stopped over in London on my way to Naples to apprise Winston of the grave situation developing between our white and Negro servicemen in the matter of off-duty entertainment."

Jonah nodded understandingly as he hung, ambitiously, on the great man's words.

"I had presumed, and rightly so, that the London command had not broached the problem to Winston—"

"Churchill," Jonah supplied knowingly.

Wallace raised his eyebrows. "What other Winston is there?"

"The last time I saw Churchill, that is to speak to—"

But Wallace was not the one to allow anyone else to talk in his presence. "I had learned from past talks with Winston that he was desirous of being informed of every conceivable phase of our fighting forces. Of course, Winston had me down to No. 10 for dinner—"

"Downing Street," Jonah said.

Naturally this remark was too ridiculous to elicit comment.

"Before leaving London I took up the question of integration again with Ike. As I pointed out to Ike—"

Jonah caught himself before making the faux pas of saying "Eisenhower" and instead cleared his throat.

Wallace gave him a sharp look. "I told Ike that during that critical phase of the war was when it could best be accomplished. Ike agreed with me and promised to make every effort in that direction if it did not interfere with the efficiency of the forces. However, as history has revealed, the efficiency of our colored fighting men has created—"

"Brown babies!" Jonah said triumphantly.

Dr. Garrett was saying to Dr. Stone reminiscently, "We had a Swedish girl working for us one time as maid—a fine large girl who never bruised."

"Do you think Swedish girls really, ah, er, with colored people?" Dr. Stone ventured.

"Oh, yes. I'm sure of it. In Sweden, of course."

"Really? Like Joe and Moe? Fellows that black?"

"Once read a book by a young Negro. Very talented. Called it"—he leaned unobtrusively toward Dr. Stone's ear—*"The Blacker the Berry, the Sweeter the Juice."*

"Ha-ha," laughed Dr. Stone. "Ha-ha. Capital. The Sweeter the Berry, the Blacker the Juice."

A short distance away, Willard B. Overton was discussing politics with a tall, dark, exquisitely dressed white woman. "Of course, we must campaign for him because at this juncture it is vitally necessary, not to say imperative, to erect an image, if you know what I mean."

"Oh, I know what you mean," she said. "To get him erected, that is."

Mr. Overton blinked at her disconcertedly. Wit was the only thing of which he had judged her innocent. "Exactly, to get him, er, ah, erect his image. But of course, you understand, our organization is nonpolitical. We have among our sponsors persons of both major political parties, and our members come from all races—"

"I should hope so," she said. "I mean, interracial, that is."

Mr. Overton swallowed suddenly. "Exactly," he confirmed. "The purpose, of course, the one major problem—"

"Is the Negro Problem, that is." She smiled intellectually.

"Ahem! What did you say your name was?"

"Merto," she said, although she hadn't said before. She nodded toward the dapper little man who was listening to Moe Miller discussing the comparative merits of stallions and jackasses as fathers:

"Any day! Any day of your life, a jackass will take a mare from a stallion—" Will Robbins said, "Happens in the best circles." Joe put in, "But they can only sire mules." Moe laughed. "They try too hard."

"He is my husband, that is," Merto said.

"Maurice, you mean?"

She nodded brightly.

"Ah, so you're Mrs. Gordey?"

"Yes, isn't it disgusting, that is . . ."

"Er, ah, that is—" He caught himself saying it. "What is?"

"Every time I try to help he beats me." She spoke in a rapid breathless voice.

He blinked again. "Ah, yes—I'm sorry, I don't think I heard you correctly. I thought you said he beat you."

"Terribly."

He threw another look toward Maurice, who was then following Moe toward the kitchen. Maurice was a very small man with a very red face, watery blue eyes, and thin white hair, seemingly in his sixties. Merto was a head taller, ten pounds heavier, and less than half his age.

"But he doesn't seem very strong," Willard conjectured.

"He isn't. I just let him, that is—"

"Oh, that is—but why?"

"It's just because I'm interested in the Negro Problem."

"Ah yes, I see. He doesn't want you to give your time and money to our organization."

"It isn't that, my time and money, that is."

"Oh, he resents your giving, er, ah—" He looked suddenly enlightened. "Is *that* what you give?"

"Think of all the oppressed Negroes," she said.

He thought of them and was somewhat awed. "And he, er, beats you for your generosity."

"It's not my generosity. He beats me to make me tell, that is."

"Ah, er, you mean make you tell, er, that is—"

"Isn't it horrible?"

"The dirty brute, beating you like that."

"Oh, but if I haven't, then there's nothing to tell. You understand, why should he?"

"Ahem," he said. "Yes, to be sure. I have my car outside and, that is—"

"Let me say good-bye to Mamie and get my coat."

"But I hate to be the cause, that is—"

"Oh, I don't mind; he can't really hurt me, that is, and I think I should do something for the Negro Problem."

"I'll wait for you downstairs."

Mamie let him out alone and kept Merto waiting five minutes. Even so, Dr. Stetson Kissock raised his eyebrows slightly.

When Julius Mason went to the kitchen for a refill, Kathy Carter embraced him and kissed him competently.

"There! I'm tired of waiting for you to do it."

Julius looked at her with interest.

When Will Robbins came to the kitchen for a refill, she turned from Julius and embraced him and kissed him competently, being as he was bigger than Julius and also white.

"There! I'm tired of waiting for you to do it."

"You don't have to wait," Will said.

Julius's interest waned.

Moe said to Joe, "Your secretary is smacking."

Joe said to Moe, "As long as she's not shacking."

Kathy embraced Joe and kissed him competently. Mamie came into the kitchen. Joe got the hell out fast.

Julius went back to the den.

Schooley held the floor. "With men it's different."

"How so?" Art asked. "Other than the big difference, of course."

"Everybody's ain't that big," Julius said.

"It's not that," Schooley said. "It's while we're getting emptied women are getting filled up."

"You mean via the genital canals?" Art asked.

"Filled up!" Lou protested. "Let's not exaggerate."

"It's a matter of numbers," Art argued. "I've known them to overflow."

"Well, how many would that take?" Lou demanded.

"That's not the point," Schooley said. "I'm saying that's why women live longer than men."

Moe passed by on the way to the john. He locked the door. When Maurice arrived, he found the door locked. Moe unlocked the door and came out. Maurice's hand accidentally touched the front of Moe's trousers.

"Don't do that," Moe said.

"I was just admiring you," Maurice said in a hurt voice. "Don't you like to be admired?"

"That's the trouble," Moe said, hurrying back to the living room.

The hour was getting late. Lovely faces that had been carefully powdered and repowdered were now abandoned to oil and sweat. Lips that had tasted fried chicken were now sealed in cooking fat.

Dr. John Stetson Kissock was preparing to leave with Wallace Wright. Mamie helped him into his coat. When Wallace went once more to water the dog, Mamie said to Dr. Kissock, "Stay over. Joe's leaving for Buffalo tomorrow afternoon."

"Can't."

"Can too. You can leave tomorrow at midnight."

"Won't work. Anna's expecting me."

"Tell her you were held up. Something to do with justice. You had to do it justice."

A flush spread over Dr. Kissock's cupid's face and he licked his wet red lips. "I'd like very much to do it justice but it won't work. Anna's turn now. Ha-ha, too great demands on justice—" He broke off as Wallace approached and said, "You must come and visit us, my dear. Anna enjoys you so."

"Next time I'm in Washington. I promise. Give Anna my love."

She kissed him on both pink cheeks. He patted her shoulder affectionately. Light shone on his pink bald head.

"Enjoyed myself so much, Mamie dear," Wallace said.

She kissed Wallace on the mouth. "Glad, honey. Night now. Tell Juanita to call me."

When the door had closed behind them she muttered to herself, "Dirty half-white bastard didn't bring Juanita. I'll fix him."

While outside in the corridor, Wallace spat and took out his handkerchief and wiped off her kiss. Dr. Kissock regarded him with annoyance.

Wallace was a small blond man with a small blond mustache and looked so much like a white man that his white friends found it extremely difficult, in fact downright irritating, to have to remember he was colored.

"Delightful woman, eh, Wallace?" Dr. Kissock stated.

"Oh, indeed, indeed. In the forefront of the fight."

Dr. Kissock smiled to himself.

In the living room, a distinguished-looking white woman, upon noticing a dark young man staring at her, began weeping copiously.

The young dark man approached her and asked in alarm, "Why, what's the matter, madam?"

"You look just like Jackson," she sobbed. "Poor Jackson. He was so brave. In spite of everything he was always laughing."

"Don't cry, madam, we all have to die."

"Oh, Jackson isn't dead. It's my husband who is dead."

"What happened to Jackson?"

"There just wasn't enough money to keep Jackson any longer. And he was such a fine chauffeur. He had such lovely black skin."

The young dark man laughed. "And you think I look just like him?"

She dried her tears and gazed at him intently. "Maybe you're not as tall, and I don't think you're quite as stout as Jackson—after all, we always fed Jackson well—and, mmm, your features are a little different, they're not quite so smooth and flat as Jackson's. But you're"—her eyes lit with rapture—"you're every bit as black. And you're a poet too, aren't you?"

Naturally he was a poet. So they left together to make some poetry.

Dr. Oliver Wendell Garrett was preparing to leave with war correspondent Jonah Johnson. Negro novelist Lorenzo Llewellyn had planned to accompany Dr. Garrett to his hotel himself, so as to discuss with him his application for a new Rothschild fellowship. But it seemed as if someone had locked Lorenzo in the john, or else he had locked himself in and forgotten what he had done with the key. So Jonah had offered to accompany Dr. Garrett, since obviously a man in charge of fellowships could never be permitted to go any where alone at any time.

While Jonah was helping Joe and Kathy Carter look for the missing key, Mamie helped Dr. Garrett into his coat.

"Tonight?" he demanded. "After you clear out this rabble."

"Not tonight. Joe's staying in."

"Then come out and leave him."

"Can't."

"Tomorrow night then."

"Not tomorrow either. Joe's not leaving until day after tomorrow."

"He told me he was leaving tomorrow afternoon."

"He's got it mixed up. He has a conference tomorrow with the, er, Whip," she said with a slip of the tongue.

He looked at her sharply. "Did you teach him that?"

"Oh, not that whip, the Party Whip."

"Well, I am engaged the night after tomorrow, regardless."

"Come afterwards."

"Abby will be back by then."

She noticed Jonah approaching and whispered quickly, "I'll phone you."

Dr. Garrett kissed her paternally on the forehead. She curtsied.

"Thank you for coming, Ollie."

"Haven't come at all," he muttered.

Jonah gave her a big bear hug and slipped the missing key into her hand. She smiled knowingly.

Some woman was heard to confide that Joe was secretly divorcing Mamie and had named as corespondent, of all persons, Maurice Gordey. Can you imagine that? Well, darling, he's white, isn't he, and has been white a long time. But, honey, didn't you know, he likes things. So does Mamie, darling, they could share them.

Bessie Shirley made Arthur Tucker, who was sitting on the arm of her chair, feel her contact lenses.

"It's cold," he said.

"It is not," she said. "It's hot."

"And you don't feel my finger?"

"It's not in the right place."

"My, but you have nice brown skin, it looks like coffee icing."

"Wouldn't you like to taste it?"

He bent so close to stare into her eyes that his lips accidentally touched her nose. "They're gray," he said.

She pouted. "No, they are brown. It's the lenses that are gray."

His tongue accidentally lapped her pout. "Imagine that," he said.

"You're not leaving it to the imagination," she said.

"You certainly had me fooled," he said.

"I don't believe it," she said. "You could see it right away."

His hand accidentally touched the naked part of her breast. "It's just that I'm such a busy man."

"You're not lying," she said. "But your hands are cold."

"Cold hands, warm heart," he said.

"I'll just bet you've got a warm heart, you cute little man," she said and clasped him to make sure. If it wasn't warm before it got warm then.

And when he saw Maiti Brown leaving in the company of her husband, Dr. Baldwin Billings Brown, and Dr. Carl Vincent Stone, he thought of those magnificent milk tanks and it got very hot indeed.

Will Robbins sneaked out with Kathy Carter, seeing as how she was getting even more tired of waiting for him to do it, leaving Fay Corson and Lucy Pitt to shift for themselves.

Fay Corson shifted over to Julius Mason. "You have such sad eyes."

But one look at hers was enough to make him glad as hell they looked so sad. Shortly afterwards they left together to do something about it, probably to see an eye specialist.

Lucy Pitt was in no condition to shift for herself, but her plight so moved the heart of Reverend Mike Riddick he was only too happy to shift for her.

"I'll take this poor girl home, Mamie, and see that she gets properly to bed." He stopped short. "She lives alone, doesn't she?"

"Her husband's in the army."

"In camp, though."

"In California."

He sighed sympathetically. "God bless our fighting men. I'll see to it that he doesn't have to worry about his little mate."

"Be careful," Mamie warned. "She's in no condition to wrestle."

Reverend Riddick drew himself up to his full height. "I shall pray over the girl."

No one noticed Moe Miller leave. The last seen of him he was in the kitchen talking to Joe. Maurice was sitting at the table nearby. Suddenly nature played a dirty trick on Maurice and he had to jump up and dash to the john, all alone. When he returned, Moe had left. So Maurice took his departure in the company of the leading young Negro novelist, Lorenzo Llewellyn.

"Did you get to see it?" Lorenzo asked eagerly.

Maurice sighed regretfully. "No, but I've heard it's a doozie."

What was so many departures, chances were getting slim and the party began getting a little rough.

Milt Shirley took a poke at Arthur Tucker. He said white men aggravated him. Bessie Shirley said he ought to be ashamed of himself. He said he was ashamed. Arthur Tucker said his eye was swelling. Bessie Shirley said she would bathe it in cold water. They went toward the john. When they opened the door, Eddy Schooley hailed forth. He was gloriously naked, save for a garland of Mamie's printed hand towels knotted together about his neck.

"All hail to Bacchus!" he cried. "The Bacchanalia begins."

"Look how potbellied Schooley is," Brown Sugar remarked.

"Light on his feet, though," Art replied, nestling up to her.

The heavy-hammed reincarnated Bacchus leaped and twisted with such gay abandon as to cause considerable misgivings about his intentions.

"Putting or taking?" a woman's voice was heard to ask.

But one look at Schooley was enough to inform the initiate there would be no putting done.

"He's just doing a little research on alcoholism," Lou Reynolds assured everyone. "Subject of his next book."

"Don't do it over me!" Cleo Daniels said sharply, dodging as he swung within inches of her face.

Mamie interceded and danced him into the kitchen where

they had drink for drink. After giving one last waggle, Bacchus subsided quietly on the floor.

Milt Shirley and Joe Mason hauled the prostrate Bacchus to the bedroom; but Bessie Shirley had already availed herself of the bed and had taken Arthur Tucker with her to soothe his injured eye, although where she was soothing seemed indeed a very strange place for an eye. So Bacchus was laid to rest beneath a comforter on the couch in the den.

Milt Shirley disappeared.

Art had snuggled so close to Brown Sugar on the sofa in the living room as to be trying to melt her back into molasses. He gripped her shoulder protectively in the curve of his strong right arm to defend her sensibilities against the exciting realities of the fourteenth chapter of his life, subtitled *Me and Sex*. But she held on to her own, or rather to his own which she intended to take in her own before the night was done.

Mamie's maid, Aquilla, went about and shook hands with all the remaining guests and said she hoped they'd all had a good time. She staggered toward the door and turned and waved and said, "Good-bye, all," and left.

Cleo Daniels went into the kitchen and sat atop the table and took off her shoes and stockings. Panama Paul, that big impressive Negro actor who immortalized the role of Hot-foot in that famous interracial motion picture, *Read and Run Nigger,* sat beside her and took off his shoes and socks. They compared feet, white foot for black foot. He outfooted her considerably, although she was no mean foots-man herself in the women's division. She leaped to the floor and did a ballet. He leaped to the floor and did a buck-and-wing. They saw they couldn't team up on Broadway in that fashion, so they went to the den and began playing blues recordings. She sat on the couch, leaning back against the sleeping Bacchus. He sat in a chair facing her, and waggled his long red tongue. She put her white feet in his lap and opened wide her legs so he could see the vee of her black nylon panties fringed with brown hair between her fine white thighs. Needless to say he looked and waggled his tongue at her vee while she waggled her feet in his vee.

Ray Daniels came into the den and sat down and glowered at Cleo Daniels. She glowered back. They glowered back and forth in silence while Panama Paul massaged her big white feet in his big black hands and hummed the blues.

Cleo had been married to Ray for five years and he had never massaged her feet. Perhaps that was the reason she divorced him. Anyway, it was none of his business who massaged her feet now.

"Don't stare at my feet!" she snapped.

"I'm not staring at your feet," he denied.

"Whose feet are you staring at then?"

"I'm not staring at anybody's feet."

"Then quit staring at whatever you're staring at."

Panama Paul sang lowly, *"Some black snake is sucking my rider's tongue . . ."*

Ray Daniels jumped up and slapped Cleo Daniels. Panama Paul jumped up and tried to restrain Ray Daniels. Cleo Daniels tried to dash her highball glass into Ray's face, but her aim was poor and she dashed it into Panama's face instead.

Mamie came in and thought they were both fighting Panama. Mamie was not the one to stand by while her white guests fought her colored guests, unless they were getting the better of it. So she ordered Panama Paul to release Ray Daniels and leave her house. Panama Paul released Ray Daniels and sat down and picked up Cleo's feet.

Cleo said, "Mamie, you're a horrible bitch."

Mamie said, "That's because I don't sleep with cats."

Cleo had three spayed Siamese cats who lived with her in her one-room apartment in Greenwich Village and crawled over her bed and a fishnet she had hung against the wall for them to climb. They had developed strange, fat, big-bellied shapes, resembling feline eunuchs, but Cleo loved them dearly, and she was sensitive about people insinuating as to their relationship.

So she replied cattily, "No, you only sleep with rats."

"At least they're not castrated rats," Mamie said.

Milt and Bessie Shirley and Arthur Tucker said good night and left together. Mamie laughed curiously and wrote several lines in her little black mental notebook.

Finding no one to talk to after Moe had left, Joe was in the den telling Cleo Daniels and Ray Daniels and Panama Paul his elephant life. "Of course the French student chose as his subject, *Les Amours des Eléphants;* the Russian, *The Oppression of Elephants under British and American Imperialism;* the Italian, *Glories of the Past Empire of the Mastodon;* the German, *The De-Nazification of the Elephant and Other Anti-Semites;* the Englishmen, *The Elephant, a Deterrent for War, as Compared with the Hydrogen Bomb;* and the American, naturally, *The Elephant and The Negro Problem.*"

No one was listening.

Mamie had hidden the whiskey and said it had given out.

The party broke up.

Mamie was happy, but hungry. It had been a successful party. Even if she hadn't caught Juanita, she had set a trap, and she would catch her sooner or later and expose her bald-headed privacy. Mamie Mason had faith.

FOR ONE THING Panama Paul invited Cleo Daniels up to his room at the Lewis Hotel, which is situated on University Place a few blocks north of Washington Square. He invited her up to his room for the purpose of having a drink. She accepted on those grounds.

They had a drink on those grounds and then another drink on those grounds and he attempted to get chummy.

"Take off your shoes, baby."

"I will not."

So he took off his own shoes. And they had another drink.

"Take off your clothes, baby."

"I will not."

So he began taking off his own clothes.

"What are you doing?" she asked.

"I'm undressing," he replied and continued to undress until he had finished undressing.

"You're naked," she said, carefully examining his buck-naked black body, especially his private parts which were not at all private now.

"I sure am," he said.

"For what?"

"For to go to bed."

"You can't go to bed and leave me here."

"I ain't. You're coming with me."

"I am not coming with you."

"You mean you came up here and drank my whiskey and now think you're going to go? What's the matter? You scared?"

"You invited me to have a drink. You didn't say anything about going to bed."

"What else would I invite you up here to drink my whiskey for, pray tell, without going to bed with you?"

"Use your imagination."

"Oh. You thought I was going to do that?"

"Well, what else did you keep showing me your tongue for? What was that supposed to mean from an accomplished thespian like you?"

"Well, get ready, girl, I can't through your clothes."

So she took off her shoes and stockings and garter belt and panties and pulled up her skirt and sat in the arm-chair with her naked white legs hooked over the arms and it was ready.

And was he astonished. "It's red-headed!" he exclaimed.

"It is not," she said. "It's just red hot."

Naturally this was his cue to demonstrate his virtuosity.

And before he knew what was happening she jumped up, snatched up her shoes and stockings and garter belt, and ran out into the corridor, slamming the door behind her.

He was so mad he finished the bottle of whiskey all by himself and fell into a drunken sleep and dreamed he was in a heaven filled with naked white angels, but when he tried to fly in their direction he found that his testicles were weighted down with anvils.

And for another thing, Milt and Bessie Shirley and their guest, Arthur Tucker, went gaily into their suite of rooms in the Thomas Hotel and gaily closed the door behind. And what with all the people moving about in the corridor, it was some time before one had a chance to peek through the keyhole. And, well kiss my foot, all three of them were stark-naked.

Bessie Shirley was hanging head down from a walking stick stuck through the chandelier with her long hair hanging to the floor, and embracing Mr. Tucker, who stood confronting her. And were they having a ball! Where was Milt Shirley? He was standing to one side looking on, having his own private ball. The last thing one saw before some people came down the hall, interrupting one's enjoyment, was the chandelier gradually pulling loose from the ceiling.

Then, of course, Merto guided Willard B. Overton to the apartment on the West Side where she lived with Maurice Gordey, who was not really her husband, she confessed, and where Eddy Schooley had been guest of honor during his broadcast, but not since.

When all was in readiness she took out a small tape measure and measured Mr. Overton. Mr. Overton was not accustomed to being measured in such circumstances and became so chagrined that his measurements abruptly changed. However, when Merto revealed her purpose, his measurements were restored. It had nothing to do with his capabilities, as he had assumed.

In her spare time she knitted a record of her accomplishments. Being as Merto was an expert knitter, they were identical to the subjects, which they represented, so naturally measurements were required for the accuracy of the data.

Afterwards she opened a drawer and showed Mr. Overton her filing cabinet. It was filled to the brim with data of all sizes and colors except white. Obviously she had done well by the poor oppressed Negroes.

Mr. Overton was immensely impressed. He thought she had made a commendable contribution to the Negro Problem, but poor Maurice must be getting worn out from beating her.

However, it evidently suited her, for she looked nice and rosy and in the pink of health, sitting crosslegged on the bed.

She promised to knit his record in duplicate and mail him the extra copy for a souvenir. But he convinced her that it was unnecessary, as much as he adored her generosity. If she would just phone him, at the office, that is, he would come and get it. There was no telling what might ensue should Mrs. Overton open the package and examine its contents and recognize the measurements.

Naturally Dr. Brown drove slowly and carefully down the dangerous New York City streets to their hotel at 34th Street and Eighth Avenue, being as he was responsible for the person of Dr. Carl Vincent Stone, his white boss as you might say, who was sitting in the back seat of Dr. Brown's Chrysler sedan relentlessly crowding Maiti's big hams into her corner.

So, when on their way up to their rooms Dr. Brown invited Dr. Stone to stop in for a nightcap of real eight-year-old Kentucky bourbon whiskey and a sandwich of real Smithfield ham, how could Dr. Stone refuse, as desirous as he was by then for some ham?

But when Dr. Stone discovered that the ham was really Smithfield ham and not the ham which he had anticipated, he recorded a black mark against Dr. Brown's dog-in-the-manger character, and soon afterwards bade them good night.

However, before retiring he called the night bell captain and ordered some of the common Eighth Avenue variety of ham to assuage his appetite.

"Good and black," he instructed.

"Black, sir?"

"You heard me."

"Oh, yes sir, black, sir," the bell captain stammered, wondering where he was going to find any black ham in that vicinity that late at night.

As forty-nine-year-old leading young Negro novelist Lorenzo Llewellyn and his companion, dapper Maurice Gordey, were scouting about, they came upon a house in Brooklyn where a whole bevy of big strong gaily dressed colored women were having themselves a ballll! But being as they didn't have any women's clothes to join in the ball-ing, the women were considerate enough to take off their own; and lo and behold, underneath they were actually mennnn! Suddenly Maurice was heard to squeal delightedly, "Don't you dare pull that big thing on a little girl like me!"

On the other hand, one might have sworn that Jonah Johnson would get himself a Rosenberg fellowship by driving Dr. Garrett, president of the Rosenberg Foundation, all the way from 155th Street downtown to the Waldorf-Astoria Hotel. Especially as Jonah talked all the way at the rate of three hundred words a minute, giving Dr. Garrett a detailed synopsis of his intended book on, er, ah, the Russians.

"Mmmmm, quite fetching, the little brown ones," Dr. Garrett said, jerking himself awake from time to time. "Mmmmm, and they liked to be whipped, did you say?"

"Well, I didn't say they would like it exactly, sir, but I'm sure we can do it if we keep prepared."

"Mmmmm, they all like it, my boy."

"Well, sir, they would certainly resist."

"Mmmmm, I like them with spunk, but I'm worn-out tonight."

So when they stopped in front of the hotel, Jonah asked hopefully, "What do you think of that as a book, Dr. Garrett?"

"Book!" exclaimed the startled Dr. Garrett. "Book, did you say?"

"Yes sir, my book about the Communists."

"Communists. I thought you were discussing the Romanists."

"Er, why no sir, I was telling you about my book—"

"Oh, ah, quite interesting. Quite! Read it just last week."

"But I haven't written it yet."

"Haven't? Ha-ha, better get started, Mr., er, ah—No time like the present."

"Johnson, sir," Jonah said desperately. "Jonah Johnson. I was thinking that with a Rosenberg fellowship—"

"Ah, yes, Mr. Johnson, remember you now. Never forget a Rosenberg fellow. Showed great promise—"

The Waldorf-Astoria doorman hastened to the rescue of Dr. Garrett and whisked him safely into the confines of the Waldorf-Astoria Hotel.

Jonah turned his car around and drove back uptown to his apartment on the third floor of a walkup on 139th Street. His light-complexioned ever-loving wife asked crossly where he had been all night. She already had one black eye and he promptly gave her another, whether she liked it or not.

So what happened to the unidentified distinguished-looking white lady and the young dark Negro poet who looked like Jackson? They left Mamie's to go somewhere and make some poetry, and, oh, brother, they are making it, white and black poetry, that is.

This poetry is not only being made but it is being said, between pants and grunts and groans, that is.

HE: Birmingham.
SHE: Oh, you poor lamb.
HE: Ku-Klux-Klan.
SHE: Oh, you poor black man.
HE: Lynch mob.
SHE: Oh, you make me sob.
HE: Little Rock.
SHE: Oh, what an awful shock.
HE: Jim Crow.
SHE: Oh, you suffering Negro.
HE: Denied my rights.
SHE: Oh, take my delights.
HE: Segregation.
SHE: Oh, but integration.
HE: They killed my pappy.
SHE: Oh, let me make you happy.
HE: They call me low.
SHE: Oh, you beautiful Negro.

Finally the verses ceased as the rhythm increased to a

crashing crescendo with a long wailing finale:

HE: Oooooooooooo!

SHE: Negrooooooooooo!

Which just goes to show the Negro Problem is inspirational too, for what other grave problem of our time inspires such spontaneous rhapsody?

And what did Julius find out about that fashionable East Side divorcee, Fay Corson? He found out that she lived in a seven-room apartment on the eighth floor of a very swank building in the East Seventies, and that she was an animal lover. For no sooner had they disrobed than she suggested they play dogs. So they scampered about the carpeted floor in the manner of mating dogs. Then she decided to play shaggy dog and pulled down the telephone from the bed table and dialed a number. It so happened that Will Robbins answered and she said to him:

"You sneak."

"Fay!" he exclaimed. "Where are you?"

"I'm at home, you rat."

"Doing what?"

"I'm playing bitch, if you just must know."

"Is that new?"

"With a big black dog," she said.

"Lucky black dog, you lucky white bitch," he said.

"And what are you doing, you louse?"

"If you just must know, I am sitting at the kitchen table eating oysters on the half shell."

"And what is that black slut doing you took home with you? Eating oysters too, I suppose."

"That fine brown woman is not eating oysters whatsoever."

"Then why don't you give her some oysters?"

"Her turn will come when I'm finished."

"And when will that be?"

"Soon."

"Wait for me."

"Better hurry."

"Now!" she cried.

"Now!" he replied.

"Oh, now and now again and again now," she said, quoting Hemingway.

"Not any more now," he said, sighing.

"You dirty freak," she said, and banged down the receiver.

Then she pulled away from Julius and ran into the bathroom. Julius listened to the water running. And what had he found out for real? Well, he had found out where sea urchins come from.

As for Reverend Riddick and Professor Samuels, they both wound up in the Bellevue psychiatric ward for observation.

But it is not at all like you're probably thinking. What happened was that Isaiah and Kit Samuels, leaving Mamie Mason's party at the same time as Reverend Mike Riddick, could do no less than help him get the helpless Miss Lucy Pitt downtown to her abode. Then what happened after that was when they had got the young lady home and got her undressed and safely resting atop the sheet with all her sweet brown femininity exposed, Reverend Riddick was struck by such compelling compassion that he wished to say a Christian prayer for the poor helpless girl before tucking her beneath the covers. And that is the only reason he asked Professor Samuels to leave the room, which in turn precipitated the wrestling match.

Because Professor Samuels said, "I see no reason why we both can't pray in turns. That is, if we leave my wife out of it."

"It's because you're Jewish," Reverend Riddick said. "And while I have nothing against the Jewish faith, it being the father of my own faith, still and all you can see the girl has not been circumcised and is only fit for a Christian prayer."

"I'm not Jewish," Professor Samuels denied vehemently.

"Then what are you doing with a Jewish name?" Reverend Riddick challenged.

"You've got an Irish name but you're not Irish," Professor Samuels rebutted.

"I have never said I was Irish," Reverend Riddick said.

"I have never said I was Jewish either," Professor Samuels said.

"Then what are you doing with a Jewish name?" Reverend Riddick persisted.

"That's my family name," Professor Samuels informed him. "The fact of the matter is, I am from Mississippi and all of my family are Christians and very anti-Semitic."

"If you're anti-Semitic then you're anti-Negro," Reverend Riddick charged. "And if you're anti-Negro I shall not let you pray over this helpless young Negro girl."

"I'm getting damned tired of people accusing me of being anti-Negro just because I'm from Mississippi," Professor Samuels said. "Some of the Negro peoples' best friends are from Mississippi."

"How far from Mississippi?" Reverend Riddick asked.

"It's not a matter of distance," Professor Samuels said. "We can be miles apart and still be friends."

"Then if you're not anti-Negro you're not afraid of the black rubbing off of me," Reverend Riddick said.

"As far as that goes, if you're not anti-white you're not afraid of the white rubbing off of me," Professor Samuels said.

"Then if you're not afraid of the black rubbing off of me, I'll wrestle you buck-naked," Reverend Riddick challenged.

"I'll wrestle you buck-naked with the greatest of pleasure," Professor Samuels accepted his challenge.

So that is how they came about wrestling buck-naked.

But one look at Reverend Riddick's fine black body with its big impressive limbs inspired Kit Samuels to rip off her own clothes and begin wrestling buck-naked also. She wrestled about the room in circles, as though she were wrestling two buck-naked electric wires.

"Oh, oh, big black Riddick," she cried in spontaneous rapture and began throwing her white body about as though to demonstrate its potentialities, in case anyone might be interested.

"Put on your clothes, you bitch!" Professor Samuels shouted. "You're exposing yourself."

But she must have misunderstood him because she began doing the splits and the bumps and exposing herself from all directions, shouting in reply, "Oh, big black Riddick, I'm a bitch! I'm a bitch! Oh, big black Riddick, I'm a bitch in heat."

"You're a frantic slut," Professor Samuels screamed.

Naturally Reverend Riddick resented Professor Samuels addressing such a fine white woman in that manner, even though she was his wife. So he caught Professor Samuels' head in a nelson. Professor Samuels was not one to be nelsoned without retaliating, so he gripped Reverend Riddick's most vulnerable limb. The only thing was he was too weak to take a good hold and his hand kept slipping up and down.

And when Kit Samuels noticed this she entered into the spirit of the match with greater abandon.

"Oh, big black Riddick, I'm a frantic slut. Oh, I'm a frantic slut. Oh, big black Riddick, I'm a frantic slut."

Such behavior on the part of his wife so intensified Professor Samuel's agitation that he wrapped his legs about one of the Reverend Riddick's big black legs and began to wrestle in earnest.

"Oh, you whore!" he reviled his wanton wife.

"Oh, I'm a whore, I'm a whore," Kit Samuels cried, dancing in even greater frenzy.

"I'll divorce you, you whore!" Professor Samuels cried. "I'll throw you out!"

"Oh, I'm a whore and I'll give you cause to throw me out," Kit Samuels said and immediately launched into such frenzied cause that Professor Samuels cried out.

"I'll kill myself! I'll jump into the river!"

Which, for some inexplicable reason caused Kit Samuels to cry joyously, "Go kill yourself! Go jump into the river! Or I'll give more cause!"

Professor Samuels broke from Reverend Riddick's hold

and ran, still dripping, out of the door.

"Jesus save us!" Reverend Riddick bellowed, and ran, still dripping, to bring him back.

Just as day was breaking, Professor Samuels came running down the stairs from Lucy Pitt's fourth-floor flat beside the railroad tracks on West 10th Street, in the Village, white-baby naked. Reverend Riddick came running down behind him, black-baby naked.

Early Village risers looked up and saw a naked white man highballing down the street with a naked black man chasing him and hastened back inside their homes and locked their doors, thinking the Africans were invading.

The naked white man ran underneath the elevated railroad tracks and headed toward the Hudson River. The naked black man ran after him. The naked men ran past one big trailer truck after another big trailer truck. They ran past one freighter dock after another freighter dock. The naked white man couldn't find any way to get close enough to the river to jump in and drown. The naked black man couldn't run fast enough to catch him and stop him in case he got to the riverbank.

One of the Bowery bums who had stayed over on that side during the night, a former professor of Greek mythology at an Ivy League university, dozing fitfully on the sidewalk, looked up in time to see the fleet-footed naked runners rounding the walls of Troy, and exclaimed weakly, "History repeats itself!"

Shortly afterwards two truck drivers came out of an all-night greasy spoon and caught the runners and held them for the police.

Which just goes to show that the phallus complex is the aphrodisiac of the Negro Problem.

Speaking of phalli, what about that big-all-over white man, Art Wills? Well, Art Wills was taken home by Brown Sugar, who was really Mrs. Lillian Davis Burroughs, wife of the Harlem financier in private life. She told him that it would be perfectly all right, and she had her big new shiny Buick there, and she was a big, handsome, hefty, hammy, curly-headed, wide-eyed, smooth, brown, luscious piece herself, so naturally Art believed her. Even when she parked her car before a three-story brick house on Fish Avenue in the Bronx, and informed him coyly that was where she and her husband lived, he was so far gone it didn't bother him a bit as long as it didn't bother her.

They sat on the sofa in the living room and explored their differences until, as it should always happen when there is sufficient negotiation, her difference seemed ready to accept his difference and come to the point, or if not to the point, come anyway.

So she said, "You undress now."

The lady said undress and, being as he was a man, he undressed.

"You undress, too," he said.

Being as she was a woman with an undressed man about she undressed too. Now they were both undressed. He looked at the lady's well-inflated, curley-haired privacy that seemed about to pop from her smooth, tight, copper-colored thighs and naturally he didn't want that to happen, but the lady contended that there were more important decisions to be taken.

"You won't be afraid of the scandal?" she asked.

"What scandal?" he asked.

"I'm going to scream when you're ready."

"You can see I'm ready," he contended. "But you're not going to scream just because of that."

"Oh, I'm ready for that too, but are you ready for the other?"

"Ready for what other?"

"Why, ready for my husband to come down and catch us."

"Catch us doing what?"

"Why, catch making love. What do you think? Who else would I want to catch us making love?"

"I'm sure I don't know. The neighbors, perhaps."

"The neighbors are not in it."

"Well, I'm glad to know that. It would be a little crowded if they were. But what is your husband going to do when he comes down here and finds us making love?"

"Oh, he won't make any trouble. He's a coward. It's just for him to see it."

"Oh, he likes to see you making love with other men?"

"Certainly not. Do you think I'd be married to a man like that? That's why I want him to see it."

"Let me get this straight. You mean you want your husband to see you making love with another man because he won't like it?"

"If he liked it there wouldn't be any point. Are you stupid?"

"I'm beginning to think so. You mean to say your husband is going to hear you scream and come running down here and find us making love and he's not going to make any trouble even though he won't like it?"

"Of course not. He's not a savage. He's going to give one look and see right away it isn't anything like that."

"You mean he's going to give one look and see you're not making love? You don't know me, baby."

"I don't mean that. I mean as if you're hurting me. He's going to see right off I'm loving you too."

"The way things are going, it is going to take more than him to see that. But why are you going to scream before we even start, unless you're one of those natural screamers who start screaming just by thinking about it."

"Oh, don't be so silly. I've got to scream to get him down here to find us. Otherwise he'd just stay up in his room and keep on sleeping and we'd be making love for nothing."

"You might be making love for nothing but not me, and I don't see why some husband has got to find me making love to his wife in order for me to enjoy it."

"Please, don't try to appear so dense," she said, stroking him and kissing him. "We can't avoid the scandal."

"Do you mean to say you can't make love without making a scandal?" he asked.

"What do you take me to be, an exhibitionist?" she flared. "But it can't be avoided."

"It seems to me it could be avoided easily enough if we would just make love quietly and you didn't scream."

"But how else can we get him to come down here and find us making love! You don't know Handsome—"

"What's more, I don't want to know him—"

"He wouldn't even sue for divorce at all if he didn't actually find us making love."

Art felt suddenly as though he had gotten involved in the Cold War by mistake. "You mean he wouldn't sue you for divorce—" he began.

But she cut him off. "It's not him I'm thinking about. I know you can handle him—"

"Don't tell me there will be others?"

"It's your wife I'm thinking about," she said. "Can you make her give you a divorce, or does she have to catch us making love too?"

"But why all these divorces?" he asked in amazement. "Just for a little lovemaking?"

"So we can get married, you big wonderful white man, and make love all the time," she said.

He looked regretfully at all that ripe October-painted flesh going to waste and thought, My God, this woman is stark raving mad. Whereupon he jumped into his clothes and got out of there as fast as was humanly possible before she started screaming, making love or not.

For a natural born philanderer, he was exceptionally glad to get home to his apartment on East 54th Street where his ever-loving wife, Debbie, was waiting for him with this news:

"Darling, she did it again."

By then he was good and tired of cryptic women.

"Say what you mean," he said crossly. "*Who* did *what* again?"

"Your daughter, dear. What other *she* would I mean?"

"How would I know?" he snapped.

Her eyes widened. "And just what does that mean?"

But he refused to get involved again in women's logic.

"It means I would like to know what did my daughter do again? I know it's something bad because the only time she's my daughter is when she's done something bad. When she's good she's your daughter."

"Well, heaven knows she must have inherited it from you. No one in my family has ever done anything like *that*."

"Like *what?*"

"I just told you. She threw the cat out of the window again."

"Who do you know in my family, may I ask, who has ever thrown a cat out of a window?"

"I can't speak for the others, but *your* daughter has, twice."

Two weeks before, Art's angelic little eight-year-old daughter, Marilyn, had befriended a mangy old alley cat she'd found in the street, obviously friendless. She'd brought it upstairs to their fourth-floor apartment and had bathed it in the bathtub and her mother had had to call the doctor to treat her for scratches. Then she had fed it and pampered it until the cat became ungrateful and unresponsive, as are all fat cats. So Marilyn had picked up the ungrateful cat and had thrown it out of the fourth-story window back into the street. The cat's front legs had been broken. Her mother had had to take the cat to the cat-and-dog clinic, and it had cost twenty-five dollars to get the cat's legs set and put in plaster casts. For the past week the cat had been living the life of an invalid in the Wills' apartment. So naturally Art was only too happy that *his* little daughter had taken this commendable action and got rid of the cat.

"Did you call the SPCA to take it away?" He meant the cat's corpse, of course.

"I did not," Debbie replied indignantly. "Do you think I want anyone to know *your* daughter has inherited such a streak of cruelty?"

"Well, then, when did it happen?" he asked.

"At one o'clock this morning, while you were gallivanting around Mamie Mason's."

"Oh, then it was all right to leave it there."

"And listen to it yowling in agony?"

"What! You mean it wasn't dead?"

"Of course it wasn't dead. That kind of cat never dies."

"Then what did you do with it, may I ask?"

"I called the doctor, of course."

"What! You called the doctor at two o'clock in the morning? My God, what did he charge?"

"Why, the same as before, twenty-five dollars. The same two legs were broken."

"Wife, do you mean to stand there and tell me you paid twenty-five dollars on that cat again?" he demanded. "And do we still have the monster here convalescing in our house?"

"I know it's difficult, dear. But she's your daughter."

"*My* daughter."

"So what else could I do?"

"You could have called an ambulance and all of you could have gone to an insane asylum."

She bristled. "I believe you mean that."

"Mean it!" he shouted.

But he restrained from committing himself and went into the kitchen and drank the pint of one hundred and twenty proof corn whiskey he had been saving for such an emergency.

Speaking of emergencies, one might assume that Moe Miller, blessed with such a formidable talent and charged as he was with strong whiskey and fried chicken, would certainly have passed the night in some creative activity, such as increasing the population. But no, Moe was a home man, and even though his wife, Evie, was in Baltimore, he went straight home.

What was wrong with him? Did he have a case? Had he buried his talent and forgotten where? Not at all. Moe was writing a series of newspaper articles on the Negro Problem, mornings after parties being the best time for such creativity, and on the side he was trying to catch a rat. Not the kind of rat you're thinking about either. The rat Moe was trying to catch was a real ratty rat, a dirty lowdown thieving rat that had been stealing food from the Millers' larder for a long time.

The Millers lived in a two-story brick bungalow in Brooklyn, and when they first began missing the food they had assumed it was a two-legged rat, since Brooklyn is known to be infested with all kinds of rats. Whole loaves of bread, sacks of potatoes, bowls of fruit, tins of meat, bottles of whiskey had disappeared, along with several bags of nuts, although, in view of the ensuing events, that would not have been so farfetched as it might seem.

Moe had notified the police and had kept their doors and windows securely closed and locked. But still the food kept disappearing. Naturally Moe didn't put up with that, as well as he liked to eat. He began setting rat traps in strategic places about the house. The first traps of the common spring type disappeared also. It was then Moe concluded it had to be a mighty big rat if it could eat the traps. So he bought all of the biggest rat traps known, but the rat merely ignored these traps and continued to steal the food. So Moe bought a bear trap and baited it with a pound of the best cheese money could buy, and he chained the trap to the cold-water pipe. But the rat moved the trap over beside the door and then made a big racket, knocking over the dustpan and letting out some horrible-sounding squeals. Moe came rushing down into the kitchen, thinking he had caught the rat, and stepped into the trap. At first he thought the rat had him. By its bite he knew the rat was as big as a Great Dane. He fought the rat so furiously and screamed in such desperation the entire neighborhood was awakened and prowl cars came from all directions. For one whole week Moe was unable to walk and after that he gave up on traps. He decided to shoot the rat. He was going to shoot it in cold blood. He was going to blow that dirty rat's brains to hell and gone. He bought a double-barrelled twelve-gauge shotgun, and nights on end he laid in ambush for the rat. But the rat never appeared while he was waiting for it. Naturally, the rat had more sense than that. The rat wouldn't come out and raid the larder until Moe got sleepy and went to bed.

Besides which, it kept Evie so nervous with Moe prowling around in the black dark house with a loaded shotgun that she threatened to leave him. He compromised by promising to keep the gun unloaded until he actually saw the rat. One night he was sitting in the dark kitchen with the two twelve-gauge shells on the table at his hand and the shotgun across his knees, waiting for the rat to show its dirty head. But he dozed off, and while he was sleeping the rat came and stole the two shotgun shells. The very next morning Moe got rid of the shotgun to keep the rat from stealing it and shooting him, being as the rat already had the shells for it.

That was when he bought the big, vicious-looking, razor-sharp hunting knife. He was going to lay for that rat and catch him face to face. And it was going to be man against rat, a fight to the finish. The rat was going to find out who was the best man. He was going to cut that rat's heart out.

When he arrived home from Mamie Mason's party, he took off his shoes and entered the house as silently as an Indian. He tiptoed up the front stairs in the dark and got his knife and tiptoed down the back stairs and snapped on the light in the kitchen.

And there, in the middle of the polished linoleum floor, was a hen egg. He blinked and spun about, holding the knife ready to stab. And there, at the head of the basement stairs, was another hen egg.

Before going to the party he had bought a half-dozen eggs, a pound of butter and a loaf of bread, which he had left on the sidestand for his breakfast. Nothing remained but the empty sack which had held the eggs.

He turned on the basement lights and started downstairs. There was an egg on the middle stair and another one at the bottom. In the middle of the basement floor was his pound of butter with one corner nibbled off. At the far end of the basement was the old fuel bin which had been out of use since they had installed a new oil burner. There was a sizable hole at the bottom of the screen door to the bin. Directly in front of the hole was another egg.

Moe opened the door. Directly inside of the bin was the loaf of bread with a corner nibbled off. There, beside the big wooden box where kindling and paper had been stored, was another egg.

Moe lifted the lid of the box. The box was filled to the brim with food. There was a hole in the back of the box opening onto a network of tunnels. The box had been neatly divided into compartments. There was a compartment for eggs, one for fruit, one for bread, one for cured meat, one for bottles of whiskey, Coca-Cola, milk, ink and cleaning fluid, and one big compartment at the far end for a miscellaneous collection of nails, screws, Tampax, lipstick, perfume, chewing gum, cigarettes, a pipe, an old pair of house slippers and a stack of comic books. He could see right off that the rat loved comfort, but he didn't think much of the rat's reading habits. Poking around with a stick he uncovered some suspiciously stained towels and some used condoms. He had already realized it was a big rat, but judging from the size of the condoms, what an enormous rat it must have been screwing.

He searched the coal bin and the entire basement, but there was no sign of the rat. He went back to the kitchen, determined to search the entire house, room by room, and also looked to see if the beds had been used. But just as he stepped into the kitchen, at long last he had his wish. He and the rat stood face to face. The rat tried to get past him into the basement but he kicked the rat back into the kitchen and slammed the door.

This was it. Man to rat. The rat stood up on its hind legs and snarled at him. The man was somewhat alarmed. That rat was as big as a tomcat. It had mangy gray fur and a long bare tail that resembled the main root of a giant cactus. But what alarmed the man most was the size of the rat's teeth.

Moe clutched the broom in his left hand and held his hunting knife in his right hand. He swiped at the rat with the broom. The rat dodged and slapped him on the ankle with its tail. He slashed at the rat with his knife. The rat backed away slowly. Moe advanced cautiously. Suddenly the rat looked around and found itself in a corner. It knew it was a cornered rat. It stood up on its hind legs again and snarled a warning. Moe punched at it with the broom. The rat bit the broom and jerked it out of Moe's hand. Moe lunged for the broom and the rat lunged for Moe. Moe jumped back and slashed at the rat with his knife. The rat charged Moe and slashed open his pants with its teeth. Moe was so frightened he threw his knife at the rat. The knife missed the rat and hit the wall and bounced back onto the floor. The rat lit on the knife and grabbed the handle between its teeth. Then it charged Moe with the knife. Moe jumped on top of the table. The rat leaped up into the air and tried to cut Moe on the leg. Moe jumped from the table onto the drain. The rat leaped up into the sink. Moe jumped from the drainboard on top of the stove. The rat leaped onto the drainboard and Moe jumped down to the floor. When the rat leaped down to follow Moe the knife was jarred from its teeth. While the rat was going back for the knife, Moe had time to get the door open and run out of the house.

Shaken and exhausted, Moe went to the police precinct station and reported the rat to the police. Then he sent his wife, Evie, a telegram:

FOR GOD SAKE DO NOT COME STOP RAT HAS GOT KNIFE STOP IN POSSESSION OF HOUSE STOP I AM DROPPING THE NEGRO PROBLEM UNTIL RAT IS CAUGHT STOP LOOK FOR ME ON THE 12:10.

And right there you have the main trouble with the Negro Problem—*rats*.

Well, what about Joe? No inference intended.

Joe looked into the den at the sleeping Bacchus. All looked peaceful atop Olympus. In fact, Bacchus had Olympus to himself.

Joe went into the bedroom and took off his clothes. He was hairless as an eightball, save for the patch of dried pubic grass.

Mamie came into the bedroom and looked at Joe and laughed.

"Baby, no one will challenge your legitimacy," she said.

Joe smiled slyly. "Mama kept it for papa."

"This mama is keeping it for her papa," Mamie lied with a straight face and took off her own clothes.

And what do you know? Those catty women who were always disparaging her breasts weren't too wrong. They hung down like a nanny goat's udders, but that suited Joe fine, as much as he liked to suckle. For no sooner had she climbed astride his soft black belly in jockey fashion, holding his arms pinioned to the bed and letting her titties dangle over his face, than he tried his damnedest to suckle. The only trouble was he couldn't catch one in his big juicy mouth although he nibbled hard enough, first at one and then at the other like a fish after worms. But finally he got hold of one, looking for all the world like a big black baby suckling. Afterwards he didn't even have to change position to go to sleep.

Having that done with, Mamie donned a red quilted robe and red felt mules and carried the telephone extension from the den and plugged it in the kitchen outlet. She dialed a Chelsea number and asked to speak to Wallace Wright.

It so happened that Wallace Wright's home telephone was on the Audubon exchange and his office telephone on the Murray Hill exchange. And this Chelsea number that Mamie called was listed in the name of a very smart, middle-aged white divorcee who lived on West 23rd Street.

"Wallace Wright?" The low husky voice sounded startled. "That's you, isn't it, Mamie?"

"Yes, darling. Wallace left his notecase here when he was at my party and I found your letter in it."

"Letter? What letter?"

"The one where you asked him to divorce his Negro wife. Naturally I don't want that type of letter in my house and—" She broke off to listen to the faint sound of whispering at the other end. "What did he say, darling?"

"You are vicious, Mamie. You know damn well I've never written any such letter to Mr. Wright and if I had, Mr. Wright has too much pride—"

"Call him Wallace, darling," Mamie interrupted. "At least while he's in bed with you."

"Mr. Wright has not, is not—"

Mamie hung up. Her only regret was that she was not there to see Mr. Wright getting out of bed. But what she didn't know was that by the time she had hung up, Mr. Wright had already gotten out of bed and had gotten half-dressed.

"I'd better go dear. Better go. Best thing," he was muttering.

His erstwhile bedmate started to tell him he didn't really have to go, that she wasn't afraid of Mamie Mason. But after the second look she realized that Mr. Wright had already gone.

"I know, dear. Phone me and come when you can," she said.

Mamie would have then phoned Wallace Wright's wife, Juanita, and informed her where Wallace had been. But she and Juanita were not on speaking terms, and she would not give Juanita the satisfaction of being spoken to by her. Instead she went downstairs to have her very best friend, Patty Pearson, who was also Juanita's very best friend, telephone Juanita instead.

Patty had not attended Mamie's party because she had been entertaining a party on her own. But her party had finished and gone and Patty was alone, reminiscing over the delights of being screwed while standing on her head.

"Come on into the kitchen and tell me all about it, honey," she welcomed Mamie.

"What's that you're cooking, sugar?"

"I'm frying some salt pork to go with my grits. You want some scrambled eggs with yours?"

"You know I'm on a diet, sugar."

"I know you are, honey. Just eat one of those cold pig's feet while you're waiting."

"Enjoy yourself, sugar?" Mamie asked with the foot in her mouth.

"I blitzed him, honey. You couldn't squeeze out another drop with a steam roller. How was your party?"

"Wonderful, sugar. Schooley sobered up enough to dance naked."

"Nothing dropped off, I hope."

"No, sugar. You'll find it just as you left it."

Patty raised her eyebrows. "*That* limp?"

Mamie laughed and started on another foot.

"Wait, honey," Patty said. "I just got to do the eggs."

"Do you have some mineral oil, sugar?"

"Natch, honey, with my men. In the bathroom."

When Mamie returned from drinking a quarter of a glass of mineral oil, the feast was on the table.

"I suppose Dora Steele got Jule," Patty said.

"She couldn't come. Jimmy had a case of acute indigestion."

"When you said *case* I thought—"

"You know how careful Jimmy is."

"But indigestion!" Patty exclaimed.

"Something he et."

"Does it give one indigestion?"

They exchanged sly looks and noisily chewed their grits.

"Who did get Jule, honey?"

"Fay."

"Oh, her. Is he still trying to find out if it's true?"

"He's just hunting while he can."

"He won't win a home with her."

"Not home-hunting, sugar. Tuft-hunting."

"When's my turn coming to be shot?"

"Soon, sugar. Just keep flipping your tuft at him."

"Wallace have a nice time, honey?"

"Lovely, sugar. I want you to call Juanita for me."

"I'd love to. What do you want me to tell her?"

"Just say that being as you're her best friend, you want to

tell her before it gets all over town that Wallace has been caught in bed with a you-know-who."

Patty smiled sweetly.

And that was how it happened that Juanita first found out about what later became known in Harlem as Wallace's folly.

It turned out so well they both returned to the kitchen and drank a pint of rum to celebrate.

And why did Mamie do this thing to Wallace Wright? Simply because Wallace never brought Juanita to any of her parties. He always came alone, just as though she ran a whorehouse. She considered that a damn insult.

IT SO HAPPENED that Patty's telephone call, instigated by Mamie, so upset Juanita that she became ill and had to stay in bed that day. Juanita was an elementary schoolteacher, and when she reported her illness a substitute schoolteacher was called to fill her place.

Mamie Mason was a substitute schoolteacher, and it so happened that she was the substitute schoolteacher called to fill Juanita Wright's place. Needless to say, she was as tight as a boiled owl when she reported for duty. Mercifully, there is no available record of her day's activities, but according to the custodian's report her classroom was thoroughly aired before school began again.

The only thing that saved the day from complete devastation was the marriage proposal from Art Wills to Brown Sugar which Mamie found in her mailbox on returning home from school.

It came about from drinking too much corn whiskey on an empty stomach. Art had a bad hangover which made him feel remorseful for always being unfaithful to his ever-faithful sweet little wife, and he wanted to go to sleep and forget both wife and remorse. But after her bad night with the cat, Debbie felt very much in the need of some good old-fashioned therapeutical loving. So they stripped naked and began the therapeutics. While this was going on their daughter, Marilyn, came into the room and saw Papa bounc-

ing up and down on top of Mama while Mama was gasping and moaning and crying and trying to throw Papa off,
the way it looked to her. Naturally she thought they were
fighting. So what can you tell a child in a case like this? Art
said they were working up a sweat in order to take a bath.
So Marilyn said, Oh, goody-goody, I'll run the water.

So Art had to get up and take a bath. Then Debbie said
that being as he was already up he may as well have breakfast with them since, after all, they were his family and Marilyn deserved to see her father some mornings before going
to school.

So Art had to eat breakfast until Marilyn went off to
school. After Marilyn had gone Debbie saw no reason for
them not continuing their lovemaking, since he had already
taken his bath.

Well, just about the time they had got that accomplished
successfully and Art had given a big yawn and snuggled
down under the covers, the broken-legged cat started yowling. The cat had tried to get out of its basket and had got
itself caught, and Debbie was afraid to touch it, so Art had to
get up and put the cat back into its basket. Evidently the cat
resented being put back into its basket for it gave Art some
nasty scratches on his hands and wrists. He was putting io-
dine on the scratches and gritting his teeth against the sound
of the cat yowling when Debbie came into the bathroom
and said he must have injured the cat's broken legs and he
would have to take the cat to the cat-and-dog clinic to have
its casts reset.

That was when Art decided to run away. But it isn't as
easy to run away when one grows up as one might think.
Where can a grown man run away to? Then he thought of
Brown Sugar. He'd run away to her. She might have a cow-
ardly husband he'd have to contend with, but at least she
didn't have any broken-legged cats.

So when he dressed to take the cat to the cat-and-dog
clinic he put some stationery into his pocket and when he'd

deposited the cat with the vet, he went to the post office and wrote Brown Sugar the following letter:

> *Dearest,*
> *Want very much to marry you providing your husband doesn't yowl. Need sleep badly.*
>
> > *Lovingly,*
> > *Art*

But when he came to addressing the envelope he discovered he not only did not remember her address but he did not remember her name. So he addressed it to:

> *Mrs. Brown Sugar*
> *c/o Mrs. Mamie Mason*
> *409 Edgecombe Drive*
> *Manhattan, N.Y.*

Naturally Mamie opened and read any letter addressed in her care. How could she care for a letter if she didn't know what she was caring for?

No letter ever written in her care was more welcome than this one. She had been waiting for some time to ask Art for another favor and his letter to Brown Sugar made her realize just how happy he would be to oblige her. He had scheduled a big picture story on Wallace Wright for the first issue of the magazine he was to edit when the money had been raised to begin publication. And his proposal to Brown Sugar ought certainly to convince him just how unjust that was. Why should Wallace Wright benefit from publicity given him by her own personal friends when he wouldn't even bring his wife to her parties? And to think of assigning the story to Julius, her own brother-in-law, who would have to go into the Wrights' house and take that droopy-drawered woman's picture. There was no justice in it at all. The least Art could do would be to cancel the story and do one on herself instead.

In the meantime Art had been assailed all day long by

contemplation of life's injustices. He worked like a dog to support his wife and child and pay the rent on the apartment and he couldn't even sleep there without having to dissipate his energies on his own wife. Oh, the humiliation of it. Not to mention having to nursemaid a broken-legged cat. The only thing left for him to do was to get drunk. But how could a man get drunk without a drinking buddy? And what better drinking buddy than someone who was soon to become his employee?

So he telephoned Julius, who had just got home and gone to bed, to come out and meet him for lunch.

"I want to go to sleep," Julius complained.

"Why should you sleep when I can't sleep?" Art asked.

"Why can't you sleep if you're sleepy?"

"I haven't got anywhere to sleep."

"What's the matter with sleeping with your wife?"

"I've left my wife," Art said sadly.

Julius realized it was indeed serious if a man had to leave his wife when he was broken and exhausted, when that was the only sensible time for a man to sleep with his wife. So he promised to meet him within a half hour at Small's Paradise Inn uptown in Harlem, at the corner of 135th Street and Seventh Avenue. If he couldn't get him fixed up there it would only be because all the colored women had dropped dead. So instead of going to sleep he got up and dressed again and took several slugs of Mamie's whiskey for inspiration.

He was not a little astonished to find Art sitting in a booth talking to a big fine-looking colored man. He hadn't realized Art was that hard up. He sat down beside him and said, "I see you two know one another."

"No," said the colored man. "We haven't been introduced."

"This is Art," Julius said. "He's going to be my boss. What's your name?"

"Handsome," the colored man said.

"All right, you're handsome," Julius conceded. "But what's your name?"

"That is my name," the colored man said. "My mother was named Beauty so my father thought I should be named Handsome because I took after her."

"All right, Handsome, meet Art."

Handsome and Art shook hands.

"What's your name?" Handsome asked Julius.

"My name? Oh, that's right, we don't know each other, do we? My name's Julius."

"I'm glad to make your acquaintance, Julius," Handsome said, extending his hand.

Julius shook his hand. "Just call me Jule," he said.

"Art tells me he's going to get married," Handsome said.

"He's already married," Julius said.

"He's going to get married again."

"Oh!" Julius turned to Art. "Who to?"

"To a woman who's all woman!" Art said enthusiastically.

"I'm glad of that," Julius said relieved. "What's her name?"

"To tell you the truth, I've forgotten her name."

"Then how do you know she wants to marry you if you don't even know who she is?"

"She said she did. I was at her house."

"Well then what does she look like if you don't know her name?"

"She's a big fine-looking woman," Art raved. "Every inch a woman. They call her Brown Sugar."

"Brown Sugar!" Handsome exclaimed. "A big yellow woman with curly hair?"

"She has curly hair but I wouldn't call her yellow. Her face, of course, is lighter than the lower part of her body. I'd call her body copper-colored and, well, her thighs I'd say were a nice warm brown. Do you know her?"

"That's my wife!" Handsome said indignantly.

"Oh! Then you're her husband who's the coward."

"I am not a coward," Handsome said belligerently. "And if you marry my wife I'm going to marry yours."

"You can't marry my wife. She isn't divorced."

"Oh, you're one of those kind. You want to marry my wife but you don't want me to marry yours."

"It's not whether I want you to or not. It's just that you can't."

"I know what's the matter with you. You're prejudiced," Handsome charged.

"I am not prejudiced," Art said. "I didn't write the laws."

"If I was white you wouldn't be talking like that," Handsome said. "You'd go ahead and marry my wife and let me go ahead and marry yours and there wouldn't be nothing said about it. It's just because I'm colored that you start talking about laws."

"That's what's wrong with the whole situation," Art said heatedly. "Whenever you colored people can't get what you want you accuse us of being prejudiced."

"If you weren't prejudiced you'd be a real man and wouldn't stand in the way of your wife's happiness just because a colored man is considering marrying her," Handsome maintained.

"I'm no more prejudiced than you are," Art contended. "You can't bear to see your wife marry me because I'm white and here you are yourself considering marrying a white woman who doesn't even have her divorce."

"I know what's eating you," Handsome said. "You're just worried because you know I'm a better lover than you."

"I doubt that very seriously," Art said, bristling.

"You ask my wife," Handsome said.

"I don't need any favoritism," Art said. "She'd choose me."

"Why don't you go in the john and make comparisons?" Julius suggested.

"And have everyone think we are fairies?" Handsome said. "They know me around here."

"Oh, in that case you'd better not," Julius agreed.

"If we could find some impartial woman," Handsome suggested.

"Do you know Mamie Mason?" Art asked.

"Of course I know Mamie Mason," Handsome said. "Have you made love to her?"

"She'll tell you I'm not prejudiced," Art said.

"All right, I'll take her word," Handsome conceded.

So instead of eating lunch, the three of them started walking up Seventh Avenue in the direction of Edgecombe Drive to get Mamie to prove to Handsome that Art wasn't prejudiced.

But on the way they met Kathy Carter, Joe Mason's secretary, who had quit work early to get some sleep too, and they put the proposition to her.

"I like a drink when I'm talking politics," she said, so they retired to the nearest bar.

"Now that you ask me about Art," she said, sitting on her high stool at the bar and blinking her eyes in his direction, "I think it's all just a matter of white and colored people getting together and then we can judge."

"How can we get together with white people if they're too prejudiced to get together with us?" Handsome demanded.

"Well, that's just what I mean," Kathy said. "Once we've gotten together with them in a real good way then they're not prejudiced anymore."

"That's just what I've been saying," Art said. "I might have been prejudiced once but I've gotten together with such fine colored women I'm not prejudiced anymore."

"That's just what I mean," Kathy said. "Once you get to know what it's all about, it's just a question of congenitally, if you know what I mean. Just like colored men are always thinking they're so much, but if you take colored men and white men, man for man, it's the expansion that counts. I've known some white men who can take a colored girl away from a colored man just like that." She snapped her fingers to demonstrate. "If you know what I mean."

"But would you want to marry a white man?" Handsome persisted.

"Would I!" she exclaimed, rolling her eyes at Art. "Better not one ask me."

Handsome looked disgusted. "That's what's wrong with

you colored women. Colored men ain't good enough for you. That's the whole trouble with the Negro Problem. Here my wife is, wants to marry some white man—"

"You colored men are just jealous," Kathy said. "You make me sick." She was beginning to feel frisky and snapped her fingers exhilaratingly. "Given enough time, I bet I could solve this whole Negro Problem by myself.

Art looked as though he would like to suggest there was no better time to start than the present, but Handsome had gotten so disgusted he said, "Come on, I thought we were going up and discuss this thing with Wallace Wright. He'll back me up."

So all four of them left to see Wallace Wright, who lived at 555 Edgecombe Drive. But as they were crossing 145th Street they bumped into Eddy Schooley, who had such a miserable hangover he thought he was going through the change of life.

"That's another thing that affects the Negro Problem," Kathy said. "The change of life."

"How so?" Art asked with interest.

"Colored men are so easy to get humiliated," Kathy said. "They keep trying and trying to satisfy their fine white women and don't nothing happen. The ladies keep wanting more and more and when colored men get worn out they get evil and want to take it out on the Negro Problem."

"Men go through the change of life just the same as women," Schooley contended.

"That's what I mean," Kathy said. "It works both ways."

"Colored women got more stamina," Handsome said.

"Colored men too," Julius supported him.

"They eat more," Kathy said.

"Eat more what?" Art asked.

Kathy gave him a coquettish look. "I have to have a drink when I'm discussing sociology," she said, so they retired to the nearest bar.

Kathy began with, "Of course what the change is really like is a long cheap drunk. Lovemaking just tickles."

Schooley said, "No wonder I'm always drunk."

Julius said, "I thought you were going to say ticklish."

Kathy said, "Of course, with white women they're more ticklish to begin with."

Art protested, "That doesn't prove they're more prejudiced just because they're more ticklish."

Handsome argued, "Nobody said the change of life made white people any more ticklish. What I said was—"

All of a sudden a perfect colored stranger interrupted the conversation to say, "ladies and gennulmens. I'd like your opinion on this question. Is it right to jump on a white man and beat him half to death just because he tries to kill himself?"

"Why a white man?" Art asked.

"Well, he was the one who had the money," the perfect stranger said. "And we was scared that he might die."

"That reminds me," Schooley interrupted. "I've got to phone Lou."

So Schooley telephoned Lou Reynolds, his white editor, thinking of money, and asked him to come uptown to the bar right away. "It's very important," he said. "I can't tell you over the phone but it has something to do with my next book. A matter of, er, ah, genetics. Do white people have greater suicidal inclinations than colored people due to, er, ah, being broke?"

Lou assured him he would rush right up.

So while waiting for Lou they discussed whether more white people, percentagewise, killed themselves than colored people, and why.

"It comes from masturbation, whether you's a white man or a colored man," the perfect stranger said. "Every time a man masturbates a little piece of his brain comes out."

"Some people I know ought not to have any brains left, if you know what I mean," Kathy said.

"Colored folks drink themselves to death," another perfect stranger said. "Keep so drunk they can't even diddle."

"Every drink of whiskey is a nail in your coffin," the first perfect stranger said.

By the time Lou arrived everyone's coffin was well-nailed.

"My God!" Lou exclaimed. "Where's the body?"

"Well, it ain't hot air filling out these bones," Kathy said, shaking herself to prove it.

"Give him a triple so he can catch up," Schooley ordered the bartender. After all, he wasn't paying for it.

"We're not drunk, we're just chummy," Kathy said, blinking her eyes at him. "Come sit on my other side."

"No wonder you're cummy," Schooley said. "Piled up with white men."

"It's old white people who are more prejudiced than young white people," Handsome said.

"People are just naturally more understanding when they're drinking," Kathy said.

"I understands everything," the first perfect stranger said slyly.

"I could solve the whole Negro Problem with enough whiskey, used judiciously, if you know what I mean," Kathy said.

"To oil the tools," Art offered.

Kathy gave him a knowing look.

"I mean mathematically," Handsome said. "Take for instance if you add it up, allowing so much prejudice per person per year—"

"You can't do that," Art objected. "Prejudice is acquired."

"Comes from all this education," the second perfect stranger said. "If didn't nobody know nothing there wouldn't be no prejudice."

"Naw it don't," the first perfect stranger contradicted. "It all comes from genitals, excuse me, miss. If didn't nobody have any genitals there wouldn't be all this trouble about prejudice."

"It's parasitical, like moss," Lou said.

"Moss!" Kathy echoed. "That's just what I mean. It's all a matter of hair. If colored people had straight moss and white people had kinky moss, it would make everybody equal, I mean."

"I thought we were going to go and see Willard B. Overton, if you want to know something about prejudice," Handsome said, looking at the gathering with disgust. "If you don't, I'm going home."

Willard B. Overton lived at the corner of Edgecombe Drive and 163rd Street, eight blocks north of where Mamie lived and five blocks north of where Wallace Wright lived. So they all started staggering up the Drive toward the residence of Mr. Overton. By this time there were three perfect colored strangers added to the group and they were still discussing the origins of race prejudice.

"One of the things white folks got against colored folks is colored folks is always buying big Cadillacs when they can't even pay their rent," one of the perfect strangers said, looking enviously at a big green Cadillac sedan they passed. "Course I'd rather have me a red convertible," he added.

Suddenly they found themselves in front of 409. By that time everyone had completely forgotten Mr. Overton and Mr. Wright.

"Well, here we are," Art said. "Mamie's probably just getting up."

In fact Mamie had just got home from teaching school and had just had time to read his letter to Brown Sugar when the invasion took place.

NATURALLY, everyone was amenable to any suggestion, so long as there was whiskey to be drunk. Besides which, Joe had gone to Buffalo.

So Mamie suggested to Art that he phone Wallace Wright at his office and arrange to meet him at Patty Pearson's so they could discuss plans for the coming picture story in the coming picture magazine.

Art thought that was a fine suggestion and phoned Wallace immediately while Mamie stood by, lending moral support, not to mention telling him what to say.

"He wants to know why at Patty Pearson's," Art said, covering the mouthpiece with his hand.

"Tell him because you don't want me to know you're meeting him and he can stop by there on his way home from work," Mamie said.

Wallace was delighted by that explanation. "Fine, Art, I'll be there in forty-five minutes," he said.

"Oh, we forgot Juanita," Mamie said. "She'll be hurt."

"I haven't forgotten her," Art denied. "I just haven't thought about her. But I'll phone her and tell her to come too."

"She won't come," Mamie said.

Art looked at her. "How do you mean that?"

Mamie laughed knowingly. "She won't come to Patty's."

Art sighed. "Then I'll call Wallace back and tell him not to come."

"No, don't put anything off," Mamie said. "You go and see Juanita now before Wallace gets here, it's only a couple of blocks, and get all this done right now while you're thinking straight."

"I don't know whether I'm thinking as straight as you think I'm thinking," he said. "Why can't Julius go and see her. Maybe she'll come with him."

"I'm sure she'd love it," Mamie said. "But it's you who has to see her. You're the boss. I'll send Julius for you when Wallace gets here."

Art went, but he didn't want anyone telling him it wasn't a woman's world.

After which Mamie said to Julius, "You go ahead and entertain your friends. I have a little run to make."

She ran downstairs to Patty's and had her phone Wallace Wright's you-know-who downtown.

"Tell her to come up and see you right away and you'll tell her how to stop me from meddling in her affairs."

"I don't know her," Patty said.

"That doesn't make any difference, you just tell her what I said and she'll come all right."

Mamie was right about the lady. She came. We'll call the lady Peggy, to keep from embarrassing Mr. Wright, which of course wasn't her name.

Peggy arrived two minutes behind Wallace, and were they surprised to see one another.

By then Mamie had long since returned to her own apartment upstairs where she was giving a little impromptu party, and she didn't know anything at all about what was going on downstairs in Patty Pearson's apartment. In fact, Patty Pearson didn't know what was going on in her own apartment, because the moment Peggy arrived she had had to dash out for a minute to keep an appointment with her dressmaker.

It happened, however, that on the way to her dressmaker she dropped into Mamie's to borrow a hat to wear when she tried on the dress and, finding a party in progress, felt she had to stay long enough for one drink at least. It was the polite thing to do. The only thing she regretted was that Julius was leaving just as she arrived. He couldn't even stay long enough to say a good old-fashioned hello, because Mamie had sent him posthaste to get Juanita and Art. Naturally Patty didn't know one single thing about that but just what she had heard and what she guessed and what she made up out of her own little imagination for future reference.

As far as Julius was concerned, it was strictly business, being as Art had got there first. So he was very businesslike when he brought Juanita and Art back to Patty's apartment to confer with Wallace on the picture story.

By then Patty had returned from her dressmaker and was reassuring the nervous couple, Wallace and his white paramour, Peggy, that they were as safe in her apartment as they would be in Peggy's own apartment and they could do all the same things if they wished, and there wouldn't be anybody there to see them but herself, when who should arrive unexpectedly but Wallace's colored wife, accompanied by Julius and that big fine white man, Art Wills. Was Patty surprised, not to mention the nervous couple.

It goes without saying that Juanita was speechless with fury. She turned about to leave but Wallace, like a fool, tried to restrain her.

"This is not at all as it appears," he said. "There is a very simple explanation."

Everyone looked at him expectantly. But Wallace made the grave mistake of not presenting his simple explanation with the urgency the situation demanded, no doubt because he hadn't thought of one.

So Art rushed to his rescue. "Naturally. These things just don't happen."

"What things?" Juanita demanded furiously.

"You can have two guesses," Patty said maliciously.

"This is all Mamie Mason's doing," Peggy said.

Like a drowning man, Wallace grabbed for the straw. "Undoubtedly."

"I came here to discuss a project with Mrs. Pearson," Peggy continued bravely.

"I asked you to come," Patty supported her.

"I've never before met Mr. Wright," Peggy stated.

"I see it all," Wallace said. "Arthur phoned me to meet him here for a business discussion. Isn't that so, Arthur?"

"Indubitably," Art said. "I was at Mamie's at the time. Wasn't I, Julius?"

"Positively," Julius said. "So was Mamie."

All seemed tacitly agreed to stone Mamie and get out of the mess as gracefully as possible, being as Mamie wasn't there to defend herself. And for the sake of sweet martyrdom Juanita was willing to accept this solution and permit Wallace to take her home.

"How that woman hates me," she sighed.

But Wallace committed the unforgivable offense of saying good-bye to Peggy, whom by her own admission, he had never before met.

"I thought you didn't know her," Juanita said.

"Why, I don't, my dear," Wallace said.

"Then why are you telling her good-bye?"

"Really, my dear, you're splitting hairs. I don't know this woman from Adam's tomcat."

Maybe if he had said a Persian pussy, Peggy might have overlooked it. But a tomcat, and old enough to belong to Adam. "I resent that allusion very much, Wallace," she said furiously.

"So she calls you Wallace, does she?" Juanita stormed. "And in public at that. I wonder what she calls you in private."

"My dear, you're becoming hysterical," Wallace said in a manner he felt to be soothing. "She doesn't call me anything in private."

"She just whistles, I suppose," Juanita said scathingly.

"Well, at least that is more than you can do, I'm sure," Peggy said.

"This is so uncalled for—" Wallace began in his highly commendable manner of understating the case, but Juanita cut him off.

"Well, you just stay here with her, uncalled for or not. Arthur will take me home."

"I'll not stay here another instant and be insulted," Peggy said. "Julius will take me home."

"I've got to remember that technique," Patty complimented them. "That was slick."

So Art took Juanita home and Julius took Peggy home, and both ladies were so mad at Wallace they gave their two unprotesting escorts some mad loving, and no other loving is so responding and so embracing as mad loving.

Patty was already at home but she took one look at Wallace and took herself away from home. Wallace didn't have any home he wanted to go to at that time, and if he had he wouldn't have found any loving waiting, so he stayed where he was.

Patty went upstairs and told Mamie about all the exciting things that had happened in her apartment. And was Mamie surprised!

Art came from taking Juanita home.

"There goes your story on the Wrights," Mamie consoled him.

"What happened to him?" Art asked, it so happening that by then he didn't remember a thing that had happened at Patty's, such being the effect of mad loving on the brain.

"They've separated."

"Who?"

"The Wrights."

"Why, I just came from Juanita's and she didn't say anything to me about it," he said. "And we had a long fine get-together."

Mamie began getting furious. "You were down there when it happened."

"Down where when what happened?"

Mamie became so furious she ran to her bedroom and got the letter he had written to Brown Sugar.

"If you publish that story on Wallace I'll show this to your wife," she threatened.

Art tried to focus his blurred vision on the letter. "What's that? It looks like a letter."

"It *is* a letter."

He fumbled in his pocket and got his glasses and put them on. Then he stared at the scrawled words:

> *Dearest,*
> *Want very much to marry you providing your husband*
> *doesn't yowl. Need sleep badly.*
>
> > *Lovingly,*
> > *Art*

"Why, it looks like my handwriting," he said, surprised. "And it looks like my signature too."

"Now do you recognize it?" Mamie demanded.

"Who is it addressed to?" he asked.

Mamie showed him the envelope.

"Brown Sugar. Why, I remember her quite well," he admitted. "Who do you suppose has been writing to her in my handwriting and signing my name?"

"You won't get out of it that easy," Mamie threatened. "I'm going to phone Debbie right now."

"Debbie. You mean my wife, Debbie?"

"Yes, and I'm going to tell her to come up here right away."

"Then I'm going to leave."

Art left.

That made Mamie so doubly furious she hid all the whiskey and said it had given out.

Lou said he would go out and buy some more whiskey. He left.

Schooley protested that the party was getting dull. Mamie asked him to leave. He left.

Art remembered he was going to marry Brown Sugar

and decided to go see her. He had forgotten about the letter Mamie had just shown him. So he hailed a taxi and told the driver to take him to the Bronx.

"What address?" the driver asked.

"I'll show you the street," Art said. "You just get me to the Bronx."

The driver drove him to the Bronx.

"It's a street with trees on it," Art said.

The driver drove about the Bronx looking for a street with trees on it. After all, he wasn't paying the fare. But he couldn't avoid all the streets with trees on them, big as the Bronx is, so whenever he accidentally came across a street with trees on it, he asked courteously, "Is this the street?"

After carefully studying the street Art would say, "No, too many trees," or else, "No, not enough trees."

Finally they found the street with just the right amount of trees to satisfy him. Then he had to find the house. He found the house, but by that time it was night and the house was black dark. He rang the bell until a light came on. A big black man in a bathrobe came to the door. Art saw right away the man wasn't her husband: he had seen her husband. So he supposed the man must be her brother.

"I'd like to speak to your sister," he said.

"She ain't my sister," the man said.

"Oh, I thought you were her brother," Art said.

"You got the wrong house, buddy," the man said. "It's the house across the street."

Art looked at the two-story frame house across the street and shook his head. "That's not the house. It's a brick house."

"No it ain't," the man said. "It's a frame house."

"It isn't a frame house," Art contended. "I remember it very well. It's a three-story brick house just like this."

"It's not this house," the man said. "It's that frame house across the street. You're thinking about some other house."

"I know the difference between a frame house and a

brick house," Art said. "Even though it was dark."

"I'm telling you, buddy," the man said patiently. "I wouldn't steer you wrong. You see that house across the street? Maybe if you go closer you can see it better. That's the house you want."

"I know that's not the house," Art said. "That's a frame house."

"That's what I've been saying, it's a frame house."

"But I'm looking for a brick house."

"Listen, lots of white men make the same mistake," the black man said patiently. "But don't nobody live in this house but me and my father. That's the house you want across the street. Do you think I've been living here all this time and don't know that's the house? You go over there and you'll see for yourself it's the house."

Art knew it wasn't the house, but he went across the street and knocked on the door just to please the man who insisted it was the house.

The door was cracked cautiously and a pair of black-ringed eyes peered at him. Then the door swung open and a heavily painted colored woman exclaimed heartily, "You got the right house, sugar pie. You come right on in, all the girls been wondering where you was."

In the meantime Lou stopped at the Fat Man's to get a drink. He hadn't said he was going to take any whiskey back to Mamie's. All he had said was he would go out and buy some more whiskey, and that was what he was doing.

Two cute brownskin girls one seat removed at the bar looked him over in the mirror. At least to Lou they looked like cute brownskin girls.

"Do you like fried chicken?" one of the cute girls asked him.

"I sure do," he said, giving her the eye. "Fried nice and brown."

"You can't get none here," she said.

"Naturally not," he said. "Where can we go?"

"You can get some at Maggie's," the other cute girl said.

"All three of us?" he asked.

"Sure, if you're sure you like fried chicken," the first cute girl said.

"I like fried chicken," Lou said cautiously. "But not too much at one helping."

"You won't get too much."

"Just one leg and some potato salad," the second cute girl added.

"Just one leg!" Lou said in amazement. "How is that done?"

"Why, they gives the other leg to another customer," the first cute girl explained.

"Come on, let's all go to Maggie's," Lou said. "This I got to see."

But when he got to Maggie's he found out they were right. He only got one leg and some potato salad.

Maggie had a big seven-room apartment on the top floor of the adjoining building. In one room a three-piece combo was trickling out the blues while couples sat about blowing weed. There was no one in the dining room until they went in. Lou never found out who was in the other rooms, one-legged chickens or otherwise. It made him wonder if chicken meant the same in all tongues.

While all this was going on, Schooley was sitting in the kitchen of an apartment on the fourth floor rear of 409 eating stewed chitterlings with great relish. He didn't remember how he had gotten there but everybody seemed friendly. There were only four of them, a couple and a single woman and himself.

"Well, well, so you're the famous writer Edward Spooling," the single woman was saying. "When I saw you staggering around out there I said to myself I bet he's somebody important." She was a dark-brown, heavyset, muscular woman who didn't look as though she would care to be disputed about what she had said to herself.

"I've been to a party at Mamie Mason's," Schooley said.

"I always wanted to go to a party at Mamie Mason's,"

the woman said wistfully. "But she's so uppity I ain't never been asked."

"Come on, I'll take you with me," Schooley said.

"Why, bless your sweet little heart. Ain't he the sweetest thing?" she appealed to the others. "Just call me Viola, honey-bunch, and let's go."

Naturally the party at Mamie's was still going on. Patty had borrowed two bottles of whiskey from the janitor's wife, who came with the whiskey. Handsome called up a friend who came over with three more bottles of whiskey and two more colored women. One of the perfect colored strangers called up another perfect colored stranger and she brought over four bottles of whiskey and two perfect white strangers, one of whom was a meter reader and the other a truck driver. There was plenty to drink but nothing to eat.

So that was why Schooley was welcomed with such warmth. Because Viola brought along a dishpan of stewed chitterlings.

After that the party got a little redolent.

One of the perfect colored strangers went to sleep and burnt a hole in the arm of Mamie's almost brand-new over-stuffed armchair. Needless to say that didn't throw any water on the fire.

Art returned with two highly spiced ladies of the evening. By right they were dark ladies, but they had put on so much white face powder they looked bright purple.

That didn't help much either.

One might have thought Lou would have done likewise, being as he had bought some fried chicken for those two cute brownskin girls whom he had first mistaken for fried chicken themselves. Instead he brought back the three-piece combo from Maggie's. They started right in serenading Mamie with a bop rendition of "I'll Be Glad When You're Dead You Rascal You." The only thing was they kept stopping from time to time to ask for a little sweet wine to dampen their throats. No one had any sweet wine, so their throats remained dry.

And who do you think Julius brought back? Why, Fifi, the girl in show business who had thrown him over for Art. Sad to say, when she spied Art among those present, she tried to throw him over again. But Art's ladies of the evening resented her encroachment. Some words were exchanged between them which some of those present had never heard before. Lou told the combo to play louder to drown out the noise.

All the noise got drowned out except that made by the police hammering on the door. But the police saw right off how everything was. Just perfectly respectable people having a little fun. All they did was advise Mamie to keep it low.

"How low can you get?" Handsome muttered, watching Kathy's hand creep inside of the white truck driver's fly.

But the cops ignored him. "Don't worry, ma'am, we know Joe," one of them said.

Which caused Kathy to let go of the truck driver and suddenly exclaim, "My God, I was supposed to go with Joe to Buffalo!" thereby cooking her goose for good with Mamie.

Mamie got so mad she had the cops throw out everyone. Julius went too and that made her madder. Her own brother-in-law deserting her. But Julius had no intention of permitting Fifi to go home by herself; he had more sense than that.

Mamie was so mad she sat down and ate all the stewed chitterlings that were left in the dishpan. But no sooner had she got through eating than she ran into the bathroom and stuck her finger down her throat and got rid of them.

Mamie Mason had faith.

WHEN WALLACE AWAKENED that morning and found himself in bed with Patty Pearson, who, after all, had to sleep somewhere, he was so horrified he jumped up and went home. It was bad enough to be untrue to one woman, but to be untrue to two women was unthinkable. Wallace hadn't really been untrue. Patty had tried to make him untrue, but as drunk as he had been, she hadn't succeeded. But he didn't know that, and Patty was not the one to tell him.

In the meantime Juanita had had the lock changed on their apartment and she had locked Wallace out and had gone home to mother.

On finding himself locked out and his wife gone, naturally Wallace phoned Peggy. But Peggy was still so mad at him for drawing a parallel between herself and Adam's tomcat, as much as she despised cats—and a tomcat at that!—she would have refused to accept his apology if he had offered one. But Wallace was so miserable he didn't think of offering an apology for the cat. Instead he apologized for his wife. Being as Peggy wasn't having an affair with his wife, she didn't see how the apology was pertinent. So she told him she was through, and he could go back to his wife for all she cared. Naturally Wallace didn't tell her that he had already tried to go back to his wife, but his wife wasn't there. So he went and ate some breakfast. All the whiskey he'd drunk had left him with a mighty appetite and he ate two orders of fried country sausage, Southern fried eggs and hominy grits. Then he went to get a shave.

When Wallace didn't phone right back, Peggy got to

imagining him jumping off the top of a high building, as women always hope will happen in such circumstances, and she tried desperately to reach him by telephone to stop him. But no one knew where he was, for the simple reason he had checked into a hotel under an assumed name so he could take a bath. After that everyone knew that his white paramour had phoned to make last-minute arrangements for their flight.

And that was how word got about Harlem that Wallace Wright had left his middle-aged colored wife, who had slaved and sacrificed for him all those twenty years of their marriage, for a frisky young white woman half his age. Word had it that Juanita had jumped into the Harlem River and had drowned and Wallace had fled to Canada with his white paramour. Responsible people had seen them boarding the train. And of course the hundreds of anxious colored people lined up on the bank of the Harlem River saw for themselves the boats dredging the river bottom for Juanita's body. Little difference did the fact make that the dredging was for the purpose of deepening the channel, being as they didn't know it.

Naturally race pride came to the rescue.

Women's organizations adopted such slogans as:

Be Happy That You Are Nappy. . . . Be Proud That You Are Black.

Following which drugstores did a land-office business in bleaching creams and hair straighteners. One smart joker bought himself a solid gold Cadillac from profits he made by selling a bath called Black Nomore. True, it didn't have much effect on black skin other than to turn it battleship gray, but it turned hair white. This proved very embarrassing for young ladies trying to get married. One prospective husband, desirous of engaging in prenuptial ceremonies with his bride-to-be, was startled out of his wits to discover her pubic hair was snow white from old age.

Not to be outdone, street-corner orators and store-front ministers exhorted their audiences with such reassurances as:

Black People Are Faithful. . . . Black People Are True.

Nevertheless, specialists in voodoo sold out their entire stock of love potions, dried menses to mix with cake batter, vaginal oil guaranteed as infallible love bait, all types of amulets and wax images with white surfaces and blond hair. Nathan, the root man, became rich. Cats disappeared from the streets in the wake of an outburst of hucksters hawking rabbits' feet. And there was no end to the minor incapacitating accidents to the genital organs of suspected husbands and fiancés.

Obviously greater reassurances were sorely needed. As a consequence, colored historians stated unequivocally that:

(1) Cleopatra was black.

(2) The Queen of Sheba was black.

(3) Dido was black. She was the first queen of Carthage, and Carthage was in Africa, wasn't it?

(4) Fatima was black. She was the only daughter of Mohammed, and everyone knows that Mohammed was black.

(5) Aphrodite was black. Pictures of bronze statues were exhibited to substantiate this fact.

(6) Eve was black. If not pure black, at least she was dusky. If she wasn't dusky, why did the Lord name her Eve, which everyone knows is dusk? And even Webster defines dusk as "moderately dark."

(7) Original sin was black, and what was original sin if not the first lovemaking between man and woman?

Colored poets were inspired to write impassioned verses, such as the now famous poem, "The Whiter the Face, the Blacker the Disgrace," which is so universally known as to need no quoting. However, another fine poem not so well known was "If i had my rathers":

> if i had my rathers
> i'd rather be a woman black
> in a shack
> away back
> in hackensack

than be a woman white
in the light
so blind i might
think it a delight
to excite
Wallace Wright.

It was perfectly natural that race resentment followed in the wake of race pride. Rumor had it that various colored ladies began boycotting milk because it was white.

However, the most revealing incident occurred on the subway between Columbus Circle and 125th Street. A white lady standing in the aisle noticed a bedbug crawling about the collar of a colored lady's dress, who occupied the seat beneath her. With the utmost surreptitiousness, to avoid attracting notice, the white lady reached down and carefully removed the bedbug with her thumb and forefinger. The colored lady noticed the white lady withdrawing her hand, and asked suspiciously, "What's that you're taking?"

Solemnly and silently the white lady exhibited the big fat bedbug.

"Where did you get it?" the colored lady asked.

Diffidently the white lady pointed to the colored lady's collar.

"Put it back!" the colored lady shouted belligerently. "That's what's the trouble now, you white folks want to take everything we got."

Does all this mean the colored ladies of Harlem were losing their faith? No-no-no! This proves that their faith was stronger than ever. Without great faith they would never have gone to such extreme measures to hang on to their men, being as colored men are known to love white women, faith or no faith.

It goes without saying that the colored ladies took Juanita's side against Wallace and they might have given him some lumps if they had found him. No need of putting too much faith in faith when a good old-fashioned whipping will do the job as well, if not better.

When Patty saw the way everyone was going, naturally she went with them. After all, it was Mamie Mason who had engineered the business. That was all Patty ever said. She never said that Mamie had got this white lesbian to go after Wallace at one of her parties just because Juanita had remarked that Mamie loved white men so much she had segregated the sexual capacities of her own body, reserving the best for white men, and giving the leavings to Negroes. That was something that *those* people she talked to make up themselves. What else could you expect? Getting all those frantic white and colored people all mixed up together at those drunken orgies that took place at Mamie Mason's. If the truth be known, girl, there were plenty of other sheets in that same wash that hadn't yet been bleached. But that was what *they* said, not Patty.

When this story got about everyone got down on Mamie instead of Wallace. If it hadn't been for that Mamie Mason deliberately sicking that white prostitute on him, Wallace would have still been true to all the colored women in Harlem, true as he could, bless his sweet heart, they said. After all, Wallace was just like any other simple-minded colored man, even if he did look white, thinking it was so different. But Mamie was a woman and she knew all of it was the same in the dark.

What made Mamie so furious was that of all people, Patty Pearson, her very best friend, would be such a dirty double-crosser as to try to ruin her annual Masked Ball. Just because Mamie had nosed it around that it had been in Patty's apartment that Juanita had caught Wallace in bed with the white woman wasn't any reason for Patty to attack the biggest social event of the year, because after all, she and Patty Pearson had been friends too long for Patty to get mad about a little friendly lie. Who was one to lie about if not one's friends? One never knew enough about anyone else, one might be telling the truth.

Of course the Masked Ball was Mamie Mason's own affair

and it was soon to take place, at the Savoy Ballroom, naturally, from ten o'clock at night until dawn of the next day. But for the sake of history, Mamie being a firm believer in the democratic processes, it was given out to be sponsored by *La Société des Mondaines du Monde de Harlème,* of which Mamie was founder, organizer, president and dictator.

And what made it such an important social event was that all of Mamie Mason's white friends would be there, and scores of other white people who would dearly love to be her friends.

It was really disgusting of Patty Pearson, who was a charter member herself, to endanger its success by saying that she, Mamie Mason, who was to be the Masked Queen, had separated the Wallace Wrights with a white woman. Because Patty knew darn well no white woman would dare show her face in Harlem as long as there was such an uproar about them stealing all the best colored men. As lief ask a white woman take her life in her hands as to come up to Harlem to the Savoy at such a time and cut the rug with some suspicious colored lady's husband.

And Mamie knew if things kept on as they were going, Wallace Wright would become such a great martyr that Art Wills would have to do the picture story on him for the first issue of the proposed magazine, Brown Sugar or no Brown Sugar. Which would be the worst thing that could happen to white and colored race relations. When by rights the feature story in the first issue of the proposed magazine should be on her Masked Ball, not to mention herself, any way one looked at it. Because at no other time or place in Harlem were better race relations achieved, or more of them, than then and there.

So that was how it came about that Mamie told everyone but her very best friends that she was going to Chicago that very afternoon on the 1:15. Then she got on the telephone.

First she phoned Mrs. Ann Kissock, wife of Dr. John Stetson Kissock, the chubby chairman of The Southern Committee for the Preservation of Justice, at the Commodore Hotel where they were staying for the week.

All she wanted Mrs. Kissock to do was to get Wallace and his white paramour, Peggy, to meet in some discreet place and reach an agreement to give each other up. Being as she and Dr. Kissock were Wallace's best friends, Wallace would listen to her.

Mrs. Kissock was certain that he would do so, and she thought it was a splendid idea. "Oh, I've wanted so much to do something about it," she said. "I've been so worried. Wallace was here last night to see the doctor and I so wanted then to suggest that he give her up. If only for his health. I can't imagine what she does to him, but the poor dear looks so haggard and tired."

Mamie was so grateful that Mrs. Kissock would go out of her way to do this fine thing for the Negro Problem that she consented for them to meet that afternoon in her own apartment, after she had left for Chicago. It would be the very last place anyone would think of looking for them, and therefore insure them against any further gossip. Mrs. Kissock heartily agreed and she was delighted to be of use in such a delicate situation. So if Mamie would leave the key to her apartment with the doorman, she would come early and be waiting.

Following which Mamie telephoned in turn her very best friends of both races:

Stark-colored Alice Overton, wife of Willard B. Overton, president of NAI (which Harlem cynics called Negro Antics Integrated), who was Juanita Wright's best friend;

Dark-colored Dora Steele, wife of Brooklyn M.D. James Steele, who wanted to show Julius her, er, ah, hat;

Freckly white Debbie Wills, wife of that great white man about the publishing world, Art Wills;

Slightly colored Maiti Brown, possessor of the fabulous bosom and wife of colored professor Dr. Baldwin Billings Brown;

Rosy-blond Kit Samuels, wife of white professor Isaiah Samuels, who had come to town alone for some of Reverend Riddick's, er, ah, blessings;

Bright white Merto, collector of artificial doozies, wife, er, ah, passing as the wife of Maurice Gordey, the financier;

Shit-colored Bessie Shirley, trapeze artist and wife of Milt Shirley, the Negro newspaper publisher and passionate peeper;

And high-yellow Evie Miller, wife of coal-black Moe Miller, newshawk and renowned rat fighter, although to reach her Mamie had to phone Baltimore, where the Millers were rat-bound.

Mamie said the same thing to all of them:

"Girl, you've just got to come to my house this afternoon. The most dreadful things are happening to Wallace Wright and we simply must do something to save his reputation." She didn't say what dreadful things, but oh, how one could imagine.

Then she made all of them promise not to tell a soul where they were going, not even their husbands, or anything about it because it just had to be kept secret or she couldn't imagine what might happen to Wallace's reputation. She had even told everyone else but just the few of them she was going on the 1:15 to Chicago, and for the remainder of the day she wasn't even going to answer her telephone, that was how secret it was.

Naturally they came. They dropped whatever they were doing and came. How could they possibly stay away when such dreadful things were happening to Wallace Wright in such dead secrecy that not one of them had heard a thing about it?

Maybe he'd turned into one of those. Nooooo! You never can tell, dear, he was always a little on that side. Wouldn't that be the lick that killed Dick, race leader becomes turnabout? Maybe it's all for the best, dear, as little as his was. Hush, girl, what a dirty mind you've got; imagine him running off with a white *man*. . . .

Of course Evie Miller had to tell Moe before he'd permit her to return to their rat-infested house. But when he heard of the dreadful things Wallace was doing in secret, he decided to return with her.

"I'm going back and stand by friend Joe," he said. "Rat or no rat."

All he did was wire his city editor:

PUT TAIL ON WRIGHT STOP STINK ESCAPING

The only thing was he telephoned the message to Western Union and the girl misunderstood. So when his city editor got his message, PUT TAIL ON RIGHT STOP STINK ESCAPING, naturally he was indignant. Just what was Miller insinuating?

Everyone else followed Mamie's instructions to the letter, concerning their husbands, that is.

Of course Alice Overton had to phone her best friend, Juanita, and tell her that something fishy was going on at Mamie Mason's. How could she do otherwise, with such dreadful things happening to Wallace? She suggested that Juanita get over there as fast as she could and station herself at the Judas window of the door in the apartment across the hall from Mamie's so she could at least see who was coming and going. Juanita thanked her effusively and said she would bring Big Burley, the famous colored detective, whom she had engaged to get evidence for a divorce, just in case.

"That's the spirit, girl," Alice said.

Dora Steele phoned her best friend, Daisy Perkins, wife of the Brooklyn undertaker, and said she was off to Mamie Mason's where a brand-new scandal on the Wrights was cooking. And she wouldn't be a bit surprised if it wasn't something that Julius Mason had found out about Wallace's illegitimate child, because nobody could tell her Wallace would throw over his whole career for one of *those* women if there weren't a child to hide. But she warned Daisy not to tell a soul.

What kind of friend would Daisy have been if she hadn't phoned her best friend, Mrs. Lillian Davis Burroughs, known to her intimates as Brown Sugar, to let her know they had got real pictures of Wallace in the act, girl, doing things I wouldn't even mention, because she was smart enough to know it was really Art Wills, that big fay editor Brown Sugar liked, who had taken the pictures. She just wanted Brown Sugar to know what kind of man that Art Wills really was, taking those pornographic photos of Wallace, because after all, she and Brown Sugar were from the same little town of Piney Ridge, Tennessee, and she wouldn't want Brown Sugar to get herself photographed too, not in that position.

Maiti Brown told her hostess in Jamaica, Long Island, whom she was visiting before returning to her husband at the college, if she wasn't back in time for dinner it would be because she was held up at Mamie Mason's where a group of civic-minded women were getting together to sift the facts of the Wright scandal to determine what effects it would have, in the long run, on the male Negro's virility.

Kit Samuels phoned Reverend Mike Riddick and said, "Oh, Reverend Riddick, it's the hottest thing in town."

"Good Lord, Mrs. Samuels, I'm on my way!" he exclaimed.

"Oh, it isn't *that*," she said, giggling. "It's just that Mamie Mason is entertaining her club this afternoon, and that made me think of you. You're well, I trust."

"Very fit, Mrs. Samuels," Reverend Riddick said, "And ready to club temptation wherever I find it. How is Professor Samuels?"

"Very well, thank you. He couldn't come this time."

"Poor man. No doubt he's overworked. But if I may say so, I'm always ready to come to your assistance."

Mrs. Samuel's laugh tinkled with pleasure. "I'm sure you are," she said. "You thoughtful man."

Since Maurice Gordey was not really her husband, Metro felt free to tell him she was going up to Mamie Mason's that afternoon to sit in on the Negro Problem. Maurice told Lorenzo Llewellyn, to whom he was telling everything then, that Mamie Mason was holding a forum on the Negro Problem, and did he think, by any chance, Moe Miller might be there? However, Lorenzo advised him against it, saying the competition would be too great.

Bessie Shirley told the Theresa Hotel bellhop to tell the numbers writer when he came to get her day's play that she was going to Mamie Mason's to dig some dirt, and if it wasn't too much trouble would he run up there, because she figured this might be the day to get down on 409, but she wouldn't know what combination she wanted until she saw who else was there. She might want to lead with the zero, such as 0-9-4.

The hell of it was that nobody told Joe. He had to find out the hard way. Arriving home from Buffalo at exactly the same time Mamie was supposed to be taking off for Chicago, he phoned home. No one answered, so he phoned Patty Pearson to ask if Mamie was there. Patty was very sweet and told him that Mamie had gone to Chicago, not mentioning a word about her concern over the noise coming from Mamie's apartment above.

So no sooner had all Mamie's guests got together over tea and tittle-tattle, laced with rum and bourbon, than Joe arrived. The trouble was that Joe had brought his secretary, Kathy Carter, and he had unlocked the front door and had ushered Kathy into his domicile ahead of himself like the gentleman he was, before he caught sight of the assembled ladies. Otherwise he would have quickly slammed the door in her face and hastened into his wife's outstretched arms like a bustling businessman returning home from an arduous trip, alert for any contingency.

Not that his wife's arms were outstretched at the moment. In fact, she had her back to the door and was considerably amused by the sudden amazement of the assembled ladies. Maiti Brown's eyes seemed to be popping from her head.

Mamie thought it was only Mrs. Anna Kissock entering with the key she had left for her with the doorman, so she said, "All of you know Mrs. Anna Kissock," which inspired even greater amazement before she turned about to greet her distinguished guest.

Needless to say, Mamie was not a little amazed herself.

"I had no idea you were here," Joe said needlessly.

"You didn't?" Mamie said dangerously.

"I phoned but no one answered."

"You did?"

"So I brought Katherine along to give her my notes."

"What notes, dear?" Mamie asked acidly.

"Why, his own notes," Kathy said.

"I didn't expect them to be your notes, dear," Mamie said. "As hard as you may try."

"Well, you don't have to be so catty," Kathy said defensively. "I've got to take his notes sometimes, don't I? After all, I can't take them while he's away, can I?"

"With your reach, dear, that wouldn't be so difficult," Mamie said.

"If he's got notes I'll take them," Kathy said defiantly. "After all, that's what I'm paid for."

"I don't doubt it, dear," Mamie said. "If you'd put together all the notes you've taken you'd have a New World Symphony."

"Well, maybe if I played the flute like you do, honey, I'd be bursting out with notes," Kathy said.

"Does Joe write music too?" Maiti Brown asked in astonishment. "What kind of notes has he got?"

"That's what I'd like to know, with both of them after them, that is," Merto said.

"I've got my notes with me," Joe said. "They're right here in my bag."

"It'd be awfully embarrassing if they weren't," Metro said. "I mean, if she came to take them, that is."

"His notes?" Maiti Brown asked, hovering on the verge of shock. "You mean if he had brought his secretary up here to take his notes and found they weren't in his bag."

"I realize you haven't brought your secretary up here to take dictation without your notes," Mamie said. "But just what is wrong with your office?"

"I just thought it would be more comfortable here," Joe said. "My trip was awfully hard."

"If you're so worried about your husband's notes, you can take them yourself," Kathy told Mamie. "There is plenty of corn in the field that's never been shucked."

"No one blames you for it, dear," Mamie told Kathy. "You've shucked all your stalks."

"Well, if you want to be like that," Kathy said to Mamie. "If I was going on a vegetable diet I'd want more than asparagus tips, if you know what I mean."

"I'm sure you'd stick to bottle gourds and watermelons, dear," Mamie said to Kathy.

"Well, I must say I feel relieved to hear them talking about gardening," Maiti Brown confessed to Dora Steele. "For a moment I thought they were talking underneath Joe's clothes."

They were saved from further discussions along these lines by the entrance of the bona fide Mrs. Anna Kissock who, needless to say, was no less startled by sight of the assemblage. "Oh, Mamie dear!" she exclaimed in dismay. "I expected only Wallace."

"Wallace, did she say?" Maiti Brown inquired in a shocked whisper. "My God, is she after him too?"

"We're all his friends," Mamie assured her.

"Yes, of course," Mrs. Kissock conceded. "But you informed me that you would be away, and I expected us to be alone, with her, too, of course."

"My God, at the same time!" Maiti Brown exclaimed in rising horror. "Both of them?"

"And I never got to know him," Merto said regretfully.

"At the last moment Evie Miller arrived from Baltimore," Mamie explained to Mrs. Kissock. "And the girls thought I should stay and we all get together with Evie and tell her what happened because of the importance of knowing just where to start."

"Yes, I can understand that," Mrs. Kissock said. "But won't Wallace be rather embarrassed? He's only expecting two of us. I talked to him on the phone and explained just what we wanted. I mean, would he want to do it with so many others present?"

"But we all love Wallace," Alice Overton said.

"Leave me out of it!" Maiti Brown exclaimed.

"This Wallace," Merto said. "Maybe just one of us could

do more with him. If I got together alone with him, where we wouldn't be disturbed, that is—"

"We thought afterwards we should talk to one of them at a time," Mamie explained.

"Was there more than one?" Mrs. Kissock asked in a shocked tone of voice.

"Will someone please tell me what everybody is talking about?" Kit Samuels complained.

"You know Wallace Wright, dear," Mamie said. "We're trying to decide what to do about her."

"Her! Wallace? Has he had one of those operations?" Kit asked.

"What we ought to do is send *her* a delegation," Dora Steele said. "Give *her* an ultimatum."

"Wallace?" Kit asked in bewilderment. "You mean order him to make them put it back. Could it be done?"

"A delegation to her?" Mrs. Kissock questioned. "But what about Wallace? I don't see how we could get Juanita to take him back under such circumstances."

"Frankly," Kit said, "neither do I."

"Personally I think it's just that Juanita wants one too," Bessie Shirley said.

"Then give her the one Wallace had," Kit said.

"She isn't like that," Alice Overton said indignantly. "She doesn't want one to do to Wallace what he's done to her."

"Well, why not?" Kit said. "If she liked it he might like it too."

"As soon as one gets one everyone else wants one too," Alice Overton said bitterly.

"I certainly don't," Merto said. "Not for myself, that is."

"What is this *one* everybody is talking about?" Maiti Brown asked in perplexity.

"My God, are you that naive?" Bessie Shirley said. "In France most men have one if they can afford it."

"Good Lord, don't they all!" Kit Samuels exclaimed.

"All colored men are just alike," Dora Steele said scathingly. "If it's white they think it's something special."

"White men are just the same if it's black," Bessie Shirley said. "Ain't it wonderful!"

"You're telling me," Maiti Brown said. "One of them tried to rape me right here in this room."

"Merciful heavens!" Mrs. Kissock exclaimed shudderingly. "With what?"

"Anthropology says opposites attract," Kit Samuels said.

"My husband, Mr. Overton, says it's just psychological," Alice Overton said. "That once we get over the idea of forbidden fruit—"

"Oh, I thought I recognized your name," Merto said. "You're Mrs. Willard B. Overton. I know your husband, but he didn't say anything to me about it's being like forbidden fruit."

"And just what did my husband say to you, my dear?" Mrs. Overton asked.

"Oh, he just talked about the Negro Problem and sacrifices and how good it was, that is," Merto said.

"And I suppose these conversations took place in the privacy of your boudoir when your husband was absent," Mrs. Overton suggested.

"Oh no, they weren't in privacy at all," Merto denied. "What good is it talking then, that is?"

The chances are an old-fashioned hair-pulling rumpus was avoided at that moment by the arrival of Patty Pearson, juiced to the gills and demonstratively affectionate.

"You sweetie-pie!" she exclaimed, embracing Mamie and kissing her. "Who're you frying?"

Patty was not one to sit down below in her own apartment and worry over whether it was herself.

Mamie was furious. "What do you mean by coming to my house uninvited?" she stormed, disengaging herself from Patty's clutches.

"Why sweetie-pie, wasn't that you who just telephoned me to come up to your house? It sounded so much like you talking on the phone, I couldn't understand a word."

"Just don't think you're not going to be talked about be-

cause you've come," Mamie warned her. "Because I consider you a traitor."

"Sticks and stones may break a traitor's bones," Patty said
drunkenly. "But all I said was nobody but you knew that
Wallace was in my house with her and me."

"My God!" Maiti Brown exclaimed. "Another two! He
must be a goat in sheep's clothing."

"Before I let you lie out of the fact that you started all this
scandal just to ruin my Masked Ball, I'll get all three of you
women together with Wallace at the same time and then see
what happens," Mamie threatened.

"That I'm going to see too!" Maiti Brown stated.

"If you accuse me of starting all this scandal I'll get Wallace here with all of us together," Patty threatened.

"Don't think I haven't thought of that too, dear," Mamie
said. "He's coming here this afternoon."

"Oh dear," Mrs. Kissock said. "If Wallace comes that will
set the Negro Race back twenty years."

"All of us!" Maiti Brown said in an awed whisper. "So
what's twenty years?"

WHEN WORD GOT ABOUT that a committee of colored women was meeting at Mamie Mason's to figure out some foolproof way of keeping colored men from running off with white women, there were spies everywhere. Not that this ambitious undertaking didn't have the support of one and all the colored ladies of Harlem, but you know Mamie Mason, child, she just loves white folks.

Naturally Juanita Wright was stationed at the Judas window of the apartment across the hall where she had an unfailing view of Mamie's door and could see everyone who came and went. In addition she had availed herself of the services of the famous colored private eye Big Burley, in the event of there being evidence forthcoming suitable for the divorce court.

The only trouble was, Big Burley was a busy man and impatient for Wallace to come on and get himself caught. So every time a new arrival entered Mamie's apartment he turned to Juanita and asked impatiently, "You want I should burst in now?"

The only person in the whole vicinity seemingly safe from spying eyes was Joe. That was because he had gone to bed.

ABOUT THAT TIME Dr. Kissock was suddenly inspired to phone Mrs. Kissock to find out how the negotiations were coming along. However, as a precaution against eavesdropping and scandalmongering, he addressed his wife thusly:

"Has the party of the first part been convinced as yet of the expediency of renouncing the party of the second part and has the party of the second part consented to a reconciliation with the party of the third part?"

It so happened that Bessie Shirley was nearest to the kitchen extension when the phone rang. She would never have forgiven herself for not taking advantage of finding out who might be calling Mamie at a time of day when Joe was usually absent. But when she heard Dr. Kissock speaking in such a cryptic manner, she thought it was her numbers writer referring to the three figures in the day's number as "parties" in case there might be police present.

So she told him, "Everything is cool, cousin, what's the leading party?" Meaning, of course, what figure in the day's number had come out first, since she always took the long odds and bet that a certain figure would appear first.

"By Jove, that is cryptic enough to confuse anyone," Dr. Kissock said admiringly. "But what the devil does it mean?"

"I might ask what the devil do you mean, cousin," Bessie said. "What's buzzin?"

"Buzzin!" Dr. Kissock echoed. "That's taking cryptogra-

phy too far, dear. Speak a bit more intelligibly and the devil
if it's deciphered."

"Speak more intelligently yourself," Bessie said. "Who do
you think you are?"

"Who do I think I am?" Dr. Kissock said. "I know very
well who I am, but just who the devil are you?"

"I'm Bessie. And if you're not Candy the Dandy numbers
man, just who the devil are *you?*"

"Bessie!" Dr. Kissock sputtered. "Just what the devil is
going on up there, may I ask?"

"Just some of us girls got together to fry some fish," Bessie
said. "Whomever you are whom wants to know so much
about our business."

Dr. Kissock was alarmed. Being a Southern gentlemán, he
took her statement to mean what it would mean in the
South whenever a group of women got together and said
they had some fish to fry—that some shenanigans were
going on. Immediately he tried to phone his good friend
Wallace to warn him to keep away from the trap. But Wallace had already left his hotel and couldn't be located. Dr.
Kissock recalled that Art Wills, the editor, and Wallace
were as thick as thieves, well, no, not actually thieves, that is
to say he meant that Wills was editing a book of Wallace's,
or perhaps it was a book about Wallace, something to do
with editing, he couldn't recall what, but no doubt Wills
would know exactly where Wallace could be found night
and day as editors were known to keep close track on their
authors. So he phoned Art's office. But Art wasn't in his
office, for the simple reason he was at home nursemaiding
his daughter and her broken-legged cat in the absence of his
wife, whom as we know was at Mamie's, although Art himself was in the dark about this. So Dr. Kissock left word with
Art's secretary for Art to have Wallace Wright telephone
him immediately; and to insure she carried out his request
he added that it was a matter of great importance concerning Wallace's book.

Art's secretary knew beyond all doubt that if any person-
age such as Wallace Wright was writing a book it could

only be about himself. So she phoned Art that some fellow calling himself a Dr. Cassock had given her a tip that Wallace Wright had finished his autobiography and Art had better get in touch with him immediately before he took it to another publisher. Naturally in a matter of such importance, duty came before such miserable chores as nursemaiding his gabby daughter and her constantly complaining cat. So Art phoned Baby Sitters Unlimited for a dependable baby sitter, and went searching for Wallace. But first he phoned Lou Reynolds to find out if Hightower Publishers had got the jump on him.

"What do you know about Wallace's life, Lou?" Art asked discreetly.

"Look here, Art, don't get me involved in that scandal," Lou warned. "I don't know anything at all about Wallace's wife. I've never met the lady."

That satisfied Art. So he said, "Well, thanks anyway, Lou. I'm off to the races."

"Have a good ride," Lou said, knowing that what Art meant was he was headed up to Harlem to Mamie Mason's where there were always races of all kinds.

As for his part, Art didn't mean any such thing. It was just that common sense told him if Wallace was anywhere, being as he was colored, it was more likely he would be in Harlem than anywhere else. And if Wallace was in Harlem, it stood to reason that he would be at Mamie Mason's, because that was where Art wanted to look for him.

Now that Dr. Kissock felt assured of Wallace being warned in time of the danger of visiting Mamie Mason's, he felt called upon to warn the woman, Wallace's white paramour, which was only the human thing to do. So he phoned his good friend Dr. Oliver Wendell Garrett, who was fortunately in the city that day, to permit him to share in the honor of helping their mutual good friend, Wallace, in his hour of need. Dr. Garrett was dutifully appreciative of the honor and expressed no doubt of being able to carry out the mission successfully with the large staff at his command.

"If you will give me her name and address," he suggested.

"By Jove, what *is* the woman's name!" Dr. Kissock said. "Woogie? No, not that, that's, er, ah, what they call their own kind I believe. I'll boogie your woogie, I believe they say. But she's, er, ah, one of us, our species, not kind of course."

"Is she really?" Dr. Garrett said. "Imagine! But surely Wallace must know her name. He must call her something, you know, when he is, er, ah, topping her. Perhaps something like, er, ah, pinktoe, I've heard it said."

"Pinktoe! By Jove!" Dr. Kissock said. "I've heard it said they call them silks. Of course, in their, er, ah, sweaty sessions."

"Silks!" Dr. Garrett echoed. "Think of that. But it would seem to be a bit distracting to have one saying to one, you know, as that fellow, you know, who writes this war pornography, such things as, er, ah, no silk oh silk now and now silk spin and spin silk again and again silk come silk me my silk until I come silk like you come silk again and again come silk. Ahem. Of that sort."

"It does sound a bit like cocoons propagating, doesn't it?" Dr. Kissock said. "But would, er, ah, pinktoe be less so? As, er, ah, licktoe my pinktoe, or would they say blacktoe my pinktoe until my pinktoe is blacktoe with, er, ah—well, on those lines?"

"We must leave it for the anthropologists," Dr. Garrett said.

"Indeed," Dr. Kissock agreed. "They might come up with, er, ah, sable."

Dr. Garrett was not a man to be selfish with honors, so his first thought was to share this honor of helping Wallace with some deserving person of Wallace's own kind. And what better person than that eager Rosenberg fellow who drove him home from one of Mamie's parties recently. By George, what *was* his name, wrote a book on whales—Moby, no that wasn't it, that was the name of the whale. *Jonah,* by George, that was it, Jonah Belly, but that might be a pseudonym. Sounded pretty fishy for an author named Jonah Belly to write a book on whales. He'd have to turn the matter over to his secretary.

"The fellow calls himself Jonah Belly," he said. "But if I know these fellows it might just as well be Jonah Johnson."

So it was easy enough after that tip for his secretary to locate Jonah Johnson in the files, the famous colored war correspondent who was in the process of thinking about a book he was planning to write about the Russian people if his application for a Rosenberg fellowship was accepted. She informed him that Dr. Garrett would like for him to get the name and address of Wallace Wright's silk dealer, because she knew that Dr. Garrett could not possibly mean Wallace Wright's silk, it didn't make any sense, and she had become accustomed to supplying words lacking in Dr. Garrett's dictation.

Now if some compatriot in Harlem had asked Jonah for the name and address of his own silk dealer Jonah would have sent him to the same house where he could meet some white women, being as in Harlem white women are known as silks, due to the legend that their pubic hair feels silky to the skin. But it never occurred to the Jonah Johnson who so badly wanted a Rosenberg fellowship that the president of the Rosenberg Foundation, who could get all that kind he wanted free, not to mention the busloads of the colored kind he had to turn away, would think of dealing through Wallace Wright. If Dr. Garrett employed the word *silk,* Dr. Garrett meant the *cloth* that was woven from the glossy secretion of silkworms. And if Dr. Garrett was desirous of getting in touch with Wallace Wright's silk dealer, it was for the sole purpose of having some silk shirts made. Jonah Johnson was not the man to keep the president of the Rosenberg Foundation waiting for his silk shirts.

So he set off immediately for Mamie Mason's, because there was one thing for sure, if Mamie didn't know the name and address of Wallace Wright's silk dealer, no one else would; and what was more, anyone out on an important mission for Dr. Garrett would certainly be welcome to a drink or two at Mamie's, and who knew but what one might find something interesting there, perhaps one of those fine silks who were always visiting her.

Meanwhile Reverend Mike Riddick had been sitting down contemplating the fate of that great race leader Wallace Wright, and considering the temptations of the flesh that had led the poor sinner astray, and in so doing had developed a strong desire to pit his Christian valor against some similar temptations. And where was one more likely to find such similar temptations than at Mamie Mason's, who at that very moment was entertaining, among others, Mrs. Kit Samuels, than whom he knew no greater temptation to challenge. So he put his faith in the Lord and hastened over to Mamie's.

"Good afternoon, dear lady, may the Lord bless thee and keep thee," he greeted her warmly. "And though I am aware that I have not been called I do not believe you will obstruct a man of the cloth in his duty to fight temptation."

"Temptation!" Mamie said, startled. "When did you begin fighting temptation?"

"I have always fought temptation long and arduously," he declared. "Makes no difference that I've never won."

"I hate to disappoint you," Mamie said. "But we're not having temptation today, we're having fried fish."

"Fried fish!" Reverend Riddick enthused, sniffing the air like a hound dog on a hot trail. "What is more tempting than fried fish?"

"Furthermore," Mamie said, "there's barely enough to go around."

"Barely enough fish to go around!" Reverend Riddick exclaimed. "That's incredible! There is more fish in the world than there is bait."

"But it's not here," Mamie maintained.

"Not here! With all your guests? Surely if our Saviour alone could supply a whole multitude with just five little fish, you and all your guests can put out enough for me."

"That was the Saviour," Mamie said. "Besides which, we

don't want any men in here. We women are having a private affair."

"Affair! Among women?" Reverend Riddick was scandalized. He drew himself up to his full height and demanded sternly: "Is there anything immoral taking place in this house full of women that you wish to hide from a minister of our Lord?"

So there was nothing left for Mamie but to invite Reverend Riddick to inspect the innocent little gathering for immorality. Reverend Riddick entered and inspected and as soon as he saw Kit Samuels he was assured he'd have his fight with temptation at last.

"How do you do, Mrs. Samuels?" he greeted her. "May the Lord protect you in your innocence and strengthen you for the temptations which lie in wait for us."

"Oh, Reverend Riddick," Kit Samuels said. "Would you care for some of my fish?"

"I would like nothing better than to have some of your fish," Reverend Riddick said solemnly as he squeezed down beside Kit on the bench of the kitchen table, pressing his big hard thigh staunchly against her small soft thigh, no doubt to alert her to the great temptation nearby. "Now let us bow our heads and give thanks to the Lord for the fish we are about to receive."

Reverend Riddick thanked the Lord with such inordinate fervor for the fish he was about to receive that Maiti Brown was heard to whisper, "My God, that man loves fish!"

"I like a man who loves fish," Merto said. "If a man loves fish he's dependable; I mean you don't have to beat about the bush trying to find out what he loves, if he loves fish, that is."

"If you love a man who loves fish so much, go find one for yourself," Kit Samuels said.

"Well, I'm sure I'm not trying to take any man from you who loves your fish so much," Merto said. "I mean you can do just as you wish with your fish and I'll do the same, that is."

"Ladies, remember it is more blessed to give than to receive," Reverend Riddick said. "Allow me to bless you both by accepting some fish from each of you."

"You know," Maiti Brown was heard to whisper, "I believe there's double-talk going on here."

Of course, Mamie saw right off that if this preoccupation with fish continued, there was going to be more fishing than she contemplated. So she was about to dispatch Kit Samuels on an errand that would require the assistance of a strong fisherman when, lo and behold, Art Wills arrived looking for no one less than Wallace Wright.

Needless to say, Debbie was not a little put out to find her husband in so compromising a position as to confess associating with a man of Wallace Wright's character. For all she knew he might even be trying to help Wallace get another one. And besides, just what had he done with her child? Art assured her he had gotten a sitter for *her* child but if *her* child threw the cat out of the window again just don't call her *his* child, because as hard as he worked to support them both he didn't feel called upon to have to wear the skirts.

That made Debbie furious, insinuating she was that way. She said if he paid more attention to the skirts in his own home *his* child wouldn't do such things.

Naturally Art bitterly resented being charged with the truth. So he reiterated by saying that if she had told him where she was going instead of saying she was going to Far Rockaway to visit her aunt, he wouldn't have come up there in the first place, maybe he would have gone to Far Rockaway himself, or even farther. All he wanted was to read Wallace Wright's autobiography.

"My God! Wouldn't we all!" Maiti Brown exclaimed.

If it hadn't been for Jonah Johnson arriving at that juncture, Art's linen might have been exposed.

But when Jonah announced he was looking for Wallace Wright's silk dealer, shock prevailed.

"What!" Bessie Shirley cried in astonishment. "Is he

buying it, with all that's going for free?"

"It's not that kind of silk," Jonah said. "This is silk for shirts."

"Good Lord!" Mamie said maliciously. "Don't tell me Wallace is dealing in hot silk too."

All the colored people present knew just what she meant. If Wallace was dealing in hot silk it could only mean he was offering it to selected customers as contraband, but which everyone knew was stolen.

However, the majority of the ladies had gone over to Wallace's side since they had learned of his insatiable desires, and Patty Pearson was smart enough to see this.

"I think it's perfectly all right morally for Wallace to sell contraband silk," she said. "Because I'm sure the only reason Wallace does it is to help the colored Asians who are up against the silk problem like we are up against the Negro Problem."

"I have to agree with Patty," Alice Overton said. "As you all know, I have many social acquaintances among white people of good intentions. But whenever one of our own goes out of his way to help colored people, he has my admiration, I don't care if they are Asians."

"Far be it from me to accuse Wallace of stealing silk, if he can't get it any other way," Mamie said.

"And just to think, I can't give enough away," Merto said.

"No one thinks he's actually stealing it himself," Patty defended him. "Just because he's dealing in it."

"Isn't everyone doing it?" Alice Overton said.

"I'll say," Bessie Shirley said. "Ain't it marvelous?"

"But how does he get so much silk?" Kit Samuels asked.

"Don't ask me," Maiti Brown said. "If it's what I'm thinking."

"Certainly Wallace is only trying to do his bit for the Asians," Alice Overton said.

"But should we bring in the Asians with Wallace?" Mrs. Kissock ventured doubtfully.

"Bring on them all," Bessie Shirley said jubilantly.

"But so many of them are Red now," Mrs. Kissock continued. "The Asians. For instance China, all of China is Red."

"But what is there to be ashamed of, it's so natural, that is," Merto said.

"As everyone knows, I'd be the last person in the world to blacken Wallace's character," Mamie said. "But if he can get silk from Red China, how do we know he's not a Red himself?"

"I do wish Wallace would come and explain all this himself," Mrs. Kissock said. "I am certain he would know the difference, and he would also know the latest consensus of opinion concerning Reds."

"That's another thing wrong with the Negro Problem, always calling colored people Red just as though they can't be black to steal something out of the ordinary," Kathy Carter said.

"It makes no difference whether it's red, white or black," Reverend Riddick said. "Temptation is temptation."

"What's he talking about?" Maiti Brown asked. "Women or Reds?"

"Well, I know one little thing," Mamie said. "When colored people start defending their own traitors they certainly can't expect to be invited to my Masked Ball."

"Oh dear," Mrs. Kissock said. "I must telephone Dr. Kissock and tell him I'll be late."

"I think what Kathy meant," Art said, "is that we should hesitate before condemning a great man such as Wallace Wright as a Red just because out of loyalty to his people he is accused of stealing a trifling bit of silk."

"That's just exactly what I meant, honey," Kathy said, snapping her fingers triumphantly. "It ain't what you do, but it's the way that you do it."

She seemed on the point of giving a demonstration, but was restrained by the presence of Debbie Wills who, after all, was not expected to just sit by and applaud.

Of course Mamie was furious with Art for taking up for Wallace, as good as she had been to him in more ways than just two.

"Naturally you can't expect the pot to call the skillet black," she said dangerously.

"That isn't what I meant," Art said. "Some of my best friends are black as the ace of spades."

This time he was saved by the ringing of the doorbell announcing the arrival of Eddy Schooley and his editor, Lou Reynolds. Afterwards, both denied emphatically that they had come together, because on entering Schooley said, "Holy Moses, this place is full of spooks." Of course he swore to the bitter end he had been invited by Mamie in person to attend a seance and he had only been referring to the spooky feeling aroused by the cracking of the doors all up and down the corridor and the peering of eyes from the dark recesses when he and Lou got off the elevator, and not in the least to the fact that there were more dark ladies present than white.

But the colored ladies felt he was referring to them, being as *spooks* is a term sometimes applied to darkish people, and they resented it bitterly and in such language as to cause the white ladies to blush so vividly Reverend Riddick was reminded of cherries. Reverend Riddick loved cherries and it had been a long time since he had gotten a fine cherry, but he didn't feel that the moment was propitious to comment on his love for cherries, being as he had a profound respect for colored ladies when they had gotten their color up.

Not so with Art. He not only did not know the colored ladies had gotten their color up, but he thought it was a shame for Schooley's own colored ladies to denounce him in such a manner for what seemed to him a perfectly natural mistake.

"Everyone's taking it wrong," he said. "Schooley didn't mean live spooks, he meant dead spooks."

"Well now, if you think there's anything dead about me,"

Kathy Carter said, snapping her fingers indignantly, "you certainly won't hear any bones rattle when I shake, if you know what I mean."

It would happen that Mrs. Kissock would choose this moment to return from telephoning Dr. Kissock, armed with all the pertinent facts of Wallace's narrow escape, and commend Art for warning Wallace to keep away from Mamie's that afternoon.

But Art was so happy to at last find something he could deny in all truth that he launched into such an eloquent denial no one believed him.

Needless to say, Mamie received this good news with blinding fury. "Snakes who come into my house and eat my fried chicken and drink my good whiskey and repay me by stool-pigeoning are what I call a disgrace to the white race," she raved.

"I haven't seen Wallace Wright since the night of the big party you gave in his honor," Art denied in all sincerity, having no memory of confronting Mr. Wright in Patty Pearson's apartment in the company of Mr. Wright's wife, Julius and Patty, not to mention Mr. Wright's white paramour. "And it's a good thing I haven't," he went on. "Because I would certainly have warned him against Greeks bearing gifts."

"That just proves you're a liar," Mamie said. "I've never in my life given a party in Wallace Wright's honor."

"Mamie's right," Schooley said. "The party was in my honor."

"I had understood it had been in Dr. Kissock's honor," Mrs. Kissock said.

"I certainly wouldn't hold anything back from these Greeks," Merto said. "If the gifts were really gifts, like diamonds and things, that is."

"I knew a woman who got knocked up from eating in a Greek restaurant," Bessie Shirley said.

"My God!" Maiti Brown said. "From eating?"

"What's more, Art Wills is the Judas who betrayed Wallace Wright in the first place, if the truth be told," Mamie said.

"It's impossible for me to have betrayed Wallace because I don't even know what he's guilty of that we all haven't done," Art said.

"My God!" Maiti Brown exclaimed. "Him too!"

"I will not stand by and see you persecute Brother Wills in such a manner," Reverend Riddick said. "Makes no difference if he is white."

"It's Brother Wallace who is being persecuted more than me, just because he isn't white," Art said.

"In the name of Brotherhood let that woman cast the next stone at Brother Wright who has no rocks in her own bed," Reverend Riddick said.

"I can point my finger at some people present who're trying to be so almighty virtuous, when if the truth be told you could call *his* bed the Rocky Mountains," Mamie said.

"I might not be so virtuous, but I have my own virtues, if you know what I mean," Kathy Carter said, snapping her fingers and giving her hips a twist to accent what she meant.

"The truth is we are all brothers under the skin," Art said.

"My God!" Maiti Brown exclaimed. "Do we have to unskin?"

"If you want to start throwing the truth around, I can pitch a few strikes myself," Mamie said. "And if the truth be known, everyone may as well know right now that Art Wills sat right here in my house and phoned Wallace Wright to meet him at Patty Pearson's and then lured Juanita to Wallace's love nest and betrayed him," Mamie said.

"To tell the truth it seems to me as if Wallace's only sin was being caught," Art said.

"Ain't it the truth?" Bessie Shirley said.

"I can make anyone tell the truth by hypnotizing them," Schooley said.

"Well, don't just sit there doing nothing," Mamie said. "Make Art tell the truth."

And that was how it came about that Eddy Schooley exercised his powers of hypnotism over Art Wills.

Art lay on the sofa and Schooley sat in a chair beside him and stared down into his eyes while passing his hands slowly back and forth across his vision, repeating in a low hypnotic voice, "Sleep . . . sleep . . . I command you to sleep . . ."

Art had had a very wearying day, including everything, and it was comfortable on the sofa and Schooley's droning voice was a welcome relief to all the jaybird chatter of the women. So Art thought, what the hell, he may as well take advantage of the opportunity and catch himself a little nap, which certainly no one could find fault with since they had practically forced him to submit to Schooley's foolishness. Which is what he did. He closed his eyes and went to sleep.

"He's asleep," Lou Reynolds said.

Schooley peeled back one of Art's eyelids and saw that he really was asleep, and he was the most astonished person present.

"Holy Moses," Schooley said. "He's asleep."

"That's what I said," Lou said. "Make him stand up."

"Stand up," Schooley commanded.

Naturally Art paid no attention to his command, as hard as he was sleeping. Instead he began to snore.

Schooley was so disconcerted by this turn of events that he failed to notice that Mamie Mason stood up from her chair on his left hand and Patty Pearson stood up from her chair on his right hand.

But Schooley was not one to be defeated by minor setbacks, especially after having discovered how to put a subject to sleep. So he laid his hand gently on Art's forehead and spoke to him with the openhearted candor of a brotherly cop asking a halfwit yegg what he had done with the loot: "Where lies the truth, pal?"

But on the one hand it was Mamie who answered, staring straight ahead from a deep hypnotic trance. "It is in the kitchen, O master."

And on the other hand it was Patty, likewise in a deep hypnotic trance. "It's in the bedroom, O master."

Mamie flicked Patty a dangerous look out of the corners of her hypnotized eyes and Patty flicked Mamie a defiant look out of the corner of hers.

"My God!" Maiti Brown exclaimed. "He's got his wires crossed."

Schooley was so dumbfounded by this unexpected revelation of his really tremendous powers he sat there gaping like a goof.

Not so with his subjects. Neither of those smart ladies was dumb enough to get herself hypnotized without keeping in full command of her wits.

So on the one hand Mamie prompted the hypnotist thus: "O master, I will do as thy thoughts biddest me and go henceforth and get it from the hidden place and bring it to thee for thy inspection."

And on the other hand Patty prompted the hypnotist thus: "O master, if thou wilt come with me I wilt lead thee to them so thou mayest see the truth with thine own eyes."

At this point the occult powers impelling the subjects entered into such furious conflict they looked daggers at one another, and each took hold forcibly of one of the master's arms.

"Go thou not with that lying bitch, O master, the truth is not in her," Mamie said.

"Be not deceived by the falseness of that double-crossing witch, O master, or you'll never get to the truth," Patty said.

"Lord in heaven! Those women need exorcising," Reverend Riddick said wistfully.

"Turn him loose, you bitch!" Mamie shouted at Patty

in a sudden rage and began pulling the master toward the kitchen.

"I got as much right to him as you have," Patty retorted furiously and began pulling the master toward the bedroom.

"Lord in heaven!" Reverend Riddick said in an awed voice. "The devil himself has got into those women."

"My God, unhypnotize them quick!" Maiti Brown cried in horror.

The trouble was the master had not yet learned how to release his subjects from their trances. All he could think to say that in any way might prove efficacious was to shout, "Awaken! Awaken!"

Neither of the two subjects bent on tearing him in two paid the slightest heed, but the third subject who until then had been sleeping peacefully on the sofa came suddenly awake, and the first thing he saw was the big brute, Eddy Schooley, manhandling two women. He leapt to his feet, shouting, "Unhand those women, you fiend," and promptly knocked the master unconscious.

"My God!" Maiti Brown exclaimed in even more horror. "The devil has got another one."

Being as the master was now lying on the floor unconscious with no one to release the subjects from their trances, Mamie ran into the kitchen and returned waving the letter Art Wills had written to Brown Sugar.

"The master bids me present this to thee, O my sister," she said, thrusting the letter into the hands of Debbie Wills. "So thou, the wife of this deceiver, may open thine eyes to the truth."

Art wasn't paying any attention to Mamie's shenanigans at the moment as he was kneeling on the floor beside poor old Schooley trying to bring him back to consciousness so he could apologize for acting so hastily.

So when Debbie had finished reading the letter and turned on him, shouting, "You beast!" naturally he thought she was referring to his violence.

"I am not a beast," he protested. "I would do the same

thing for any woman whom I admired, whether I was right or wrong."

This brazen confession of his infidelity was such a profound shock that Debbie became hysterical. Reverend Riddick was not one to stand by and see a hysterical woman.

"Leave it to me, I'll wrestle the devil out of him," he offered, looking about for Mrs. Samuels whom he knew appreciated a good wrestling match.

Meanwhile Patty Pearson had rushed to the back of the apartment and peeped into the bedroom. Finding Merto conversing intimately with Joe Mason, who was clad only in his pajamas, she took the key from the inside of the bathroom door and quietly locked the bedroom door from the outside.

And how did it happen that Merto was in the bedroom with Joe in such a compromising position at such an inopportune time? Well, it brings us back to the subject of fish.

Just before Schooley began to hypnotize Art, Merto went to the john, and as she was leaving the john to return to the scene of the activities, Joe Mason cracked the bedroom door and said, "Pssst!"

It goes without saying that Merto was instantly intrigued by this manner of greeting, especially as it came from a colored gentleman clad only in pajamas standing in a doorway to a bedroom with a bed clearly visible in the background.

"I know it's an imposition to appeal to a guest," Joe said with a sweet imploring expression, "but I'd like awfully to have some fish."

Having been lying there all that time, smelling the tantalizing aroma of fried fish, it was perfectly natural that Joe had developed an uncontrollable desire for some.

But without even knowing that, Merto could understand perfectly. "But it's hardly the time or place," she pointed out. "I mean with the whole house full of people and everybody all around, that is."

"That's why I asked you," Joe said. "Dressed like this,

you know, even if I put on a robe, it would still be shocking, out there among all those women, I mean."

"Well, I can certainly understand that," Merto said. "But it would be awfully exciting too, I mean, with everyone watching, that is."

"It's just that I don't want Mamie to catch me eating fish in her bed," Joe explained.

"But would she have to know?" Merto said.

"Well, she'd certainly guess if she saw me like this," Joe said.

"Well, anyone would, if they saw us together, that is," Merto said.

"I've been wanting some so badly all afternoon," Joe explained. "And now it's beginning to smell so good I wouldn't care who was around once I got some."

"Frankly, I wouldn't either," Merto said.

"But I don't want to impose on your generosity," Joe said.

"Oh, that's no problem," Merto said. "But let me come inside and think it over. I mean one can decide better after one sees the lay of the land, like a general, that is."

And that was how Merto happened to be in Joe's bedroom when Patty Pearson discovered them during her hypnotic trance.

And what occult powers guided Patty in this diabolical discovery? Well, frankly, she saw Merto go to the john, and being as Patty Pearson was curious about the whereabouts of everyone at all times, she waited for Merto to return from the john, and when Merto did not return from the john in what Patty considered a reasonable enough time for anybody to do whatever they had to do of a legitimate nature in a mere john, she put one and one together and came up with two.

So by the law of averages, Julius Mason chose that very moment to arrive at Mamie's in the company of that rich blond divorcee from the East Seventies, Fay Corson. It was reasonable enough. Julius was living there. And he was under the impression, having gotten this impression directly from Mamie herself, that Mamie would be on her way to Chicago. There was no reason for him to doubt that his brother, Joe, was still in Buffalo. So, naturally, he assumed he was bringing Fay Corson uptown to an empty apartment. For what? Well, for what anyone in their right senses would think.

The only trouble was that Big Burley was on watch by himself in the apartment across the hall when Julius arrived with Fay Corson, and from the combined reasoning of policeman's logic and long experience, he assumed that Fay Corson was Wallace Wright's white paramour come at last. Because, first of all, she was the only white woman whom he'd seen arrive since the advent of Mrs. Anna Kissock, and secondly, she was accompanied by a strange colored man, it being that Julius was a stranger to him, and thirdly, it stood to reason that Wallace Wright's paramour would not get some colored stranger in Harlem to bring her up there unless Wallace was already there waiting for her. But they couldn't fool Big Burley.

"They're here!" he shouted to Juanita, who had gone to the kitchen to get a drink of water, nearly causing her to strangle to death. "I seen her come!"

"Oh!" Juanita cried, gasping for breath. "Beat me on the back."

"This is no time to be beating you on the back, ma'am," Big Burley said. "We got to be quick."

With that he rushed across the hall like a battering ram and hurled his massive weight against the Chinese red door, bursting it from its hinges.

The sight that greeted Big Burley's eyes was enough to curdle the blood of stronger men than he.

Mamie Mason and Patty Pearson were pulling each other's hair.

Reverend Riddick was wrestling Art Wills all over the living room, grunting like a hog rooting for acorns, and shouting to the devil lodged within the person of his adversary, "Turn loose, tough mouth, turn loose."

Kit Samuels was wrestling buck-naked electric wires, handicapped, no doubt, by her own clothes.

Debbie Wills was having crying hysterics. But Dora Steele was embracing her in an effort to console her.

Bessie Shirley was having laughing hysterics, watching all this hot flesh performing for nothing.

Eddy Schooley, having regained consciousness, was crawling about on his hands and knees, trying to avoid the wrestlers' feet.

Lou Reynolds was halfheartedly trying to restrain Kathy Carter from joining the hair-pulling contest.

Jonah Johnson, taking advantage of the general confusion, was trying to take Fay Corson away from Julius, but Julius was valiantly holding on to her.

Mrs. Kissock was murmuring in obvious terror, "Oh dear! Oh dear! They're running amuck. Just like in *Gone With the Wind*."

Maiti Brown was sitting in a grandstand seat on the sofa, looking on the chaos in indescribable horror. "My God!" she was shouting. "The devil has got them all!"

Naturally Juanita didn't follow Big Burley into such a den of iniquity. Not that she minded the iniquity, in fact she was delighted by the iniquity, being as it was taking place in Mamie's where one could expect such carrying on. But she had vowed she would never set foot in that woman's house. So she stood in the hall and directed her forces through the broken-down door.

"Get the woman!" she called. "Get the woman!"

However, Big Burley was a man to do his duty as he saw it, so he grabbed Reverend Riddick and Art Wills in a bear hug and shouted triumphantly, "I got you both red-handed!"

"Not them, you fool!" Juanita screamed from her headquarters in the corridor. "Do they look like women to you?"

Big Burley released his culprits and scratched his head. "No, ma'am, they doesn't," he confessed. "But you never can tell. I was thinking I was still on that case investigating crooked wrestling, and if ever I seen any crooked wrestlers, these is them."

Patty Pearson saw the nature of things at once, being as she knew Big Burley from a similar occasion where he had confused the *loot* with the *lute,* and she screamed, "They're in the bedroom, you idiot!"

That was right down Big Burley's alley. Not for nothing was he known as Bed-eye Burley. If they were in the bedroom, they had had it. So when he arrived at the bedroom door and found it locked, it was all over but the hanging as far as he was concerned. He dashed back to the living room and broadcast to HQ in the corridor, "I got 'em dead to rights, locked in the bedroom."

Instantly:

Mamie Mason and Patty Pearson stopped pulling each other's hair; Reverend Riddick and Art Wills stopped wrestling; Kit Samuels stopped still and shook down her skirt; Debbie Wills stopped crying hysterically; Bessie Shirley stopped laughing hysterically; Lou Reynolds released Kathy Carter; Jonah Johnson and Julius Mason released Fay Corson simultaneously; Eddy Schooley got to his feet; Mrs. Kissock said, "Oh dear! Now what?" Maiti Brown stopped being horrified and started being scandalized. And all of them converged on the bedroom in a reconnaissance in force.

It was just too much to expect Juanita to remain at her post in the corridor while such dead-to-the-right scandal was brewing in the bedroom. Besides which, it was her own husband involved. So she came tearing into Mamie Mason's apartment, vow or no vow, and was just in time to join the awed forces watching Big Burley crash through the bedroom door.

And there stood poor old Joe, looking as buck-naked in his flimsy pajamas as the first cave man, facing Merto beside the unmade bed, and giving such an improvisation of innocence as to appear downright obscene.

"What's this!" he demanded indignantly.

Mouths popped open.

"It looks awfully like an assignation," Bessie Shirley said.

And did that great crusader against adulterous miscegenation when engaged in by one Wallace Wright burn at this defection by her own black Joe. "Cover yourself!" she said furiously, as though he were exposing his private parts on purpose.

But it was left to Maiti Brown to state the impropriety of the situation. "My God!" she exclaimed in a shocked voice. "In his wife's own bed!"

For his part, Joe was superbly righteous. "Who locked that door?" he demanded.

No matter how pertinent this question may have seemed to him, it struck others as shockingly inadequate for the occasion, to say the least, and inspired a great deal of embarrassment among his good friends who desired to support him.

"That's not *my* husband," Juanita denied quickly before anyone got the idea it was herself married to such an imbecile.

Needless to say, with everything going wrong, this last snide remark by her archenemy was the bitter end for Mamie.

"He certainly isn't, dearie, from what I last saw of *your* husband's little needle," she stormed. "What does he do with it, sew you up?"

However, Big Burley was not one to be cheated out of his glory by a hen fight, especially after having broken down two perfectly good doors. "That ain't my business, ma'am, whether you're married to him or not," he said. "You hired me to catch 'em, and can't nobody say I ain't caught 'em."

"Caught doing what?" Joe protested virtuously. "I was just trying to get some fish."

"Good heavens, man!" Reverend Riddick exclaimed in amazement. "You mean you didn't get it?"

"Well, no one thinks otherwise," Mamie fumed.

What made her so mad was he wouldn't come right out and admit it, or at least confess to it even if he hadn't, instead of humiliating her before her guests by insisting he hadn't got any under such normal conditions for getting some, as though she were married to some abnormal kind of man who wouldn't even take it when it was offered on a silver platter, or at least a clean bed.

"Let's not jump to conclusions," Reverend Riddick said, coming to Brother Joe's defense. "Maybe he didn't have the time."

"I agree with the Reverend," Art seconded. "Appearances can be deceiving."

"Well, after all, who does anybody think is being deceived?" Merto said.

"Well I'm certainly not," Mamie raged.

"All I can say, Mamie dear," Juanita said, "if the shoe fits, wear it."

"I mean what's deceiving about a poor man asking for some fish?" Merto said. "If he really wants some fish, that is."

"Where there's so much fish there's bound to be some fishing, if you know what I mean," Kathy Carter said.

"I'm going to get out of here," Maiti Brown said. "This house is full of fishhooks."

"Well, there's one hook I'm going to file the point off right now," Mamie threatened.

"All I want to know is, who locked that door?" Joe said plaintively.

Everybody winced.

At this juncture the proceedings were interrupted by the ringing of the telephone.

"That must be Wallace," Mrs. Kissock said. "I think I should speak to him."

But it was only Moe calling to give Joe the good news about the rat who had been occupying his house. So when Mrs. Kissock picked up the receiver, expecting to hear her dear friend Wallace, and wondering what words of encouragement she could convey to bolster his morale through these trying times, it was indeed a shock to hear a raucous voice that sounded for all the world like a gangster saying triumphantly, "By God, Joe, we won't have to worry about *that* rat anymore. I killed him with a meat cleaver."

Poor Mrs. Kissock fainted dead away.

Juanita Wright began screaming and ran from the house.

Debbie Wills became hysterical again.

Maiti Brown became horrified again.

Bessie Shirley rushed to the telephone to play the combination of numbers called "Death Row" in the night house.

Reverend Riddick offered to wrestle the devil out of any sinner present. Kit Samuels accepted his offer, as sinful as she felt.

Joe Mason began putting on some clothes, ladies or no ladies. Big Burley stood by, patting him on the shoulder, and saying proudly over and over, "Sweetest catch I ever made."

And there was poor Mamie, in a blazing fury, trying to restore order. She put Mrs. Kissock in the bedroom and Debbie Wills on the couch in the den. She kicked Big Burley so hard on the shins that afterwards he gave up collecting evidence for divorce cases.

Schooley was still raving over his success as a hypnotist. "You've got to give me my due," he kept saying.

Mamie bopped him on the noggin with her shoe heel. "That's your due," she raved.

Schooley was later heard to complain that women didn't make good subjects for hypnotism on account of their being too impetuous.

When Alice Overton saw Merto leave in the company of Bessie Shirley, she rushed home to protect Willard.

Kathy Carter said she was all for Joe because, after all, if you left your bull in a pasture full of cows you had to expect calves.

Mamie ordered Kathy to leave her house.

"If you mean me, dear, I wasn't invited here anyway," Kathy said indignantly. "I just came to take Joe's notes."

"Someone beat you to them, honey," Patty Pearson said slyly.

"My God!" Maiti Brown exclaimed. "What a day! From fish to notes!"

Mamie said she would appreciate it if everyone got the hell out of her house.

By this time Julius and Fay had already gone about their business, presumably the same business they had come for.

Several others had business on the mind also.

Kathy and Art Wills left together on their business. Kathy was consoling Art by telling him she might not be in high society like Mamie Mason, but she knew she was better at taking notes. Art had to admit later that this was a fact.

Reverend Riddick and Kit Samuels were going down the street about their business, wrestling no doubt.

"That's how I lost my wife," he was telling her. "It was me or the devil."

"But you're a minister," Kit said in astonishment. "With all your knowledge of sin, couldn't you hide it any better?"

"Good Lord, child, it had nothing to do with sin," he said. "She never caught me at *that*. It was just my wrestling the devil out of her girl friends when they came to visit her. Once I'd wrestled the devil out of them they kept coming back for more."

"And she resented that? She must not have been very religious if she resented your wrestling the devil out of them. After all, you're a minister, and it's your duty."

"Good Lord, child, that was the trouble," Reverend Riddick said. "She was too damn religious. She jumped to the conclusion that I was trying to save their souls. Hell, I just like to wrestle with women, that's all."

Dora Steele said to Lou Reynolds, "Isn't it awful?"

"Terrible," he agreed.

"It's always got to be black and white," she said.

"Awful," he said.

"But it can't be worse than being married to a man who's impotent," she said.

"That's a fact," he said.

"But it doesn't have to be as bad as it would seem if such were not the case," she said.

"One must avoid preconceptions at all cost," he said.

"Oh, you're so intelligent," she said. "I'd like for you to meet a very intelligent friend of mine who doesn't live far from here who enjoys intelligent conversation. If she's at home."

"I hope she's at home," Lou said. "I like intelligent conversation, if she knows when to go."

"Oh, intelligent people always know when to go," Dora said. "And when to come."

"You've got something there," he said.

"I know I have," she said. "It might look burnt, but it's juicy."

They left together, looking for some intelligent conversation with plenty of juice.

And what happened to our good friend, Wallace Wright, while all this fish was being caught and fried? The fact is, Wallace had better sense than to go up to Mamie Mason's that afternoon, regardless of what Mrs. Kissock had said about Mamie going to Chicago. He knew damn well Mamie had no intention of going to Chicago or anywhere else as long as there was someone to fry at home, himself in particular. So after graciously conceding to Mrs. Kissock's great plans for his future, he merely went to another hotel and took another room under another assumed name.

And what happened to Peggy? Absolutely nothing. No one told her about anything and she didn't know anything. So she stayed in bed and passed the time being hot and bothered and wishing Wallace would phone.

And what happened to Joe after he'd departed so hastily from his happy home? He hastened to his office on 125th Street and thought things over. After which he phoned the florist and ordered a big bouquet of red roses sent to Mamie with his card. Then he phoned Grand Central Station and made reservations on the night train to Buffalo. When it was much too late to do anything about it, he felt in his bag and discovered he had forgotten his notes. And with the business he had in mind he needed his notes.

And what did Mamie do, now that all her scheming had resulted in such a monstrous fiasco? Well, Mamie Mason could salvage some tiny bit of satisfaction from even the worst of fiascos. At least she'd gotten that droopy-drawered sewed-up Juanita Wright to come into her house, and without even being invited. And just that little bit of satisfaction made Mamie so hungry she called her butcher and ordered the biggest ham he had, because what she wanted now was a big piece of real solid meat with a bone in it, so there couldn't be any doubt about it being meat and not fish. She believed if she could sit down peacefully and eat just one big solid ham, everything would be all right again.

All of which goes to prove faith may be two-faced, but it is sure as hell potent.

IT WAS A PRECOOKED HAM weighing sixteen pounds. Mamie ate two big fat slices cold to cool her rage while she was frying two fat ham steaks to take the edge off her hunger while waiting for the hock to boil, being as boiled ham hock is known far and wide for its therapeutical qualities alleviating chagrin.

By the time the rest of the ham was baked to a turn she could sit down and eat it for the pure sensuous pleasure of eating hot meat. Following which she staggered to the living room and flopped into the big armchair and enjoyed the most wonderful sense of satisfaction she had experienced since she had first started dieting.

She wasn't even mad at Joe anymore. He could have Merto or whatever white woman he desired if she could just have one big ham each day. She had practically forgotten all about Wallace Wright. He wasn't hammy enough anyway. She didn't give a damn at that moment whether Juanita came to her parties or not. In fact, she wasn't interested in giving any more parties. For a time she seriously contemplated changing her Masked Ball into a ham bake. Everyone was running about talking about interracial relations and desegregation and the like when the fact of the matter, when you came right down to it, the only real solution to the Negro Problem was ham.

It may be concluded from this that she was in no disposition to discuss trifling matters when Mrs. Kissock recovered and asked where the body of Wallace Wright would be taken so that she could send a wreath.

Mamie solemnly advised her to simply give Wallace some

ham if she really wanted to do something for the Negro Problem.

"Hams!" Mrs. Kissock exclaimed. "Are we talking about Wallace's remains?"

"Naturally," Mamie said in the slurred voice of stupefaction. "And I am suggesting that you give him hams. The poor man must need some desperately by now."

"But hams! Can you be serious?"

"I was never more serious in my life."

"But is it the custom of the Negro people here to bury their loved ones with hams?"

"Not with hams, in hams," Mamie corrected. "I love nothing better than to bury my loved ones in my hams."

"Oh, dear, I don't believe I understand. Do they feel they must prepare the body for a long journey?"

"The longer the better."

"But it sounds so barbaric, really positively loathsome."

"It feels better than it sounds," Mamie slurred evilly. "You should try it sometimes, in fact regularly."

"I should certainly never bury a loved one of mine in hams," Mrs. Kissock said, shuddering.

"You don't know what you're missing," Mamie said.

Mrs. Kissock grimaced. "I detest ham," she said vehemently. "I can't bear to eat it. It has such a strong flavor and the meat is dark, some of it is positively black."

"Your husband certainly won't agree with you," Mamie said maliciously. "That's what he likes. Strong-flavored black meat. If you had black hams yourself, he would love nothing better than to bury himself in them."

"Oh! Oh! Well, I never!" Mrs. Kissock said, finally getting the drift. "You nasty, vulgar woman. I shall never speak to you again."

She left hastily, shocked to the core to learn of Dr. Kissock's defection to colored hams; and she vowed she would never again set foot in Mamie Mason's house or attend another Mamie Mason affair.

Naturally, when Debbie Wills recovered she wanted to know more about this Brown Sugar person with whom her husband was having an affair.

Mamie looked at Debbie through her glazed satiated eyes and said, "It's just a matter of ham, baby, Brown Sugar has big brown juicy sugar-coated hams which your husband loves, being as he's tired of seeing your small white uncured-looking hams. Do you understand, baby?"

Debbie left in a huff, swearing never to return. And what was more she went straight downtown to their apartment and got her daughter and went straight home to her mother, leaving only the broken-legged cat to keep Art company when he returned.

And that's how word got out that distinguished Negrophiles by the score were deserting white wives of long standing for brownskin Hammettes supplied by that fabulous purveyor of pussies, Mamie Mason.

Needless to say, more pandemonium broke out among the second white sex than was aroused by the desegregation of condoms in Little Rock, Arkansas. Many white ladies known to have frequented Mamie Mason's parties came down suddenly with Negrophobia, panicking their doctors, who diagnosed the malady as hydrophobia but couldn't find the dog-bite, much less the dirty dog.

Of course, everyone knows how *Word* despises *Truth*. *Word* couldn't let up with the story of two or three score great white ladies going on a dinge binge, or with the story straight from the horse's mouth that Mamie had gone into the black slave trade and was getting a thousand dollars a head from white men for black women and, shhhh, man, the same amount from black women for white men. That stuff was too trite for *Word*. That was the kind of risqué parlor stuff good only for tepid titillating and warming soup, which could be culled by the chapter from any realistic American novel. What *Word* wanted was something to milk the genetics and churn some political butter, something to scorch the genitals of the racists and curdle the blood of the heretics. *Word* wanted something to make the Negro Problem resort to rape. *Word* was on a bender that would make a hurricane look like a blowfly. Makes one wonder what that stuff was *Word* was drinking; one could use some of that stuff oneself if one had some.

So *Word* came up with a script that Mamie Mason was the leader of an organized colored cult that was plotting to mongrelize the whole white race. According to *Word,* the blueprint called for massive raids by black women on all white men foolish enough to be over forty, and on all white men under forty who: (1) liked chocolate pudding; (2) dug jazz; (3) preferred coffee to milk; (4) patted black pussies; (5) believed in changing their luck; (6) had once had or still had black mammys; (8) ate dark meat; (9) listened to the blues. Great guns alive, who was left to man the "Hate Buses"?

The white ladies did not take this lying down, descendants of the pioneers who conquered the Redskins, as they were. They knew enough in this instance to fight fire with fire.

That is how the great sociological phenomenon of the twentieth century came about when absolutely normal and sensible white ladies tried their damnedest to get black.

Of course everyone knows that white ladies by the millions have been doing this for decades in such places as Florida and the Riviera, but in those instances it is perfectly acceptable on the grounds that white people who pay such fabulous prices to roast themselves black in absolutely free sunshine so hot most people wouldn't want it as a gift must be given the benefit of the doubt. But these white ladies combating Mamie Mason's plot to blacken the entire white race were as sane as you and me.

Consequently there was an immediate run on suntan lotions and ultraviolet-ray lamps. But it was soon discovered that these were incapable of doing a competent job. When white ladies set out to be black, they don't fiddle around with shades of red or tan.

Naturally, many unscrupulous people capitalized on this situation. The cosmetic firm that had been turning a standard profit manufacturing that reliable skin bleach known as Black Nomore, guaranteed to whiten the blackest skin, immediately issued a new product for the white market called Blackamoor, advertised to blacken the whitest skin, which in reality was the same product with printer's ink substituted for the chlorine bleach.

Also the manufacturers of those two renowned products to straighten kinky hair, Burr Breaker and Kink Killer, both being the same mixture of potash lye and potato paste, only scented differently, followed the example of the manufacturers of Black Nomore. Lard gravy was substituted for the potash lye and when mixed with the potato paste was issued on the white market as Burr Maker and Kink Filler, advertised to make the straightest of hair kinky.

Seeing as how these hair preparations created a whole new market, a smart furrier, on the verge of bankruptcy from overstocking black sheepskins intended for Persian lamb coats, began manufacturing those fabulously fashionable Snappy Nappy and Burr Head wigs for the bald-headed casualties of the hair kinkers.

Then an enterprising salesman began selling a powdered bath salts guaranteed to turn white skin into a beautiful dark brown color with daily immersions, and at ten dollars a pound. The only trouble was, his bath salts looked and smelled and tasted so much like instant coffee that husbands made the mistake of drinking it, and it was too damn expensive to drink.

When word reached Harlem of this lucrative business, every black cat who could get hold of a salesman's satchel got in on the deal.

Nathan, the root man, sold roots to chew to make the gums blue. Another man sold eyedrops to make the eyes red. A third sold nutcrackers to crack the fingernails to make the half-moons dark. And there was a team of pedicures, Dr. Foot and Dr. Black, who specialized in stretching and flattening white feet.

It occurred to one tall black dancer named Slim that he had been rendering white women a service free of charge for which they would gladly pay him. So after a little discreet promotion, mostly by cautious exposure of his equipment, he launched his career as an accommodation enlarger, being as white women are known to need considerable enlarging of their accommodations to compete on equal terms with black women's accommodations.

Unfortunately, before making his fortune his health gave out, and he had to retire to the Harlem hospital and take shots for anemia.

Then there was also the sad case of Biting Joe, who had perfected a technique to curl straight pubic hair by certain highly stylized applications of the tongue, and was going exceedingly well, but he couldn't resist the temptation to bite and his clientele dropped away—in fact some of them ran like hell.

Quite a number of store-front preachers did a discreet business in teaching white ladies how to follow the rhythms of the Georgia Grind, the Rabbit Patch Roll and the Parson's Hump, but the difficulties arising in restraining the white ladies until the lessons were completed limited their income, being as they were charging by the hour.

The most enterprising prospector was a Harlem shoeshine boy called Blue who looked into the mirror one day and realized his coal-black skin was pure gold. Equipped only with a hypodermic syringe he went from door to door in the fashionable apartments downtown selling blood to those ladies who wished to insure the permanence of their change. Naturally he didn't have to make any sales talk because everyone knows that one drop of colored blood is all that is required to make a person colored, and as black as he was he got fifty dollars a drop for his blood. One white lady bought five drops with the money her husband had been saving for their vacation, and when he came home that night she grabbed him in her arms and said, "Oh, honey, look at me, I'm so nice and black." If she wasn't black enough before, when her husband found out what she had done with their vacation money, she was black and blue enough afterwards to sing the gospel.

Needless to say, this phenomenon provoked incalculable confusion among women visitors from the Deep South who, in all good faith, had taken their Northern aunts and nieces and female cousins to be as white as they were. Many of them remained for the duration of their visits behind bolted doors in hotel rooms and would not allow any maid to enter unless she had an affidavit from the original Uncle Tom stating that she was not only a bona fide Negro but could trace her ancestors back to Africa.

But Northern white ladies soon found out there were many other advantages in being black other than keeping their husbands: (1) Sharks would not eat them as it is a known fact sharks will not touch black meat; (2) dirt would not show on their skin, therefore they would not have to bathe; (3) they could have black lovers without eyebrows being raised; (4) they could do the housework and pocket the maid's salary; (5) they could at last have sexual intercourse with their husbands in the broom closet without having to entertain guests and worry about him; (6) they could wear all of the loud colors they wished without their friends laughing behind their backs; (7) they could forget the Negro Problem and hate all the Negroes they disliked without feeling guilty; (8) and if times got too tough they could go to heaven without having to die—to one of Father Divine's heavens.

The paradoxical part about this situation was that the colored ladies in Harlem became equally upset when *Word* put it out that the white ladies downtown had launched a devastating counterattack along with an infallible psychiatric therapy, spearheaded by such fighting slogans as: Fight Back— Get a Black . . . Feel Low—Try A Negro . . . Hubby on the Lam? Telephone Sam. And when *Word* whispered it about that even the great Mamie Mason had lost her own Black Joe to a young Pinktoe, the same panic prevailed among the black ladies of Harlem as had previously struck the white ladies downtown.

The situation became so critical as to cause great alarm among responsible people on both sides of the issue. Educational campaigns were hastily initiated to give reassurance to all and were broadcast on national hook-ups.

Noted anthropologists assured a jittery public that, for all practical purposes, the ancient bones of all races, barring a few dissimilarities of the craniums, could be considered very much alike, and they were definitely of the same color, that color being white. Needless to say, that failed in the desired effect on both races. Black women bitterly resented being told their revered forebears had white bones. And white women scornfully rejected any concept ascribing white bones to the black race.

After this dismal failure, noted evolutionists appealed to the atheist element, hammering away at the evolution of man, stating unequivocally that one amoeba could not be distinguished from another, therefore all the agitation about racial differences in the descendants of amoebas was sheer nonsense. The reference to amoebas was very understandable to the white people who had never been able to distinguish one colored person from another, but what was this nonsense about being unable to distinguish a white person from a colored person, descendants of amoebas or not?

Noted ministers were hastened to the breach. They bypassed both the amoebas and the bones and made a beeline for Eden, reiterating again and again that all people are descended from Adam, every last mother's child, be they blue, black, white, yellow or brown, therefore all persons are cousins in the sight of the Lord. But that only served in the end to agitate the situation when black sports from uptown began accosting dignified white ladies on Fifth Avenue with such intimate greetings as, "Hello, cuz, how's your fuzz?"

At this juncture the nation's greatest physicists were rushed to the rescue and presented overwhelming scientific evidence to the effect that a thousand years hence, in the full flower of the atomic age, all human life would be transparent, and there would be no way of determining the participants in sexual intercourse except by vocal utterances such as, oh, daddy, it's so good, oh, daddy, I'm strictly in the mood, or by other related sounds such as whining, groaning, screaming and such carryings-on. But this threw the racists into sheer panic. Overnight white citizens committees sprang up all over the South advocating the immediate elimination of all branches of atomic research, Russia or no Russia.

It was then the great Negro leader, Wallace Wright, was appealed to, and requested to appear on a national radio hook-up and give the public the benefit of his long experience on the interracial battle front for civil rights for Negroes.

"And Mr. Wright," the master of ceremonies prompted, "can you think of one word which will express your optimism concerning the betterment of race relations?"

Mr. Wright grabbed the microphone like a drowning man clutching at a straw and loudly pronounced the word which he felt epitomized the optimism of all races: *"Help!!!"*

AND THAT was exactly the way Mamie Mason felt also when she learned that all of her distinguished white friends were planning to boycott her Masked Ball.

Because how could a great social event, dedicated to the sole purpose of improving relations between the white and black races by promoting goodwill and tolerance by means of conviviality, spiced, one might say, with a dash of concupiscence and concubinage, achieve its noble end if no one showed up but some black folks? After all, what was interracial about the black race? How could the Negro Problem be served if only Negroes sat down to eat? Who was to serve it? Who was to eat it? It smacked of cannibalism. And who, may one ask, were to be the judges and the jury? Who were to be the guests of honor? Who were to occupy the reserved seats? Who were to shake the hands of the black toadies? Who were to delight in the wit and vivaciousness of the darker brother? Who were to marvel at their laughter and appreciate the lovely colors of their skin, the crispy crinkle of their hair and the pearly whiteness of their teeth, if no white people were there? There was no telling what might happen to the Negro Problem.

Did Mamie drop dead?

Not so! She took a purgative.

Then she sent for her best friend, Patty Pearson, to come upstairs and give her aid and comfort.

"My God, honey!" Patty exclaimed at the sight of her bloated figure. "I had heard you were with child, but I didn't realize there were so many of them. Who is the family's father?"

Mamie had to laugh. "Ham, I guess."

"It had to be a Ham, honey," Patty said. "But my God, what a Ham."

No one can expect a girl to hold out against this kind of talk forever, so Mamie let Patty persuade her into taking a peek in the mirror. She looked as though she had been putting off her children's birth to allow them to grow up. But Patty was not the kind of lukewarm friend to let her just stand there and stare in horror. She got her onto the scales so she could see exactly what she had to suffer. The wheel spun. And great leaping catfish! She had gained forty-two pounds and her Masked Ball was only one month away!

She gave Patty a wrestler's hug and a big fat slobber in the mouth usually reserved for Joe.

"Sugar," she said evilly, "you always do it to me so good I'd marry you if you had things, but I'm afraid our children would be eunuchs."

"Anyway, they'd have to be mine, honey," Patty said. "You haven't got space for any more."

Mamie gave a nasty laugh and said, "Sugar, you run on downstairs and polish off that man you've got waiting and if you say a word about me to anybody I'm going to sew you up."

Then she telephoned her doctor and gave him the ultimatum of getting rid of her forty-two pounds of fat in thirty days; telephoned Reverend Riddick and requested that he come up to her apartment immediately as she was badly in need of spiritual guidance; and telephoned Peggy, Wallace Wright's erstwhile paramour, to ascertain if she was at home —when Peggy answered she hung up.

Reverend Riddick was not the one to keep a woman waiting who was in need of his spiritual guidance. And such was the power of his religious perception he saw right off that there was a devil lodged in the body of his gracious hostess. But Mamie warned him dangerously he had jumped to the wrong body, and if he started wrestling in her house there would be no holds barred. So he took another look, and it was enough to convince him that her devil, fortified with all of her evilness and forty-two pounds of fat besides, had him outclassed.

But when Mamie pointed out the urgent Christian need for some minister of great faith, not to mention other great equipment, to go downtown to the house of Wallace Wright's paramour and invest her with the spirit of Christian charity so that she, as a singular service to the Negro Problem, would give Wallace Wright back to his lawful colored wife, he was again reassured that he'd get his devil yet.

"There is no need to look further," he replied solemnly. "If the woman is possessed of a devil, I will cast him out."

Mamie advised him to make certain that the devil was separated from the woman before any casting began, because the woman lived on the fourteenth floor.

Reverend Riddick demanded to know if Mamie thought he couldn't distinguish between a woman and a devil.

Mamie said that better men than him had tried and failed.

Reverend Riddick said that was because they weren't sufficiently equipped for such deduction.

It so happened that in addition to being sufficiently equipped, he was positively ardent when he arrived at Peggy's 23rd Street apartment, it being that some time had passed since he had exorcised the devil of a white woman.

So it was not at all astonishing that he immediately perceived a wild, wanton and untamed devil of formidable proportions beneath her voluptuous breasts, despite the fact she seemed such a nice plump demure white woman.

The only thing was he had not anticipated the wiliness of her devil, for, after one good look at big black handsome Reverend Riddick her devil inveigled her into serving him some tea. Evidently this tea was brewed from the dried bodies of Spanish flies, for the next thing he knew their clothes were strewn all over the floor and he was exorcising her devil with all his Christian zeal.

He wrestled relentlessly and unceasingly with her devil the whole night long, refreshed by sandwiches and more tea when the tide of battle turned against him; but by the evil horns of Lucifer, her devil was as strong and wild and fresh as ever when day broke.

Seeing as how he would need an abundance of nourishment if he were to last through the long formalities of exorcism, she prepared him a hot savory breakfast of scrambled eggs, buttered toast and fried country sausage. Undoubtedly this sausage must have been seasoned liberally with powdered hashish, for the next thing he knew, as exhausted as he had been previous to eating it, he was again exorcising her devil as zealously as from the start.

He exorcised her devil with all his Christian spirit, drawing from his long experience in exorcising devils, and by evening he was so weak he could barely stand.

"Stubbornest devil I ever wrestled," he admitted to himself and was on the verge of throwing in the sponge.

But she fixed him a tremendous dinner of steak, mashed potatoes, vegetables, cheese, strong coffee and a big slice of apple pie liberally sprinkled with what appeared to be cinnamon powder, but which unquestionably must have been the powdered bone tissue of rhinoceros horn, which is known for its great powers of instant reviviscence. For the next thing he knew he was at that devil again.

He wrestled that obstinate devil all that night and half the next day, and when he was too weak to wrestle more, becoming increasingly gray-colored and decrepit as she became increasingly bright-eyed, fresh and rosy, she nurtured him back to strength with such enthusiasm he began to wonder whether she really wanted her devil exorcised or exercised.

But Reverend Riddick was not one to give up to a devil, as fine a devil as this one was, no matter how weak he had become, and seeing as how he would need considerably more time than he had anticipated, he proposed marriage to the woman.

"By the holy heavens, I'll dedicate the remaining years of my life to the exorcism of your devil," he vowed.

"No one will challenge your conscientiousness where the devil is concerned," she said. "Of course, as desirous as I am of having my devil exorcised, nothing would please me more than having it done legitimately, not to mention regularly. But you will have to stand up at the wedding."

"It is just that that devil has hexed my legs," he confessed, struggling vainly to arise. "But if you'll pass me down that phone, I'll give Mamie Mason the news, and also ask her for some kind advice."

It might have seemed like news to him, but it wasn't news to Mamie. She was not the one to waste such a sterling opportunity for the propagation of such prophetic interracial news, despite the news not being news at the time. So no sooner had Reverend Riddick put his foot in Peggy's apartment than Mamie had phoned her very best friend, Patty Pearson, and told her all about it. However, not without first swearing her to secrecy, for how else could she start the propagation of such secret news?

And did the wires begin to burn! Because Patty could scarcely wait until Mamie hung up to pass the secret news to her own best friend, swearing her to secrecy in turn.

Did you say Reverend Mike Riddick, girl? The wrestling preacher?

No one less, child.

With that pssssst woman of Wallace's?

The same, child. Holed up in her apartment and having themselves a session.

You don't mean it, girl! What's he going to tell his faithful black flock?

He claims he's exorcising her devil.

Lord, the names men give to it.

It wouldn't surprise me, child, if he made her forget all about Wallace's from what I've heard of his.

Does Wallace know?

Little good 'twill do him with his little thing once she gets a taste of Riddick's secret weapon.

Taste? Is she like that?

You know these pssssst women, child. They don't believe anything can be that good unless they taste it.

And this very best friend couldn't wait until Patty hung

up to phone the secret news to her own very best friend.

You don't think Wallace is there with them, sugar?

Don't ask me, honey, I'm not the one to comment on Wallace's tastes.

So this best friend couldn't wait to phone her own best friend, who said:

Ask Mamie, sweetie, she's the only one I know who can look through stone walls of houses on the other side of town.

So when Mamie answered the phone a few short hours after phoning Patty, a perfect woman stranger asked in a voice easily recognizable as Negroid: "Is it true that our finest black preacher is jazzing the pssssst woman of Wallace's down on 23rd Street while Wallace is standing there paralyzed?"

So for three days and nights Mamie's phone rang continuously with Harlem women wanting a play-by-play account of the goings-on in that apartment down on 23rd Street. Naturally Mamie gave it to them, from imagination of course.

But what can they be doing all this *time?*

Maybe they've discovered new ways.

Don't be so Russian, darling. Tell me. Don't keep me in suspense.

There are sixty-nine ways of doing it, on the best authority.

That's you, Mamie darling, the best authority. But they've been at it two and a half days. And you said last night they had passed the sixty-seventh.

That's what I mean, baby, they've run out by now.

But according to the specialists they can't do it any more than twenty-three ways in a single day.

Don't you believe those specialists, baby, they don't know Mike Riddick.

But how will he get her to the alter, if she pops the question?

Don't worry about him, baby, he's got a wheelchair.

And was Mamie surprised when she finally heard the startling news, being as just that morning she had decided to hold the wedding reception in her own apartment and had just ordered the invitations printed.

And how did Juanita, that long-suffering and abandoned colored wife of Wallace Wright, take his news that her husband's erstwhile white paramour was marrying that big black wrestling preacher? Naturally she was humiliated over the fact it had been a colored brother who had beat Wallace's time with that white woman, even though he was a preacher. But she didn't waste any time placing her black, er, ah, accommodation again at Wallace's disposal knowing how well off she was with a husband who was at least sixty-three/sixty-fourths white, black as she was.

And how did that notorious Ham connoisseur, Art Wills, react when he heard they were really *marrying* Hams? He got his big white self over to Hoboken and took his little freckly white wife, Debbie, back home as fast as he could before she ran into some big fine Ham and married him too, such as Handsome.

So now, that by a stroke of her evil genius, not to overlook the spectacular assist by black Reverend Riddick's really extraordinary though not quite superhuman devil's exorcisor and rosy white Peggy's indefatigable devil, Mamie had reconciled that great Negro leader Wallace Wright with his droopy-drawered wife, and reunited Debbie Wills with her luck-changing husband, it behooved her to allay the doubts and fears of other squares who had so recently disrupted interracial tolerance, justice and love.

And what better way than have this interracial marriage, loaded with all its tremendously significant political and sociological, not to say mythological, implications, stamped with the approval of the most important white people available.

So naturally she appealed to her own three distinguished doctors of philosophies and humanities, Dr. Oliver Wendell Garrett, president of the board of the Rosenberg Foundation, Dr. Carl Vincent Stone, president emeritus and chairman of the board of the famous Negro college where Dr. Baldwin Billings Brown held a professorship, and Dr. John

Stetson Kissock, chairman of the Southern Committee for the Preservation of Justice, discreetly of course, to attend the reception, in the company of their wives, because of its incalculable importance to the Negro Problem. Of course, these gentlemen, with their profound concern for the Negro Problem, were indeed acutely interested, especially when they heard her describe how that big black Riddick gave it to that plump demure white woman, Peggy.

You don't say? Won her, did he? The big black preacher with the tremendous, er, ah, teeth?

By two lengths, dear. Must come to the wedding.

The *wedding!* Well, er, ahem! Deem it a great honor. Happy that you asked. But the, er, ah, truth of the matter, must attend a high-priority conference on, er, ah, desegregation of, er, ah, public toilets in Birmingham, Alabama.

Understand, dear, but you can fly back for the reception. Can get a good look at them.

Really? But, er, ah, dressed . . . But could I venture to propose . . . no, it wouldn't be possible . . . er, ah, *un*-dressed I mean. . . .

Hardly the occasion, dear, but no end of other blacks. . . .

Oh, ah, quite. A reception, yes. Formal and all that.

Must, dear. Think of my Masked Ball. Can't risk it.

Oh, er, to be sure. But, er, ah, must move slowly. No public places, hotels and such. Must avoid publicity at all costs. Can't have the snoopers, wrong time. Old saying, you know, discretion the better part of valor.

Don't worry, dear, it'll be at my place.

Oh, er, ah, quite. I see what you mean. But, er, ah, the ladies are attending the centennial of the fall of Fort Sumter in Charleston. But we men, well, er, civic duties come first.

Yes, dear, I understand. But you might mention to Wallace to bring Juanita. It's very important. Demonstrate the unity of the fight against bigotry, her and him together, I mean.

Ah, yes, no doubt quite right. Solidarity in the face of this, er, ah, calamity, well, not that, but, er, ah, delicate situation, you know. Was his, now another's. But, er, ah, must avoid scenes at all costs. How would she react to, er, ah, the pinktoe?

She knows already, dear. It's all over town. Took them three days and nights, the loving couple, I mean.

What! Indeed! Three days and nights! By Jove, sounds like the siege of Vicksburg. How did their, er, ah, colors stand up?

Nothing rubbed off. But he paled considerably.

Really? Indeed? Debilitated, eh? And she?

Pinkened. Fresh as a daisy.

Well, by Jove. Ha-ha! The old race has still got its stinger. Must drop in by all means. Just for a few minutes, of course. Ha-ha! Cheer-hos for the pinktoes!

EXCEPT for the rosy red and pale gray faces of the bride and groom there was little to set his wedding reception apart from all other wedding receptions except the ultra-respectability.

Due to her cognizance of the delicate sensibilities of the bride and groom, Mamie had insured this ultrarespectability by inviting only husbands and wives, those who successfully passed as husbands and wives, and couples of the same race who could be construed as affianced by simple flights of fancy. No interracial couples other than the bride and groom appeared to detract from their shining glory.

Nor was Mamie one to stand on ceremony where respectability was concerned. She phoned Joe in Buffalo and ordered him to get himself back home in time to assume his husbandly role, with or without his notes. After which she gave her attention to brother Julius' sadly neglected respectability, and unbeknownst to him wired his wife, Judy, in San Francisco, to take the next plane to New York if she had any imagination. Judy had lots and lots of imagination and it had been working on a twenty-four-hour shift ever since Julius had entrained for New York. So she took the next plane as advised and arrived in plenty of time before having to dress to lavish Julius with the wifely attention he had been so sorely missing. Since no one had warned Julius beforehand of the return of such marital bliss, he had scarcely the vigor to receive such hot gushing adoration and, during the reception, Dora Steele was heard to whisper in amazement that Julius looked as old and decrepit as the groom.

Knowing as they did that the eyes of the world were on them, the colored guests conducted themselves with an unparalleled refinement. The little fingers of hands holding tea cups were rigidly extended at right angles from the other digits, somewhat in the manner of insect antennas, according to the strict dictates of etiquette. In expressions of greetings, all syllables were enunciated distinctly, so that instead of saying, "Howdy do, Moe, how's Joe?" one said, "How do you do, Moses, how is Josephus?" In fact, correct usage was so mandatory that one very proper lady was heard to refer to her husband's "dickerson." It is scarcely necessary to state that excess mucous was squeezed silently from the nostrils into the palm and disposed of by a quick furtive lapping of the tongue, and anything smacking of outright nose blowing was definitely a *faux pas*. When it became necessary to fart, the anus was clamped tightly until a cloud of tobacco smoke was raised and then the weight was shifted onto the left buttock to permit the offensive gas to ease out in a muted whistle drowned by a loud heartfelt sigh. Both the acts of sitting and standing were executed with such dignified deliberation that afterwards it could be verified that not one colored rump was flopped carelessly into one of Mamie's chairs. Naturally laughter was ruled out as positively uncouth, and even undue smiling was frowned upon, especially if blue gums were exposed. Voices were so genteelly modulated it ofttimes became necessary to identify the speaker in a conversation by the flapping of lips.

Of course the white guests were conducting themselves in the most cultivated manner also, being as they were beholden to set an example for their darker brothers and sisters in the social graces. As a consequence they imbibed their cocktails with the studied surreptitiousness of secret drinkers and kept their faces screwed into the polite limestone smiles of British royalty in Black Africa.

However, despite this oppressive omission of sound, there was an alarming wealth of movement provided by the constant shifting of guests seeking to avoid embarrassing encounters. Naturally there were numerous cases of temporary amnesia and mistaken identity.

When Wallace Wright arrived without his wife, Juanita, Mamie must certainly have mistaken him for some strange whore hunter, for she said, "You've got the wrong house, you two-dollar John."

Undaunted by such a vicious greeting, Wallace pressed forward courageously to greet the bride and groom, as social convention dictates. It was indeed a delicate situation, and was attended by all with bated breath.

But Wallace would certainly have mastered the situation had he not slipped on a chicken bone which had fallen unnoticed from the groom's pocket which contained the carcass of a roast chicken he had been nibbling on to allay his weakness. And such are the natural laws governing the compulsion of matter that he was impelled violently forward, and it so happened that he punched the bride in the belly with the very hand he had extended to greet her; and indeed punched her with such force as to knock her on her plump fanny, where she sat with her legs opened, revealing the nylon-clothed cave where her devil was suspected of hiding.

"My God!" Maiti Brown was heard to exclaim. "Seize him!"

Not one guest was so malicious as to assume she meant seize Wallace just because he lay flattened on the floor in front of her outstretched legs with his lips drawn back in a manner suggestive of biting. Everyone knew that Wallace was too much of a gentleman to bite, no matter how justifiable the provocation.

Nor did anyone assume she meant seize Reverend Riddick, who stood staring at the small black Vee of her nylon panties as though he might resume his duties of exorcising again, not as weak as he was.

Therefore, under the circumstances, the only thing which could be construed was that she meant for one and all to seize Peggy's devil which was evidently trying to escape from its cave. And from what they had heard about the magnificence of that devil, they crowded closely about her, open-mouthed and pop-eyed, if not to seize it at least to see it.

But so powerful was the prevailing force of good breeding, dead silence maintained throughout this watchful waiting, except for the slight rustling of skirts caused by sudden palpitations and the muted grinding of teeth brought on by indomitable restraint. Not one single guest was impolite enough to laugh. In fact, dark faces remained in such rigid gravity as to raise grave doubts whether they expected to see *her* devil or *the* devil emerge from its cave.

The only voices to penetrate the prolonged and intense silence were those of Dr. Stone and Dr. Garrett, whispering in a subdued manner.

"Gave her quite a bop, eh, what?" whispered Dr. Stone, his shining white face quivering from excitement as he bit his lips convulsively.

"Quite. As beautiful a straight right to the belly as I ever saw," replied Dr. Garrett, his white mane bobbing and shaking and his goatee bristling suggestively.

"Deserved it, no doubt," whispered Dr. Stone.

"Oh, undoubtedly. They all do," whispered Dr. Garrett. "Stout fellow, Wallace. Should have followed through, however."

"Right-ho. Made certain nothing of his was left," agreed Dr. Stone. "But, er, ah, should have applied a few good bites in strategic places. Once he had her down."

"Quite. A good serving of the old whip," added Dr. Garrett. "Spare the rod, spoil the woman. Stirs up their juices."

"That reminds me, what was the title of that poem about, er, ah, juice?" asked Dr. Stone, laughing silently.

"Ah, yes, by the young black poet. 'The Blacker the Berry the Sweeter the Juice,' " said Dr. Garrett, leaning unobtrusively toward Dr. Stone's ear.

"Ha-ha, capital. The sweeter the berry the blacker the juice," echoed Dr. Stone, convulsively biting his lips.

However, by the time the groom had helped the bride to her feet, the whole uncultured carryings-on were studiously ignored by a sudden outburst of polite murmuring.

One could hear such titbits as: "Did you not know, my dear, that balloons were first made from fish bladders?"

"You don't say, my darling? Did the poor fish have to go so badly?"

"I am not very scientific, my dear, but I would think it comes from all the salt in the sea."

Or:

"Honey, how do you reckon Mamie Mason breathes inside of that dress?"

"Sugar, have you not noticed? She has not breathed as yet."

"But my God, honey, how did she ever get it all into the damn thing?"

"Don't be silly, darling, you can pour fat when it's hot."

"But, honey, is it all that hot?"

"Natch, darling, with all these white men around."

However, when the photographers arrived to take a record of this memorable occasion for posterity, not to mention the society pages of the weekly Negro newspapers, Mamie's hot fat cooled off considerably. For those white men in particular; those venerable doctors of philosophies and humanities, split like a team of pickpockets on sighting the law. Suddenly reminded of previous engagements, they were heard to mutter urgently, "Must go . . . must go . . ." and every time a flashbulb went off one would have thought from their panic-stricken expressions the Third World War had begun.

Needless to say, Mamie Mason was furious with them, having visualized pictures of herself standing in their midst above the caption MRS. MAMIE MASON, THE CELEBRATED HARLEM HOSTESS, ENTERTAINS THE DISTINGUISHED WHITE DOCTORS . . . decorating the society pages of the above-mentioned Negro weeklies.

Seeing how the land was lying, or rather how the guests were flying, Patty Pearson was heard to remark cattily, "Look at Mamie trying to swallow her disappointment." Which caused her equally catty companion to say, "I thought she was warming up her throat." Which inspired

Patty to reply, "All that old suction pump needs is lots of lubrication." Which brought on the comment, "That's what I thought was stopping it up."

However, Mamie Mason was not one to accept defeat as long as she had an ace in the hole.

So while helping Dr. John Stetson Kissock into his coat, she reminded him, "Don't forget you're one of the judges."

"Judges!" he exclaimed, a startled expression inflating his pink cupid's face as he glanced furtively toward the bride. "Are we to sample it?"

"My Masked Ball, dear," Mamie said. "Don't tell me you've forgotten."

"Oh, ah, no indeed," he assured her, his face lighting up with expectancy. "Think of it all the time. All the blacks with the whites. A fine occasion for, er, ha-ha, chess."

"And be sure to bring Anna," Mamie insisted

"Couldn't keep her away," he said, his face falling. "If it weren't for that blasted European tour which falls—"

"If you go away I'll use it on somebody else," Mamie threatened.

She could have said nothing to hurt him more. "You wouldn't," he said pleadingly.

"Yes, I will too," she said adamantly. "And I've got a brand-new one."

"You have!" he exclaimed excitedly, a rosy blush coloring his shining bald head. "A big one?"

"Big and black and a foot long," Mamie tempted. "And it's never been used."

"Oh my," he said and his little rosy mouth began to quiver. "Will I be the first?"

"If you'll come," she said. "To my Masked Ball, I mean."

"Oh, I'll come," he stammered excitedly, his round face glowing in anticipation.

"To be a judge, I mean."

"Oh yes," he said lamely. "If I must."

"And bring Anna," she insisted cruelly.

"Anna!" He gulped embarrassedly.

"To my Masked Ball."

"Oh, er, ah, yes. If you promise to keep it just for me."

"All right, I promise."

"Has anyone seen it?" he asked in a whisper.

"Certainly not," she said. "I keep it hidden beneath my lingerie."

"Won't Joe find it there?"

"He'll think it's a souvenir, he won't think it's mine."

"He won't?"

"Naturally not. He doesn't know I do that."

"Oh, when will it be?"

"Come two days before the ball."

"I'll be sure to come," he promised.

She kissed him on both cheeks. He patted her shoulder affectionately and hastily departed.

Dr. Oliver Wendell Garrett had been waiting in the background to take his departure also. Naturally Mamie repeated the reminder.

And he was equally startled. "Judges!" he echoed, looking like a felon about to be tried. But when his gaze lit on the impassioned countenances of the big black groom and rosy white bride, his goatee quivered in excitement. "By Jove, are they going to wrestle?" he asked.

"My Masked Ball, sugar," Mamie said pointedly.

"Oh, that! Er, ah, I mean that splendid celebration. Have looked forward to it with, er, ah, but you see, Abby insists on her trip to Hawaii. Been promising her for years—"

"Then I'll get somebody else to use it," she threatened.

"Eh, what's that!" he said in a shocked tone of voice. "You wouldn't dare!"

"Yes, I will too," she said. "If you don't come."

"Am I to take that as a threat, my dear?" he said sternly.

"You may take it as you like," she said.

"Well, er, ah, if you put it that way," he conceded.

"And bring Abby," she insisted relentlessly.

"A terrible thing has happened," he said, his big fine patriarchal frame seeming suddenly to shrink. "I've lost mine. I didn't leave it here, did I?"

"I haven't seen it, but I've got one of my own now," she said.

"You have?" he asked sharply, carefully scrutinizing her smooth tan skin. "In use?"

She laughed slyly. "No, sugar, it's brand-new, and just for you."

His shoulders straightened and his white mane stood up like a cockscomb as he smiled down at her from behind his lecherous-looking goatee. "Er, ah, in that case, say when?"

"Come three days before the ball," she said.

Then noticing Dr. Carl Vincent Stone waiting impatiently in the background and shielding his face from the camera with a white silk handkerchief which looked gray against the whiteness of his greasepaint, he pecked Mamie paternally on the forehead and took off while she was still curtsying.

Dr. Stone had little time to wait, seeing from the corners of his eyes the photographer approaching.

"Yes, yes," he conceded in a staccato voice. "Say when."

"Day before the ball," she whispered.

She only had time to show him a small phial containing a greenish liquid which she held cupped in the palm of her hand, almost causing him to get caught with his mouth open as the flashbulb exploded behind them. But she closed the door so quickly that the developed photo showed only an alarmed hostess trying to keep out an agitated ghost.

But as it happened, two of the venerable doctors of philosophies and humanities and soon to be judges got their dates mixed up, which precipitated the most notorious scandal in the history of the Masked Ball.

ALL THAT NIGHT and the following morning the high society ladies of Harlem and their counterparts in the Bronx, Brooklyn and Westchester County had been standing over hot stoves cooking.

Pressure-steaming hogs' heads and pigs' feet; boiling king shrimp and bluepoint crabs; fricasseeing cage-raised rabbits and turkey-breasted quail; frying filet of catfish and big-legged pullets; sautéeing billy goat oysters and boiled bulls' brains; baking sugar-cured Virginia hams and Louisiana sweet potato pies; stewing alligator tails and wild rice; roasting tree-killed baby possums and milk-fed tender tom turkeys; glazing watermelon rinds and pomegranate skins.

Baked hams were scored in abstract designs, facial caricatures and hieroglyphics; roasted turkeys were accompanied on the platters by mashed-potato statuettes of Pilgrim Fathers dressed in faded black eggplant skins; filet of catfish swam in Mississippi Rivers of spoon bread through cotton-green platters; roasted baby possums curled on beds of collard green leaves. Cubes of boiled hog jowls, thin slices of boned pigs' feet, tiny rolls of sautéed billy goat oysters and boiled bulls' brains, chicken-fried frogs' legs and batter-fried clams were spitted on toothpicks which in turn were speared into halves of pumpkins so densely as to give the impression of a blushing porcupine caught red-handed with its quills full of loot.

In addition to these gastronomic delights designed to tickle the palates and tantalize the taste buds, not to mention plug up the lower colons, were those contributory and pre-

cautionary adjuncts without which one dared not venture
on such perilous pleasures:

(1) Condiments: sauces and seasonings, mustard, pickles
and relish, bottles of Red Devil and tomato catsup, mason
jars of Little Sister's Big Brother barbecue dip, chicken
gravy, ham fat, possum juice, turkey sauce, hog hoof jelly
and the like;

(2) The table service: carving knives, serving spoons,
long-pronged forks, table silver, glasses, china, cloths, nap-
kins, place cards, souvenirs, flower vases, tissue paper
streamers and the like;

(3) The beverages, not to be confused with the refreshments: jugs of black coffee, white coffee, buttermilk, sweet
milk, lemonade, fruit juices, sassafras tea, sheep ninny tea,
plain tea, and the like;

(4) The refreshments: whiskey, gin, rum, wine, beer, ale,
cider, Southern Comfort, Ruckus Juice, Red Eye, Smoke,
Coke, sparkling water, ginger ale, soda pop, and what not;

(5) Last but not least, the medications: pills for head-
aches, fainting spells, loss of voice, excess sweating and
heartburn; bottles of patent medicines for acute indigestion,
stomach cramps, nut ache, diarrhea, weak bladders, hot kid-
neys, excess gas, toothache and nosebleed; doctor's prescrip-
tions for heart attacks, black spots, delirium tremens, the
shakes and other nervous disorders; antidotes for food
poisoning, water poisoning, whiskey poisoning, air poisoning and rat poisoning; rubbing alcohol for backaches, tired
feet, sore arms, stiff necks, cramped fingers, swollen lips;
Sloane's liniment for more severe aches and sprains; ban-
dages, surgical tape, antiseptics and astringents for cuts,
stabs, bullet holes, bad bruises, black eyes and loose teeth;
mojos, love potions, amulets and herb medicines for all the
attendant emotional disorders; not to mention condoms,
French ticklers, spare panties, paper hankies, tubes of vase-
line, mouth wash, Sen Sen and other necessary cosmetics
and prophylactics for windfalls; and of course such windfall
stimulators as hashish candies, Spanish fly cocktails, marijuana cookies, and the like.

Great guns alive! Had the atomic war begun? Were the locusts coming? Was there a convention of Baptist preachers in town?

Not so.

It was the day of Mamie Mason's Masked Ball, and these high society ladies were preparing hors d'oeuvres to sustain them and their loved ones and guests, not to mention those white folks who were too good to bring anything to eat themselves but ate up your stuff all right, through all the long happy hours of revelry ahead.

And what was Mamie Mason doing while these cooking games were taking place? She was trying on that absolutely fabulous rhinestone-ornamented gold lamé costume, size twelve, she had had made months ago for her reign as Queen of the Ball, and congratulating herself on not drinking water during those tortuous days of fasting. Naturally she was alone. Do you think she wanted anyone to see the unclothed effects of that rigorous ordeal?

When suddenly there came a rapping and a tapping upon her outside door.

She smiled wanly, thinking it was her doctor with a shot of vitamin C, and wishing to congratulate him too for keeping her afoot.

But it was Dr. John Stetson Kissock, chairman of the Southern Committee for the Preservation of Justice, in a terrible state of agitation. His customarily beaming pink cupid's face was drawn up like a prune, and his pale blue eyes were distended.

"My stars!" he gasped. "I have just seen a white officer of the law brutally beating a Negro."

"I know what you mean," Mamie said. "But you were supposed to come yesterday."

"I can't wait," he cried. "Not a minute to spare."

"But I'm trying on my dress," Mamie said angrily.

"Oh, take it off, you cruel woman," he pleaded, acting as though he might tear it off himself.

Naturally she wasn't going to allow that to happen to that fabulous creation, so she began taking it off as quickly as possible while he did the same with his own sedate attire.

Needless to point out that after such a long hard fast she did not resemble a Botticelli nude. In fact, she bore a striking resemblance to a skeleton clad in a skin four sizes too large.

But without his clothes the other was not Dr. Kissock at all. It was a round happy porker fresh from the scalding pot, its pink skin glowing from a good scraping.

"Where is it?" demanded the porker, er, ah, Dr. Kissock. "You said you had a new one."

Indeed, if she had a new one it was not in evidence, if we're talking about the same thing. Even the old one was somewhat obscured by the folds of belly skin which covered it like an apron.

But she merely said, "Don't move, I'll go get it." And while he stood twitching and quivering in the middle of the living room, she put the night lock on the front door, then went back to the bedroom and got it from beneath her lingerie, which is exactly where she told him she kept it.

Great shades of Sade, it was a miniature bullwhip, black and a foot long, just as she had said, and when she began whipping the little porker with it, his face flushed with ecstasy.

"Oh! Oh! The poor Negro!" he cried, running and squealing about the room while she laid it on him.

Nor was she lacking in ardor as he jumped from foot to foot and leaped from side to side, yelping and squealing and crying: "Oh! Oh! the poor Negro!" (*Whack* went the whip.) "Oh! Oh! the poor Negro!" (*Whack* went the whip.)

She began to sweat and pant as his bright red ass began to corrugate with welts.

When suddenly there came a rapping and a tapping upon her outside door.

"Into the bedroom!" she cried, pushing the porker, er, ah, Dr. Kissock, in front of her.

Clad in her red robe and looking sweaty and disheveled, she opened the outside door.

And there stood Dr. Carl Vincent Stone, president emeritus and chairman of the board of that famous Negro college in the Deep South, sans makeup and breathing like a purse snatcher after a long desperate chase.

"I can't bear it," he groaned gaspingly, pushing her aside and closing and locking the door. "Can't bear it. I can't bear it."

"Can't bear what, dear?" Mamie asked soothingly.

"Can't bear to hear black women singing spirituals. I've been listening to the school choir and I can't bear it. Oh, how I hate the Negro."

"But you weren't supposed to come today," Mamie reminded him.

"It's those damn spirituals. I can't bear it," he snarled, slavering and biting his lips in a terrifying manner, the brown spots darkening in his white face.

"Don't tear off my robe," Mamie said in alarm, hastening to undress. "Whether you can bear it or not."

He began sniffing her in a very strange manner, sniff-sniff-sniff, from front and back. "Goodness, you're stinky," he cried and began rubbing his face in the flabby folds of her sweaty belly. "Smell just like a black bitch."

"All right, just wait here until I get it," she said, pushing him into the kitchen, then going on back to the bathroom to get the phial containing the green liquid which she had shown him at the reception, which was no more or less than essence of musk very slightly tinctured with cantharides.

By the time she returned he had undressed, throwing his clothes about the floor as though they fettered him. And Jesus save us, it was not Dr. Stone at all but an old mangy black and white dog, and judging from the manner in which it slavered it had the rabies.

Mamie gave it the bottle, cautioning: "Don't waste it, and do be careful."

Then she stood spread-eagle against the wall, arms upraised to brace herself and her rigid spine slanting outward to her protruding flabby tan buttocks.

Shaking with excitement the mad dog, er, ah, Dr. Stone, emptied half the bottle of tinctured musk on the back of her neck and began licking it voraciously, snarling and slavering and snapping his teeth as it trickled down her spine.

"Oh! Oh! I hate the Negro!" he muttered spasmodically, and began biting her with increasing viciousness.

Snarl, snap, bite.

"Oh! I hate the Negro!"

Snarl, snap, bite.

"Oh, how I hate the Negro!"

Naturally, Mamie wasn't going to just stand there and let herself be bitten until she couldn't sit down to reign as Queen of the Ball, no matter how much he hated Negroes. So she let fly a backhand wallop which caught him flush in the eye and knocked him onto his own bony backside.

When suddenly there came a rapping and a tapping upon her outside door.

"Oh, good gracious me!" she cried and shut the spotted dog, er, ah, Dr. Stone, in the kitchen before putting on her robe and hastening to answer it.

And there stood Dr. Oliver Wendell Garrett, that fine patriarchal-looking figure, president of the Rosenberg Foundation, looking down upon her with such a frightful expression of compassion as to raise the instant fear she had been sentenced to the stake.

"What have I done?" she cried.

"It is not you, my dear, but me, who has just delivered a lecture on *Brotherhood*," he said, tears swimming in his benevolent gray eyes.

"Oh, so your love has come down," she said. "But this isn't the day."

He came inside and slowly and deliberately closed and locked the door.

"Love doesn't come by the day," he said, backing her

into the living room and beginning to disrobe.

Needless to say, Mamie was becoming exhausted by this time and she watched him with extreme displeasure.

"It's no use undressing," she said adamantly. "I've lost mine."

Silently he completed disrobing and when she looked into his old liquid eyes she realized it was not Dr. Garrett at all, but an old hairy salacious billy goat.

"But I've found mine," the old billy goat, er, ah, Dr. Garrett, said.

With which he tore off her robe with one hand and with the other drew from his pile of clothing a bullwhip identical to the one she had used to whip the porker, er, ah, Dr. Kissock.

"Not too hard," she begged, as he began to flail her across the back and buttocks with an expression of incalculable glee.

She ran skipping and dancing and twisting and turning about the room, her flabby buttocks jiggling like skins filled with liquid and her breasts flopping about like the deformed genitals of eunuchs, while he flailed her with his whip, chanting gleefully:

"Oh! Oh! I love the Negro!"

Lash . . . yelp . . . shuffle . . . chuckle . . . leap . . . crash . . .

"I love the Negro! Oh! Oh!"

Lash . . . yelp . . . shuffle . . .

Her two other guests, the pink porker and the spotted dog, shut up in their respective dungeons, intently listening at their respective keyholes to the frantic shuffling of bare feet, the unmistakable sound of a whip lashing bare flesh, the muted yelps of pain, and the gleeful chant, "Oh! Oh! I love the Negro!" had begun to wonder if indeed the third visitor were not the devil himself. This they had to see.

So into the room they rushed, one from the bedroom and the other from the kitchen, as naked as they were.

And were they paralyzed by the shock of recognition? Not a bit. When they saw their big naked colleague, the old billy goat, er, ah, Dr. Garrett, gleefully chastising a sheared black ewe, er, ah, Mamie Mason, their common colored mistress, they were incited to such inordinate passion toward the Negro Problem, all of the Southern Jim Crow laws combined could not have restrained them from participating in the ritual.

The mad dog, er, ah, Dr. Stone, began biting unrestrainedly, engaging in a rhythmic duet with the billy goat who was gleefully flailing the ewe:

"Oh! Oh! I hate the Negro!"

"Oh! Oh! I love the Negro!"

But the pink porker disturbed the rhythm by dancing in eccentric circles, crying:

"Oh Oh! The poor Negro!"

Which inspired the black ewe to begin beating it again with her own bullwhip to restore the rhythm, raising welts across its bald pink head.

For a time all four were joined in such impressive mobile statuary as to be the envy of Picasso.

But the black ewe accidentally struck the billy goat on his goat piece, causing the goat to groan in such contagious anguish as to inspire a veritable symphony of groaning which rose in a moving crescendo to a sighing climax.

FINALLY the momentous hour, which had been awaited so long with such palpitations of the heart and abatements of breath, arrived.

And indeed the scene was set for an occasion of superlative magnificence. The decorations within the Savoy Ballroom were worthy of a coronation. The eye was literally bowled over by the gold and royal purple colors of *La Société des Mondaines du Monde de Harlème*. On the outside of the dance floor the boxes were completely shielded by gold and purple bunting. On the other side was a raft of solid gold floating on a royal purple sea. Overhead streamers of tissue tape extending from the center of the ceiling to the walls in all directions made a circus tent of gold and purple stripes. And in the center box, directly opposite the bandstand, stood a royal purple dais on which sat an ebony throne, commanding the attention of the ballroom from every angle.

To one side of the throne was the box reserved for the judges; to the other side the box reserved for members of the press.

On the street in front of the building a passageway had been roped off from the curb to the entrance, and was guarded by a cordon of special police on orders from the mayor, no less, and not without justification.

Long before the first guests arrived, crowds had gathered, and even the curious Harlem dogs and cats, not to mention the curious rats, slunk about to witness the commotion.

And here they come! The chauffeur-driven limousines, the big convertibles, the sedate sedans, the multicolored taxi-cabs! Bringing the white folks and the black folks to the darktown strutters ball, er, ah, this great interracial festival.

And by the hammer of Zeus, all the spicy history of the known world was represented on that great night: gods from Olympus, conquerors from the Roman Empire, kings of ancient Israel, Oriental potentates, cruel barbarian plunderers, knights from the Middle Ages, court intriguers, papal sycophants, the great lovers of all time, along with the infamous murderers, fiends and angels, devils, griffins, saints and goblins, Black Feet from North America, Black Hands from Sicily, Black Jacks from the pirate ships that scourged the seven seas, Blackguards from, er, ah, the local variety, Pinktoes from all over. Shades of Davey Jones, fish too! The great white whale Moby Dick, with a camera slung over his shoulder and notebook in his pocket—or is a whale considered a fish? And there's a huge black octopus with his arms about eight mermaids, er, an error please, that's just a Harlem character called Squatty Potty selling souvenir rag dolls. And right there before us is Ali Baba and *one* thief, in Harlem yet. . . .

All reincarnated for the triumph and the glory of Mamie Mason.

Everybody was there who was anybody.

Wallace Wright came appropriately enough as Job, but Juanita came as Lot's wife, poor fellow.

Willard B. Overton came as Buddha and his wife, Alice as Sojourner Truth, which surprised no one.

Naturally Eddy Schooley came as Bacchus, but not quite as bacchic as we last saw Bacchus, escorting Patty Pearson as Lucretia Borgia.

But Dr. Baldwin Billings Brown came as the Sphinx and his wife, Maiti, as, merciful heavens, Circe. No wonder the man came as the Sphinx.

Kathy Carter came as Catherine the Great, as if who wouldn't have guessed it, accompanied by that forty-nine-year-old leading young Negro writer, Lorenzo Llewellyn, who, fittingly enough, came as the Missing Link.

Rosenberg fellow applicant Jonah Johnson came as the

White Man's Burden, it no doubt intended as a gentle hint, but sensibly he left his wife at home.

Our Merto came as Eve, wearing a necklace of her knitted mementos, which all but their respective models thought were strange bananas, but why such big seeds, and —great wiggling tadpoles she forgot her fig leaf. No, there it is, but what a stunted fig tree it must have come from. And Maurice came as, hush, child, hush, *Cupid.*

Milt Shirley came as Nero, and his wife, Bessie, as Nana —shadows of libidos.

Light-complexioned Evie Miller and dark-complexioned Moe Miller came as the good and evil fairies.

Professor Isaiah Samuels came as Simon Legree and his wife, Kit, as Little Lisa, which inspired some raising of the eyebrows.

Reverend Mike Riddick came as, great burning bushes, Jehovah Himself, or was he supposed to be just Moses with all that flowing white beard and long white hair? And his bride, Peggy, as the Golden Calf. Moses all right.

Quite logically, many of the white folks came as black folks.

Art and Debbie Wills appeared in blackface as Uncle Tom and Topsy, which didn't sit very well with many of the natural black folks, especially the Uncle Toms.

Wills Robbins and Fay Corson appeared in blackface as the King of Ethiopia and the Queen of Sheba, which sat quite well with the natural black folks.

But when Lou Reynolds and his lady colleague, Lullabelle Talmadge, appeared in blackface as Uncle Ben, the fried rice king, and Aunt Jemima, the battercake queen, that was the bitter end for the natural black folks.

Your attention, please! Make way, please!

The Queen has arrived.

She is not in sight as yet. But listen to the thundering applause. Look at the crowd pushing toward the entrance for a better view. Notice the excitement and anticipation on their beaming faces. Regard those photographers struggling for vantage points.

And here she comes, clad in a golden gown with a crown of sparkling jewels—well, sparkling anyway—upon her raven black hair. And she is accompanied by the three venerable judges in white tie and tails, Dr. Oliver Wendell Garrett, president of the Rosenberg Foundation, Dr. John Stetson Kissock, chairman of the Southern Committee for the Preservation of Justice, and Dr. Carl Vincent Stone, president emeritus and chairman of the board of that great Negro college in our Southland.

Observe the, er, my God, is that consternation one sees on the faces of the guests? Why so?

Well great leaping catfish! *Never,* and we do mean *never,* in the long and illustrious history of the annual Masked Ball has such a select assemblage of socialites of both races, gathered to celebrate the thrilling assaults on racial bias, seen such a glorious colored Queen, and such esteemed and distinguished white judges and revered patrons of the Negro Problem, looking so beat up.

Grieving Jesus! Why, the Queen walks as though she is suffering from lumbago. And the big unseemly swellings visible beneath the heavy makeup on her neck and shoulders which even the golden crepe de Chine scarf about her décolleté cannot obscure, look shockingly like welts. And the dazed expression of her eyes raises grave doubts as to whether she is awake.

And observe the careful, wide-legged tread of Dr. Oliver Wendell Garrett. Were he anyone but the president of the Rosenberg Foundation one might think he had caught a case of the GI hazard.

And what on earth are all those ridges on Dr. John Stetson Kissock's shining bald head? One had never noticed them there before, and as prominent as they are, one would certainly have noticed. And *why* is he carrying that cushion? Doesn't he trust the seats? Or does he have a boil on his buttocks? And just what is wrong with his voice? It can't, by any chance, be that he has got a hair caught in his throat?

And do you see just what it is about Dr. Carl Vincent

Stone that causes him to so resemble the last of the Holly-wood monsters on this particular night? Good grief, it looks decidedly as though he has a shiner beneath the layers of white makeup.

Well, let us be relieved anyway that the Queen has finally made it to her throne. And there she slumps, her golden gown emblazoned on the ebony background, looking on the verge of collapse.

No wonder everyone has crowded close about her to stare in silent wonder.

But here comes a white whale approaching her. Thank God for a diversion. The whale is holding a microphone in one hand and a page of typescript in the other. But when he begins to read from the script we realize he is not a whale at all, but the Master of Ceremonies.

"Before the festivities begin," his voice booms from the PA system, "we would like to pay homage to Mrs. Mamie Mason, the founder and guiding genius of this celebrated Harlem society which is sponsoring this great occasion for interracial unification to demonstrate our reciprocal loving, er, *love,* which comes from the private parts of us all, er, *from the private part,* and who is our glorious Queen for tonight. . . ."

Deafening applause.

"And now, Mrs. Mamie Mason, or rather I should say, Your Majesty [toothy smile], will you perhaps give us a hint from your varied interracial affairs [tittering in the audience], er, various interracial experimentations [more tittering], er, ah, on ways and means of improving and perpetuating the close and frenzied ties between the races [loud laughter], er, *friendly* ties between the races which exist here tonight."

Her answer is awaited with bated breath.

The Queen looks up with a dazed expression. For a mo-ment it seems doubtful if she has understood a single word. But suddenly her eyes light up and her face assumes an expression of exultation as she looks about at all the bright and shining faces of her white and colored guests, the cream of interracial society.

She leans fòrward toward the microphone and proclaims in a gasping voice:

"More . . . interracial . . . intercourse. . . ."

"My God! Did I hear right?" Maiti Brown was heard to exclaim in unutterable shock. "Move over, Pinktoes, we're a hundred years behind."

How many of these Dell bestsellers have you read?

The Money Game by "Adam Smith" $1.25

The Madonna Complex by Norman Bogner $1.25

The Manor by Isaac Bashevis Singer $1.25

The Beastly Beatitudes of Balthazar B by J. P. Donleavy $1.25

Soul On Ice (A Delta Edition) by Eldridge Cleaver $1.95

The Hundred Yard War by Gary Cartwright 95c

The Other Side by James A. Pike 95c

Tell Me How Long The Train's Been Gone
by James Baldwin $1.25

An American Melodrama
by Lewis Chester, Godfrey Hodgson, Bruce Page $1.65

The Brand-Name Calorie Counter by Corinne T. Netzer 95c

The Doctor's Quick Weight-Loss Diet
by I. Maxwell Stillman M.D., and S. Sinclair Baker 95c

The Beatles by Hunter Davies 95c

The Movie Maker by Herbert Kastle $1.25

The Secret of Santa Vittoria by Robert Crichton 95c

Pretty Maids All In A Row by Francis Pollini 95c

**The bestselling new novel
by the author of *Another Country***

JAMES BALDWIN
Tell Me How Long
The Train's Been Gone

This is the story of Leo Proudhammer, who rose from the bitter streets of Harlem to become America's greatest black actor. It is the story of the women, and the men, in his life—a drama of a powerful, magnetic figure whose one-way path to success suddenly became an agonizing crossroads. Here is the supreme triumph of America's great novelist that tells it like it is about sex, race, and morality today.

"James Baldwin's first novel in six years is worth the wait . . . It speaks with fire, art and intelligence . . . I was swept up."　　　　　　　　　　*—San Francisco Examiner*

"Baldwin's most significant novel to date in terms of maturity and sensitivity . . . a document of infinite importance in an era erupting within the clichés of 'hate' and 'conscience' "　　　　　　　　　　　　　　　*—Denver Post*

"It is without doubt his best novel by far. Without doubt it is one of the greatest, most forceful works of our troubled epoch. Let us hope that this novel will be read by everyone in America."　　　　　　　　　　　　　*—Chicago News*

A DELL BOOK　$1.25

"BLACK POWER"—
find out just where it's at!

SOUL ON ICE
by Eldridge Cleaver

This is the voice of Eldridge Cleaver:

"Nineteen fifty-four, when I was eighteen years old, is held to be a crucial turning point in the history of the Afro-American—for the U.S.A. as a whole—the year segregation was outlawed by the U. S. Supreme Court. It was also a crucial year for me because on June 18, 1954, I began serving a sentence in state prison for possession of marijuana...."

Thus begins the book that has become one of the fountainheads of the new Black Power movement that has gained adherents from coast to coast. Here is a totally frank autobiography of an extraordinary man—and a devastating dissection of a society in the throes of agonizing reappraisal and momentous change.

"Beautifully written by a man with a formidably analytical mind ... makes you twist and flinch because he is no damned gentleman. He throws light on the dark areas we wish he would leave alone ... brilliant."
                                                          —*The Nation*

A DELTA BOOK $1.95

If you cannot obtain copies of this title at your local bookseller, just send the price (plus 10c per copy for handling and postage) to Dell Books, Box 2291, Grand Central Post Office, New York, N.Y. 10017. No postage or handling charge is required on any order of five or more books.

The Bestselling New Novel by the Author of
Seventh Avenue

"A narrative gift . . . a sure hand with character . . . convincing . . . impressive"
—*Saturday Review Syndicate*

The
Madonna
Complex

by Norman Bogner

The compelling and disturbingly beautiful love story of a Wall Street tycoon and a seductive younger woman. This is Norman Bogner's spellbinding new novel of sexual obsession, betrayal, and final strange salvation.

"A sexy book . . . all the pathos, greed and grief, longing and impatience, holiness and obscenity, depravity and creativity of human sexuality . . . an exquisite and moving, terrifying and haunting multifaceted novel"
—*Chicago Sun-Times*

"Gripping . . . compulsive readability"
—*Saturday Review*

A DELL BOOK $1.25

If you cannot obtain copies of this title at your local bookseller, just send the price (plus 10c per copy for handling and postage) to Dell Books, Box 2291, Grand Central Post Office, New York, N.Y. 10017. No postage or handling charge is required on any order of five or more books.

A Truly Provocative
and Gripping Novel

THE
MOVIE
MAKER

by Herbert Kastle

A torrid world of passion, talent and greed, the legendary producer who could turn it on and off—and the sex bomb who pulled him down into an abyss of perverse desire. This contemporary novel has everything it needs to be a bestseller; it's bursting with energy, probing deeply into the hopes, fears and sexual desires of the people behind the screen.

A DELL BOOK $1.25

If you cannot obtain copies of this title at your local bookseller, just send the price (plus 10c per copy for handling and postage) to Dell Books, Box 2291, Grand Central Post Office, New York, N.Y. 10017. No postage or handling charge is required on any order of five or more books.